CW00894726

"How sweet the moonlight sleeps upon this bank Here we will sit, and let the sounds of music Creep in our ears; soft stillness, and the night Become the touches of sweet harmony"

William Shakespeare
The Merchant of Venice Act V, Scene 1

© Kate Fitzroy 2015

MOONLIGHT IN TUSCANY

by
KATE FITZROY

round.

Lily knew so much about life in medieval Italy that it was hard to believe how little she knew about living in present-day Cambridge. Enshrouded in her research studies in the gloomy alleys of bookshelves, days would pass by when she hardly spoke. Sometimes there would be a brief exchange of greeting with Henry, the porter as she passed through the college entrance.

'Good morning, Dr Fairfax, lovely day.'
'Good morning Henry, how are you?'
'Fine and dandy, Prof, fine and dandy!'
Dr Lily Fairfax would pass on through the stone archway, give a brief glance at the bright summer sky, then scurry into the dark library to take her place at a desk between two rows of book shelves. Usually, she forgot to take lunch and sometimes she forgot to eat dinner. Until Henry came around to lock the doors, she would read, write and think, occasionally sipping from her bottle of water.

But now her book had gone to the publishers and she was sitting in a small café, alone and thoughtful. Suddenly a huge void appeared in her life. The daily routine had become pointless, at least, for the near future. There would be another book to begin, but now, right now, she was exhausted to the point of mental oblivion. Now she wanted to find out what was going on around her in the present day and not the minutiae of life in Tuscany five hundred years ago. She was an intelligent young woman, described by one of her students as a Titian beauty. What was his name? Lily frowned into her lemon tea as she tried to remember. Yes, Tristan, that was it. Tristan de Freville. Lily's frown turned to a small smile as she remembered his romantic name and how it had suited him. Did people feel obliged to live up to their names, she wondered idly? There was probably a thesis to write on that... maybe it had already been written? Lily sighed and put the idea out of her head. The time for any academic thought was over for a while. She refused to think seriously about anything, even the young Tristan, who had tried so hard to woo her. No, right now, she could surely use her considerable intelligence to sort out her life. She finished her lemon tea and paid at the counter. The barista glanced at her as he took the money and Lily felt a flutter of... well, what was it? Amusement? No, not really. Attraction? Possibly... now that she looked at him again she could feel the strength of his burning gaze.

He was very like a portrait by Moroni, yes, that was it... he had the face of 'The Tailor', 'Il Sarto', oil on canvas, c. 1570... a gentle face, slightly flushed cheeks and such a light in the eyes... yes, the barista was as interesting as a figure out of history. Her research-trained mind whirred like a computer as she began to collate and gather information to form a theory. Interesting, very interesting... that was it. Lily realised that the man was still holding out her change, smiling, his dark eyebrows slightly raised in mild impatience, his head slightly to one side as he waited to serve the next customer. Lily took the coins from his out-stretched hand, sensing and then trying to ignore the warmth of his skin as it briefly touched hers. She quickly dropped her head, her long red-gold hair forming a curtain between them and hurried from the café.

Outside, the sun shone down from a pale blue Cambridge sky. She stood a moment, blinking and hesitant as a young Bambi. Whatever should she do next?

The same café on the next day. There were a hundred different cafés to choose from in Cambridge but this one had an outstanding view of King's College. Lily sat in the window, perched on a high bar seat, admiring the Gothic architecture and the contrast of the pale stone against the brilliant green grass. Late perpendicular Gothic, she mused to herself... a feat of Tudor engineering, soaring to the grand height of twenty-nine metres, dominating the water meadows and fens of Cambridgeshire. Lily's brain was reeling back through all the knowledge she had on the subject, but there was no- one to lecture to now. The last of her students had left Cambridge a week ago. So, what should she do next? Surely not mope around in a café, trying not to think intellectual thoughts? It was all too ridiculous. The summer months stretched ahead of her... months that should be filled with sunshine... even laughter might not be too much to ask for. But the future seemed to stretch ahead like a damp rag. She had a book in her bag, well, she always had a book in her bag, but she was trying not to read it. She wanted to enter real life not escape into fiction or history. She reached out to the newspaper rack and took down the local Cambridge paper. She flicked idly through the pages, weddings, accidents and incidents... all happening to other people. She sighed and closed the paper and put it on the bar beside her. She sipped again at a lemon tea. How many lemon teas could a young woman consume a day... and then, what about the lonely nights? She sighed and looked down again at the newspaper as it lay folded in front of her. The back page was full of classified ads and suddenly she was reading a list of men who were looking for women. The dating page. Lily's green eyes widened in surprise as she realised what she was reading.

'affectionate man seeks loving companion to join his life journey'

Was this man with the sinister twisted smile seriously thinking any sane woman would answer his ad?

'man gsh wants to find lovely young woman to share cultural pursuits'

Gsh... now what could that mean? Had he missed out the 'o' from gosh? Was it an acronym? As for his photo, it looked more like a police identikit than a real person. Lily shuddered, but could not resist reading further down the column. Line after line of small print, hopeful pleas from lonely but optimistic people. Why should she ridicule their attempts to improve their lives when she was unable to solve her own solitary existence? She peered at the small colour photos, the poor newsprint quality giving each a blurred sameness. Then, her eyes alighted on a face that she recognised. The unruly blonde hair, horn-rimmed glasses and determined chin... yes, surely it was Quentin Howard from the History department. She had met him briefly, a few months ago, at a conference in Bristol. Finding they had both come up from Cambridge, they had exchanged a few words before the presentation began and they went to different seats. She hadn't seen him since but she remembered his confident, rather arrogant manner and strong voice. Why was he amongst the list of lonely people? She would never have imagined that he would need to advertise for friendship... or more.

'Cambridge man seeks interesting female companionship, no strings attached just good company and intellectual banter... and whatever that may lead to. Call.'

Lily looked anxiously around the café, suddenly aware that anyone might be watching her peering at the back page of the local paper, the dating page. She blushed, her pale cheeks turning a delicate shade of pink as she folded the newspaper neatly and replaced it in the rack. She looked around and realised that no-one was looking at her at all. She went over to the counter and paid quickly. This time there was no romantic medieval man behind the counter, just a surly young woman who gave Lily her change without a word or a smile. Outside, again in the pale sunshine, Lily hesitated a moment and then walked quickly along King's Parade and straight into a newsagent. There was no reason at all that she shouldn't buy a local newspaper... no reason at all.

Lily was waiting, her heart was thumping fast as she sipped a glass of white wine. Sitting this time, not in her favourite café but a dark and expensive wine bar. Why had she made this date? It was ridiculous and so out of keeping with her normal way of behaviour. No, she thought to herself angrily, taking a gulp of the dry, white wine, it wasn't just ridiculous it was stupid. She tapped her foot nervously and shook her wild mane of hair away from her face as she glanced quickly around the oak-panelled bar. Another sip of wine, too acidic for her taste, and she decided to leave.

'Great to see you again, Lily! To think we should meet like this!' The voice was strong and confident and close behind her. Lily turned to confront the tall, looming figure of Quentin Howard.

'Good evening, Quentin.' The few words stuck in her throat and her voice was almost a whisper. Then, Quentin's head was ducking down to kiss her. Lily quickly turned her cheek and she felt his lips brush against her skin. He had a careful amount of stubble and she was conscious of the sheer manliness of the man. Now, he was sitting opposite her and calling for the waiter. His confidence was oozing out of him and filling the area around their table. The waiter hurried over immediately and stood waiting attentively.

'I see you're drinking white but will you join me in a glass of red now? The reason I come here is for their excellent Falchini Campora.' It was a question, but Lily had no chance to reply before Quentin continued, 'Bring a bottle, nicely *chambré*, will you? And make sure it's the 2006, you know how difficult a man I am!' Quentin gave the waiter a broad smile and then turned to Lily,
'This is incredible, isn't it? Meeting again through a lonely heart's page. I remember you from that conference in Bristol. In fact, you are about the only thing I do remember,

it was stultifyingly boring, wasn't it?' Another question that hung in the air so briefly that Lily had only time to smile vaguely before Quentin carried on talking. 'Yes, I remember you were wearing a greeny blue silk dress and with your stunning red golden hair the effect was electric. I looked for you after the lecture finally ground to a halt, but I couldn't find you. In fact, it's all your fault that I ended up very drunk in a bar that night, drowning my sorrows. You will have to make that up to me somehow, sometime.' He smiled and reached over to take her hand.

Lily moved her hand out of reach and, fortunately, at that moment the waiter arrived with a bottle of wine and two glasses. Quentin immediately turned his attention to the bottle of wine. The hand he had stretched out to take Lily's was now placed lightly on the bottle.

'Excellent, young man, feels just right, not too cold from the cellar. Pour away.'

The waiter poured a small amount into Quentin's glass and waited while Quentin twirled the glass, examined the colour of the wine against the white tablecloth and then sipped and gurgled. Finally, he swallowed and flashed another wide smile of pleasure,

'Superb as ever, pour la signorina a large glass.'

Lily watched as the dark, red wine was poured reverently into her glass. Her glass of white wine stood beside it, half-finished. For a moment, she was tempted to protest and say that she didn't want to drink red wine, in fact, that she never drank red wine without food. She looked across at Quentin, registering his high-handed manner and easy way of assuming control. She knew It would be very easy to deflate him but what would be the pleasure in it? Her experience at lecturing had taught her how to handle over-opinionated students... she had no problem with it. Her own confidence was quiet but rock solid. She picked up the glass of red wine, holding only the stem of the glass between her delicate fingers and sniffed appreciatively,

'An excellent choice, Quentin, I know the Falchini vineyards and their award-winning Vermentino. This should be interesting.' She took a small sip and rolled the wine around her tongue as she looked directly into Quentin's surprised and dark grey eyes. 'Mmm, delicious, the dense blackcurrant and smoky vanilla taste lives up to the aroma, mmm... a superbly complex barrique-matured Cabernet. Well chosen!'

Quentin was effectively silenced and Lily suddenly burst out laughing. Quentin looked even more startled for a moment and then, he laughed aloud.

Their laughter had carried them through the evening and now, comfortably curled up in Quentin's very large bed, Lily smiled with satisfaction. This was exactly how she had hoped her new found freedom from academia would be. She stretched luxuriously, her muscles aching from the night of love. Quentin was a very good lover, no doubt very experienced. After their first frenzied love- making, almost an attack on both sides, they had fallen into a deep, intoxicated sleep, waking only an hour later to make love again... and again. Lily was excited by the energy and passion of this large- framed exuberant man and touched by his gentleness. Much of the night passed in talk and laughter and it was exhilarating to exchange their particular knowledge of history and art. Now, listening to the domestic noises of coffee-making coming from the kitchen, Lily felt the warmth of happiness enclose her and she drifted back into a dreamless sleep.

'I can't believe your capacity for sleep, Dr Fairfax... you are like a baby kitten. I can't believe how beautiful you are either.'

Lily opened one eye sleepily and sat up in bed, pulling the rumpled sheet over her as Quentin placed a tray on the bedside table.

'Coffee smells wonderful, thank you.' Lily said sleepily, suddenly feeling shy in the bright sunshine streaming through the tall window.

'Do you know that your hair turns to bronze in the sunlight?'

'I can't say that I did,' Lily smiled, 'but it's very nice to know. Now, are you going to pour me a coffee?'

'You look so very sweet, but I realise you're a hard woman, Lily Fairfax. What shall I do with you?'

'I thought you'd thought of most things last night.' Lily looked at Quentin with her green eyes stretched wide and with the glimmer of a smile.

'Lily, Lily, you are a wicked woman. Wicked and hard... shall we have breakfast... a little later?'

'Certainly not!' Lily wrapped the sheet firmly around herself and reached out for the coffee. 'I desperately need sustenance.'

'After the huge meal you managed to devour last night? Now there's something else I would never have guessed about you. You look so delicate that I would have thought you'd just pick at your food.'

'Good gracious, no! I love food and eat whenever I remember. Anyway, I have some making up to do. I have been so busy lately, I think I've probably been forgetting to eat properly. The food last night was simply divine. Thank you so much.'

'It was a pleasure to watch you eat. Your delight in the food was a joy... not to mention how you loved the wines. Now where did all that knowledge come from? You seemed to recognise and appreciate every one.'

'Ah well, that is because my dear old father is a Master of Wine and brought me up with a strict appreciation of the joys of the grape.'

'Really, a Master of Wine? Does he work in England?'

'Well, he did, but he's retired now and lives in Italy, enjoying some well-earned peace and quiet. My mother died just after I was born so my poor old Father, already in late middle-age, had to bring me up single-handed... unless you count a succession of nannies, housekeepers and boarding school.'

'Poor little Lily... that's so sad, never to have had a mother.' Quentin reached out and gently stroked Lily's wild hair back from her forehead. The gesture was sweetly comforting and Lily took his hand and kissed it as she said,

'Well, I suppose you never miss what you never had. I had a very happy childhood and even enjoyed going away to school. Father and I travelled together every holiday, mostly through the vineyards of France, Italy and Spain. He would be wine-tasting and writing while I... well, I suppose I took in the general cultural stuff going on around me, but mostly I read and read and then read some more.'

'Obviously to good effect. You have a reputation in Cambridge as one of the youngest and most talented dons. It just doesn't seem reasonable that you should be beautiful as well.'

'Oh, do stop now, Quentin. You're beginning to embarrass me. I think you'd better come back to bed now. I've had quite enough compliments and coffee for one morning.'

Quentin took Lily's coffee cup from her and gently began to pull the sheet away from her. She looked up at him, smiling, and then stretched out her arms and pulled him down on top of her.

Lily's affair with Quentin filled her days and nights. She had emerged like a butterfly from its chrysalis and now she was fluttering in a bright new world, Quentin Howard's world. His work as a lecturer was very different from her own. Now she spent no time in the quiet libraries but, always on Quentin's arm, she rushed around accompanying him to social events. They began to be recognised as a glamorous couple in the academic world. Lily's publishers were delighted at this new turn of events and began to suggest frequent book-signing and talks on her work. Lily's metamorphosis seemed complete... until, one morning... a letter arrived from her father.

Lily stood by the window, reading the closely-written letter in the shaft of light between the curtains. It was nearly ten o'clock and she had already had her pot of lemon tea. Quentin was still fast asleep, spread diagonally across her bed, his long arm flung out to where she had been laying. Lily looked at him critically but could find no fault. His large-boned body was well-muscled due to the time he dedicated to working out. His hair, rather long, was dark blonde, glossy with health and expensive conditioning. Quentin was certainly a handsome man and he was well aware of it. He spent both time and money on staying that way. Lily moved nearer to the bed, smiling as she thought how vain he was and self-satisfied. After a month when they had hardly been apart for more than an hour, Lily felt qualified to make judgement. Yes, he loved her and yes, he loved himself too. There was nothing wrong in that. He had certainly helped Lily enter a new, lightweight world of fun. Did she love Quentin? Lily had no idea if what she felt for this man lying in front of her, now strangely vulnerable... if it was love with or without a capital L. What she did know was that the dynamic in their relationship was changing and each day she felt he was beginning to rely on her. Nothing wrong with that either... of course. Lily hesitated, her thoughts leading to a new realisation. This beautiful man lying so deeply asleep that he didn't even know she was no longer lying beside him... yes, this extraordinary man needed her. Quentin Howard, history don and wild man of the campus was actually not so self-confident as he appeared. Lily Fairfax, the shy and shrinking violet of academia was now stretching her wings. She was about to reach out and touch his shoulder to wake him, but suddenly she drew her hand away and walked quietly from the room. She would let him sleep and she would make another pot of tea and enjoy reading her letter quietly in peace.

An hour later, sitting at a breakfast table in Carluccio's, Lily took Quentin's hand in hers and looked at him,

'I'm going to Italy next week.' Her words were quietly spoken and the noise of the restaurant almost drowned her voice. Quentin carried on eating, his mouth full of a buttery croissant, he nodded enthusiastically. Then swallowing and taking a sip of coffee, he answered.

'Did you say you wanted to go to Italy? I can absolutely understand that... being in this place, one wonders why one should be anywhere else. The food alone...' He waved an arm around enthusiastically, 'but when can we get away? I have guest lectures booked wall to wall. Crazy!'

'No, Quentin, I said I was going to Italy.' Lily let go of his hand and felt a shiver of anger. She had emphasised the small word 'I'. Surely he understood?

'I don't understand. You can't leave me. I can't get away for at least a month. In September, I do have nearly a week free. Yes, we could go then for a few days. In fact, I have an old colleague I'd like to catch up with... he lives in Venice. We could snatch a few days away.'

Lily sighed and something inside her felt slightly broken. She sat up straight and looked at Quentin, her green eyes brimmed with tears as she spoke,

'Sorry Quentin, but I am going to Italy and I think the wonderful time we have had together is very nearly over now. I need to find myself again and get down to some work. I have an idea in my head for a new book and I want to do some research in Italy over the summer. I'm sorry.' Lily wiped a solitary tear from her cheek.

'I don't understand. Why are you crying, dear, sweet Lily... you can't mean it. How can it be over between us? Of course you should write your next book, everyone awaits it. It's obvious that your publishing house is gagging for your next title. If you have to go to Italy for a while...then I shall miss you but I can join you ... weekends...whenever I'm free. It's only an hour or so away... don't talk about things being over, please.' Quentin ran his hands back through his hair, his face dark with anxiety.

'Sorry, Quentin. I've had a wonderful time with you, as I said, and yes, I am crying. It's as though a fantastic holiday has ended. But I'm not really a holiday sort of person. I'm not really the social butterfly that you have helped me to be this last month. I suppose, well, I'm really more of a bookworm.'

'Your letter brought me back to my senses, I think.' Lily was sitting with her elderly father on the terrace of his small villa. They sat under the shade of a faded canvas awning. Even though the heat of the day was dying down it was still very warm. The cicadas had just begun their strident song and small birds were fluttering among the acacia trees, hurrying to their nests.

'The swifts will be dipping down low over the pool soon' Lily's father said, apparently changing the subject, 'They always swoop in at this time of the evening. Sometimes, when I take my last swim of the day, they skim over my head to catch an insect or take a small sip of water. They're a delight.'

'I never imagined you would have a pool.' Lily looked at the small pool, almost hidden by the drop in the land.

'Did you not? You think I am such an old fossil?'

Lily laughed, 'You are an old fossil and you know it. But I'm so pleased you have put in a pool. The immense heat nearly makes it a necessity rather than a luxury.'

'So why did you need to be brought back to your senses?' Lily had been about to go for her last swim, but she stopped and looked at her father. Why did he pretend to ignore what she said and then return to the subject and catch her off guard? Why did he always do that?

'I thought you hadn't heard me, about your letter, I mean.'

'Of course I heard you, old fossil that I am apparently. I don't think there is any decline in my faculties. So?' Lily's father looked at her sternly, 'Are you going to tell me or are you going to go for a swim and leave me cliff-hanging?'

Lily sighed and sat down at the table again. Her father poured her another glass of cold white wine and waited.

'It all began with the end of my book. The last edited proof had gone to press and... well, I suppose I didn't know what to do with myself.'

'Oh dear, as a small child, you always were a little troublesome when you were bored. So what did you get up to?'

Lily relaxed and laughed and told her father nearly everything about her month long affair with the energetic Quentin

Howard. Her father listened quietly as she talked, making no comment until, finally, Lily sat silent and thoughtful.

'This Quentin certainly seems a dynamic force... but why did my letter cause you to end the affair?'

'As I said, it brought me back to my senses. Nothing in particular... it was one of your usual interesting letters and you mentioned reading about Battista Moroni. I had seen his portrait 'Il Sarto' at the National and was fascinated by the painted detail of the fabric... anyway, suddenly I had the germ of an idea for my next book.'

'Really? So soon? Don't you need an academic rest?'

'Well, that's it... I thought I did, but I really don't! I had a great time with Quentin but, suddenly, enough was enough. I was getting so bored with meeting the same people at the same functions. His life may be an academic one, but it is based on a circuit of lectures. In the autumn, he will be off all over the place lecturing... it's what he does and he probably does it brilliantly... he really is very charismatic but...'
'Look the swifts are gathering now. Are you going for your swim before supper? I've opened a rather good bottle of

Piancornello Brunello di Montalcino... you've drunk it
before and liked it... it has that intense nutty, dark chocolate
aroma and the taste is earthy but subtle, yes, a satisfying
long, intense finish... mmm. I'll light the barbecue and grill
some lamb with rosemary. You have your swim now.'

'You know what, Dad, you would have enjoyed meeting
Quentin... you could both have talked in wine language all
evening.' 'But it doesn't seem very likely I shall have that
pleasure and do you call me Dad only when you want to
tease me?'
'Correct on both points.' Lily laughed and ran down to the
pool and dived into the clear turquoise water as the swifts
dived and swooped.

Lily flexed her fingers and looked away from the laptop screen. She had read somewhere that it was beneficial to look into the distance, every so often, when working long hours at a computer screen. She sighed with pleasure as she looked across the terracotta rooftops to the distant view of rolling Tuscan hills. The sun was burning down from a cloudless blue sky but the room where she was working remained cool. On the third floor of a tall block of mediaeval houses, the shade was constant. A narrow gap in the houses opposite allowed her the glimpse of the distant landscape. It was one of the reasons she had chosen the apartment. She had known, as soon as the landlady showed her the spacious, shadowy rooms that it was perfect for the rest of her summer. Then, she had been lucky that there had been a cancellation and the landlady, a friendly woman, who Lily now knew as Signora Marelli, had been delighted with a two-month rental term. Lily had immediately signed the lease and given the deposit. Now, she had made a good beginning to her new manuscript. When she had left her father's house near Siena, she had driven north to Bergamo. Here she had spent an interesting week researching the life of Moroni... the man in the portrait that had inspired her to begin her new work. It had been one of life's chains of coincidence. Lily continued to gaze out of the window as she thought back to that day in the café. Not the day when she had read the newspaper dating advertisement, no, her thoughts hurriedly thrust away the memory of Quentin away... no, it was before that... the day she had seen the young man, yes, the barista who had looked so like the mediaeval man in the portrait. Why had he made such an impression on her? There had been something mesmeric in his burning gaze, the way he had looked at her, summing her up, his eyes so dark under his arched eyebrows. Lily allowed her memory to play back the moment, like a scene from a film. His hand outstretched toward her as he waited patiently for her to take her change. His smile, secret, slightly mocking. Lily was suddenly brought back to the real scene in front of her as she caught a glimpse of movement on the balcony directly opposite her own. She realised that she had been staring, she had no idea for how long... staring unknowingly at a young man who was looking at her from a gap between two louvred shutters... definitely looking at her. Lily looked down quickly at her table and stared at her screen, embarrassed and confused. But a voice called out, easily bridging the distance between the two balconies.

'Hi, do you speak English by any chance?' It was a strong voice with a distinctly American accent.
Lily looked up, unable to avoid replying.

'Yes, I am English, can I help you? I speak Italian.' She raised her voice but a Vespa passed at the same moment and her words were lost in the strident sound of the motor.

'Sorry, I didn't quite catch that... did you say you're English?'

'Yes,' Lily shouted and now as the road returned to silence her voice sounded unnecessarily loud, even angry.

'Wow, that's the first stroke of luck I've had since I arrived in Pis-wherever I am!' The man leant over the balcony toward her and Lily was aware that he was exceptionally tall. She just had time think that he was absolutely nothing like the man she had been dreaming about, the man so like the Moroni portrait, nor was he anything like Quentin. Yes, Quentin was tall but this man seemed to be a giant. Then, he was talking again, his soft, southern American accent, was it Texan... making him sound like a cowboy.

'Gee, I sure hope I didn't disturb you... I guess you were working... but I'm in such a fix.' He laughed then, a low soft laugh and Lily hastened to reply as she pulled herself out of her dreams.

'Sorry, I didn't mean to shout. Don't worry, I had finished working for a while anyway. What can I do to help you?'

'Well, as you have probably guessed, being typically American, I don't speak a word of the lingo. I arrived last night but my luggage doesn't seem to have caught up with me. I tried to explain to the hotel guy on reception but he doesn't speak much English. He's a nice guy and he offered to let me use the phone and all, but I had no idea what to do.' He shrugged, his broad shoulders flexing superman style muscles and then grinned. 'Don't worry, I'll sort something out later.'

'Would you like me to come down to the reception. I may be able to help.'

'Would you? Would you do that for me? That would be great.'

'I'll just put away my files and I'll be down in about ten minutes.' As Lily spoke, another Vespa passed below the balcony and her words were lost in the din. She waved and raised two hands to show ten fingers and the young man nodded and raised his hand in thanks and gave a little bow with his head.

Lily turned away from the window and began to carefully put away her work. She closed down her laptop and plugged it into recharge. All her movements were slow and careful but her mind was racing. Why had she agreed so readily to help this giant man? Obviously, it was the only polite thing to do, but she was well aware that it could lead to more than a few helpful words or a phone call to find his luggage. Anyway, she had absolutely no idea who he was or what he was doing in the quiet Tuscan town of Pistoia. He certainly didn't look like the average American tourist seeking culture. Now why should she think that? Lily lost herself for several moments wondering why the outward appearance of anyone should predispose of their nature or interests. Why shouldn't an over-muscled giant be interested in art and history? What was that thought she had the other day about someone living up to their names? Yes, it was the same theme... maybe she could work on it... Lily found herself gazing at her reflection in the bathroom mirror. Lost in her thoughts again, she had drifted around the flat, briefly washed her face and hands and now she had no idea how many minutes had passed by. Certainly more than ten, she was sure of that. She grabbed her bag and keys, ran out of the flat, down the long winding staircase and across the road.

Lily burst into the reception of the small hotel. Running in from the bright sunlight into the darkness of the small foyer she was momentarily blinded. As her eyes became accustomed to the light, she saw the tall young man sitting sprawled in an armchair at the side of the reception desk. He stood up as she entered and held out his hand to her. He really was a giant. Lily felt ridiculously small as she shook his hand. To her surprise, his large hand was cool and held hers lightly as they shook hands.

'This is truly kind of you, my name's Charlie, Charlie Woods, very pleased to meet you.'

'Lily Fairfax, pleased to meet you. How can I help?' Charlie Woods moved over to the reception desk where a small moustached man was waiting, hovering over the telephone with an anxious smile.

Lily spoke rapidly in Italian and then turned to Charlie,

'I've explained that your luggage hasn't arrived... where did you last see it?'

'Well, I landed in Rome, very jet-lagged, took an internal flight to Pisa, then took a taxi to this place... I just showed the driver the address I had on my phone... then I fell sound asleep but I guess it took a while or so... cost me a packet!

Then I fell out of the taxi here and went straight up to my room to sleep.' Charlie rubbed his eyes as though he was only just waking, 'I don't remember what happened about the luggage, except I had my backpack with me. Basically, that's it.'

'I see, well, I'm sure it will be somewhere. Anything valuable in it?'

'Not really, well, not to anyone else. All my kit is in it and I'm playing tomorrow night here. At least that's what it says on my itinerary. I thought it was Pisa... when I was first asked to play but then I realised it was this place, is it Pista something or other? Anyway, they were two different places.' Again, Charlie rubbed his eyes and then ran his fingers through his hair which was much too short to be ruffled.

'Hmm, I see...' Lily tried not to sigh as she realised she was probably talking to an American sportsman who had never travelled in Europe. What was it she had been thinking about preconceptions and judgements made from someone's outward appearance? Well, she would do her best to help the friendly giant and then retreat back to her quiet apartment. She spoke at some length to the receptionist and made several phone calls. Finally, she turned back to Charlie, who was now leaning on the reception desk, or rather, towering over it.

'Good news, we have found the taxi driver and he had already found your luggage in the boot of his car. He is very apologetic and says he will drive it over tomorrow morning as he has a fare coming near Pistoia. That's the best we can do for today.'

'Why that's brilliant!' Charlie raised his hand in a high five to the receptionist who practically cowered away. Charlie slapped the desk instead and said, '*Merci*, my man, thanks a bunch, I'm truly grateful.' Then he turned to Lily, grinning, 'Will you thank him for me?'

'Oh, I'm sure he understood you, Charlie. It's fine. He was just worried that you would need the bag tonight.' Lily decided not to mention that it was better to say '*grazie*' than '*merci*' when in Italy.

There didn't seem much point and Charlie's smile was lighting up the small reception. Even the lugubrious receptionist was now nodding and smiling. The giant then turned the full force of his dark eyes and sunny smile on to Lily,

'So, thank you, Lily Fairfax, I'm indebted to you. You just have to let me buy you lunch right now.'

'That would be great, thank you.'

Lily heard her own words with surprise. But then, she really was very hungry.

Lily looked across the table at Charlie, amazed at the amount of food he was consuming. The meal had begun with a simple antipasto of salami, thin slivers of prosciutto and olives, served on a wooden board with a basket of crusty bread. Lily had nibbled a few olives and a slice of salami and then watched as Charlie happily cleared the board, only stopping to ask her several times if she could eat more. Perhaps, she thought, he didn't realise that this was only a starter. When the large bowl of pasta arrived, redolent with a tomato sauce, Charlie had sighed with pleasure and begun to serve Lily with a large fork and ladle. He had perfect table manners and was very attentive in between his determined eating. When the main course arrived, Charlie had actually clapped his hands with delight at the sight of the large oval platter of roast meat and the bowl of green salad. By this time, Lily had given up eating and was chatting with a couple at the next table. She was pleased with any opportunity to speak Italian and found that the young couple was proud of the history of Pistoia, their hometown and interested in Lily's own studies. Finally, the waiter cleared the table as Charlie sat back in his chair with a contented grin.

'*Cosa vuole? Dolci? Tiramisu, cassata, gelati?*' The waiter looked at them hopefully. Lily shook her head firmly and was surprised and relieved to see that Charlie was also shaking his head.

'Won't you have a coffee, Lily?'

'Yes, I think I will... *un espresso, per favore,*' Lily smiled at the waiter and then looked to Charlie.

'No, no coffee for me, do you think you could order another bottle of water, though.'

The waiter disappeared with the order and Lily looked at Charlie in surprise,

'I've just realised you haven't touched the wine, do you always drink water?'

'No, I never touch wine. Don't worry, I'm not a recovering alky. I'm in training... I'm always in training but even more so this year.'
'So what is your sport?'

'I thought you'd have guessed... I'm a basketball player. In fact, this year I was nearly a basket case. I had a really bad injury on court nearly six months ago and I've been struggling to get back on form.'
Lily looked at him again in surprise. 'Well, you certainly look healthy and there's nothing wrong with your appetite. What happened to you?'

'Yeh, well, I may look fit to you but, believe me, I was struggling to walk just four months ago. I was jumping for a ball and a guy from the other team gave me a very unfriendly nudge on my shoulder. A push like that, when you're mid-air and fully stretched, makes you land real wrong. I came down like a ton of bricks and wrecked my kneecap.' Charlie winced at the memory, 'And that was curtains to my career with the San Diego Toreros.'

'That's so unlucky. It sounds like it was foul play.'

Charlie burst out laughing, 'Foul play it was indeed! I just love your English accent, Lily. You crack me up, foul play, I love it. Certainly in the bunch of big guys all going for the same ball there is a deal of rough stuff that the ref never gets to see... or take notice of anyway?'

'Goodness, how awful! I don't know how you can laugh about it.'

'Well, I guess it's the only thing to do. I mean, it's basketball, not war. Just a game. Anyway, I struggled through rehab physio and now I've come for a short tour in Italy... trying to get back to my form.'

'Well, that sounds very brave to me. I don't know how you can face going back on court.'

'I can't wait. I've been invited to play for Macerata, that's somewhere south of here but this week I'm joining them for a match here in Pistoia... or Pisa... or wherever we are.'

'Definitely Pistoia. If you want some mild exercise after all that food I could show you around the town if you like? If you don't mind the afternoon heat?'

Charlie looked at her in delight, smiled and nodded. Once again Lily had been surprised at her own words and pleased when Charlie replied quickly,

'That would be cool... I 'd really like that. Let's go.'

He called for the bill and quickly paid with a handful of euro notes that allowed for a generous tip. He brushed away Lily's attempt to pay her half and waited as she went in front of him to the door.

She was very aware of him as he followed her, but she managed to resist giving an extra wiggle to her walk.

Yes, Lily definitely liked this gentle giant who had bounced into her life.

Lily and Charlie spent a lazy afternoon wandering around the shady, cobbled streets of Pistoia. Lily soon realised that he was interested in everything although he had little or no knowledge of Italy, architecture, art or... practically anything that touched her own field of expertise.

'So would you call this mediaeval?' Charlie looked up at the bell tower looming above them. He raised his hand to shade his eyes from the bright sun and frowned. 'I've never seen anything like it... not ever.'

'Well...' Lily hesitated, wondering where to begin, 'it would have been built in the 12th or 13th centuries in Romanesque style.' Lily drew to a halt, disconcerted by the puzzled look that was crossing his face. Disconcerted, too, by a sudden strong feeling of desire as she felt the nearness of his athletic body. Was the afternoon heat and the after-effect of the wine at lunch making her like this? He was still frowning down at her,

'Do you mean this tower has been standing there for, what would that be, more than seven hundred years? Seven hundred?' Now his dark eyes were widened in amazement.

'Well, yes. I mean the whole piazza, this square, Il Duomo, that is the cathedral... all 12th and 13th century. The green and white marble baptistry...' Lily swivelled to point out the luminescent building running along the side of the piazza. Her arm brushed lightly against Charlie's shoulder and she felt a shiver run through her and a mad longing to throw her arms around him. She hurried to continue talking, 'er... yes, the baptistry is Gothic, of course.'

'Of course!' Charlie gave one of his low husky laughs and seemed oblivious to Lily's brush against him and their closeness. 'You make me die, Lily Fairfax, how on earth would I know that was Gothic. I thought Gothic was something to do with girls wearing black crosses and too much make-up. But it's too hot out here for you... we'd better find some shade.'

'We could go into the cathedral?' Lily said although every part of her body was telling her to ask him back to her cool, shady apartment.

'Go in? Would that be allowed?' Charlie was now looking slightly alarmed.

'Of course, you must see the Della Robbia terracottas and there's some amazing silver work by the master craftsman, Jacopo.' 'I knew that, of course!' Charlie laughed again and rested his arm lightly on her shoulder. 'Lead on, I am your willing student.'
Now, trying to ignore the warmth of his skin against the back of her neck, Lily resolved to remain in tour guide mode.

They walked across the square and entered the cool silence of the cathedral. Nothing stirred, it was as though the whole world, apart from them, was asleep and avoiding the afternoon heat. They walked down the long centre aisle, their soft footsteps sounding loud in the stillness. Charlie whispered,

'You know, religious places sort of spook me out. I must have a guilty conscience or something. I always feel like the hand of God is ready to strike me down. Do you get that feeling?'

Lily suppressed a giggle, 'Well, not really but then I've been visiting churches all my life. Of course, the height of the vaulted ceilings, the tall columns, the vastness... all of it was designed to create a feeling of awe or even fear. I don't think it necessarily means you have a guilty conscience.'

'I hope not. I mean, I've never knowingly done wrong.' Lily glanced up at Charlie's face. It seemed his emotions were always flickering across his face, and now he looked thoughtful and rather sad.

'Let's continue the art tour another time.' She said, suddenly feeling that maybe Charlie had suffered quite enough cultural shock for one afternoon. He stopped in his tracks and smiled.

'Okay! Now, my turn to lead the tour. I have an idea for what we could do next. Follow me!' He turned and strode back down the aisle. Lily had to run to catch up with him. She, too, had a very good idea of what they could do next.

Less than ten minutes later they were sitting eating ice creams in a *gelateria* on the other side of the piazza. Charlie slowly spooned his lemon sorbet into his mouth and sighed with satisfaction.

'I spotted this place as we came into the square. Even my poor language skills can recognise an ice cream bar, especially as it had a large cone of ice cream painted over the door. Is that what you would call a fresco?'

Lily laughed and wondered if this American giant was quite as uneducated in art and architecture as he pretended.

'Yes, Charlie, absolutely... definitely twenty-first-century fresco. Oh my, this pistachio ice is simply divine.'

Lily closed her eyes as the fragrant, cold sorbet melted slowly in her mouth and slid down her throat. When she opened her eyes, she found that Charlie was looking at her intensely. His eyes seemed darker than ever and his eyebrows were drawn together, drawing a jet-black line across his forehead. Suddenly, she knew that they would soon be in bed together.

The late afternoon sun was slanting through a narrow gap in the shutters. Lily stirred, she looked at Charlie lying stretched out beside her, every contour of his muscled body golden in the shaft of light. She rested her hand gently over the long vertical scar on his left knee, the only blemish on his body. He opened his eyes and turned toward her.

'Lily Fairfax,' he murmured, 'who would have thought it? Pleased to meet you!' He reached out a hand and gently smoothed her wild hair away from her face. Lily smiled and stretched her arms above her head,

'Charlie Woods, *il piacere è tutto mio*.'
'*El placer fue todo mío*.'
'You speak Spanish?' Lily sat up in bed and looked at Charlie in surprise.
'Did you think I just had a good sun tan? I'm half Mexican. My Ma was from Chihuahua that makes me a gringo... although I prefer coconut.'

'Coconut? How come?'

'Strong and dark on the outside and sweet and white on the inside. But you, Lily Fairfax, you're just sweet through and through.'

'Do you really think I'm sweet?'

'I do... but my, you sure are wild. That little innocent girl face, your rosy cheeks, your mass of golden red hair... that's all a cover... you're a wild tigress, aren't you? I began to see it when I looked into your green cat's eyes.'

'Me, wild? Certainly not, Charlie Wood... I live a quiet, sheltered academic life in Cambridge.'

'Then I'm sure glad I met you in the heat of Tuscany. I was feeling real sorry for myself until I saw you from my balcony.'

'Well, I'm real glad you lost your luggage or we'd never have met.'

'Exactly, but I wasn't feeling sorry about that, really. I mean, I'll be pleased to get it back, but I had begun to think that bad luck was dogging me, following me from San Diego. After my knee accident, it was real hard not to sink into gloom. Worse of all is the constant nagging thought that I am letting my Pa down.'

'How come, it wasn't your fault you were injured.'

'No, I know, but he had set so much store on my being a superstar on court. It was all going so well... I was earning megabucks... well, it seemed like megabucks to us. My Pa and I lived on the breadline for a long time. He coaches basketball at the uni, but it doesn't pay that well. He stuck it because of me, really. Basketball is his life.'

'What about your mother?'

'Oh, well, I don't remember her at all. She died when I was about four or so. A hit and run accident. Poor Pa, I guess he never really got over it... I think she was the driving force in the relationship and he was lost without her. Then he drank too much for a while and I was shipped out to live with an aunt in Mexico. One day, when I was about eight, he just drove up in an old Caddie, out of the blue, and off we went together. From then on it was just us against the whole world. Us and basketball.'

'I can understand that, my mother died just after I was born. I suppose it wasn't really the same, I mean, we weren't poor.' Lily thought for a moment, seeing in her mind's eye, the quiet Sundays she had spent with her father, reading and writing in his study. 'So it was very different... but yes, it was very much the feeling of me and my father against the rest of the world. You put it very well, Charlie. That's exactly how it felt.'

'Poor little Lily child. To be so very feminine and yet not to have a Ma to be there for you.' Charlie looked at her, his dark eyes searching her face, 'And now? Do you still struggle to make your way?'

Lily shook her head, her hair flying and catching the sunlight, 'No, not at all. I've made my own life and it is pretty much how I want it to be... especially now you have taught me how to be wild!'
Lily laughed and threw herself on top of him. She ran her fingers over his broad shoulders and he put his hands around her waist and held her close, lifting his head from the pillow and covering her neck and breasts with kisses. 'I don't know what happened earlier.' He mumbled, his voice almost lost as he pressed his lips against her skin.'

'It didn't matter. You certainly made up for a slow start!' Lily replied, her breath coming unevenly as she returned his kisses, her body aching again with desire.

'You were just too beautiful for me, you took my breath away and all my strength. Never happened to me before... for a while I just couldn't do it.' Now Charlie was kissing the soft skin beneath her breasts, one hand stroking her hair. Then, in a quick easy move, he rolled Lily over and put his other hand under her back, raising her slightly from the bed.

Lily was panting now as his hungry mouth worked its way down her body. 'It didn't take you long to recover, anyway... and you didn't stop after that...' Then she cried out with pleasure, her body arching upwards, her hands reaching for Charlie, pulling him to her as the sun went down and twilight fell.

'If my luggage doesn't turn up tomorrow, I shall have to do some shopping... and, believe me, with my size that doesn't come easy.' Charlie looked around the restaurant and grinned, 'I feel like a giant amongst Italian men.'

'You are a giant, Charlie, but I suppose your height is not so unusual in the States.'

'I sure hope there are some big guys on the Macerata team.'
'How does it work... are you playing for them now?'
'Just a temporary stretch, I hope. My manager in San Diego arranged it all. Players do get drafted and traded. My all-star status dropped to zero after my accident, but I'm lucky that they seem to think I'll climb back up again. Anyway, I just signed on the dotted, pleased to get anything. It will be a different level of play, just *Legadue*... it's really part of my rehab programme.'

'Sounds awful to me. I'm sure if I had an injury like yours I'd give up altogether.'

'Nah, you wouldn't, Lily Fairfax, you'd grit your teeth and go for it. Don't forget I know your wild tigress side.'

Lily blushed and picked up the menu to cover her embarrassment, 'I think we'd better order...'

Charlie laughed and took her hand in his, 'You're so cute, Lily, cute and wild all in one. Now, I could eat my way through the entire menu. What are you going to nibble at?

'I shall have the *insalata caprese* and then the *spaghetti alla vongole*, and I won't be nibbling, I'm ravenous.'

'I think you have that word wrong... and you a Cambridge lady, the word is ravishing not ravenous.' Charlie leaned toward her, one hand holding hers over the table and the other resting lightly on her knee. 'I could ravish you right now, in fact.'

'Behave yourself, Charlie, we'll be chucked out of the restaurant. I thought you were starving?'

Charlie sighed deeply and pulled a sad face as he sat back in his chair and picked up the menu. 'Ok, to business, I'll have exactly what you're having followed by any sort of T-bone steak and salad.'

'That will be a lot to eat, are you sure? And do you even know what I'm having, do you understand the Italian?'

'Not at all, but I eat everything, so no problem. Now, what will you drink? I guess if your father is a wine buff you must take the juice of the grape very seriously.'

'Yes, I suppose I do,' Lily hesitated for a moment, thinking about the meals she had shared so recently with Quentin, the long deliberation about which wines would complement each course. 'But you know, I am very happy with a carafe of the house wine. What about you?'

'Oh no, I never touch alcohol, just water for me, preferably not the fizzy stuff, but I don't really care. I know you'd like to get me tipsy so that you can have your wicked way with me later.'

Lily laughed and nodded, but before she could reply the waiter appeared at their table and they gave their order. The meal passed slowly as they talked and laughed, flirted and ate enormous quantities of food. The waiter was impressed with the way Charlie ate his way through the very large Florentine steak. They both refused desserts and once again, Charlie insisted on paying the bill.

'I think we should at least take it in turns or go halves.' Lily said as they left the restaurant.

'No way, I'm just an old-fashioned guy,' Charlie laughed and kissed the top of Lily's head, 'An old-fashioned guy with an expense account, don't worry, Lily my Iove, I'm no longer the impoverished gringo.'

They walked along the cobbled street toward the piazza. The moon was high in the night sky and the air still warm.

'What a night!' Charlie ran ahead, bouncing high in the air.

Lily raised her voice and called after him, "*The moon shines bright: in such a night as this, when the sweet wind did gently kiss the trees"*...'

Charlie stood still and then turned back toward her, 'That's so beautiful... how do you know stuff like that? Is it Wordsworth or something... do you know it by heart or did you make it up?'

'Shakespeare,' Lily took his hand as they began to walk together again, 'Merchant of Venice, a speech by Lorenzo, Act V, Scene I, to be precise.'

'We really don't have much in common, do we, Lily? Our lives are so different.'

'Does that matter? Maybe it's a good thing.' Lily leaned against Charlie, feeling his strength beside her, 'Shall we find somewhere for a coffee or... ?'

'Or could we go back to your apartment?' Charlie put his arm around Lily's waist and held her close to him.

'I do have plenty of coffee at the apartment.' Lily looked up at Charlie, her green eyes sparkling in the moonlight. Then, suddenly, Charlie swooped her up in his arms and ran, carrying her as easily as though she was a child. Lily shrieked with laughter, wriggling helplessly and kicking her legs. Then, realising that people were standing back and laughing at them, some even clapping, she rested her head against Charlie's chest and gave in to his overpowering strength.

Lily awoke and heard voices in the street below. She lazily
stretched out an arm, feeling for Charlie. She opened her
eyes, Charlie had gone. It was so very unlike her not to wake
at the slightest sound or movement that she could hardly
believe it. She threw back the rumpled sheets and, throwing
a cotton robe around her shoulders, she went to the window.
The sun was already high in the sky and as she peered down
through the louvred shutter, she could see Charlie standing
in the street talking to a taxi driver. Lily smiled in
amusement as she heard him enthusiastically thanking the
man in Spanish. The driver was nodding and smiling and
obviously trying to get back into his taxi and drive away.
Charlie stood surrounded by luggage, searching in the
pockets of his shorts. Then, producing a wad of euros he
pressed the notes into the driver's hand. The driver made a
good attempt at refusal and then quickly pocketed the
money. Finally, Charlie stood back on the pavement and
waved as the taxi drove away. Lily opened the shutters a few
inches and called down,

'So, your luggage arrived then.'
Charlie looked up and smiled and blew her a kiss.
'*Buenos Dias*, Lily Fairfax.'
'*Buon Giorno*, Charlie Woods, how are you?'
'I'm better than I have ever been in my entire life... *como te
va*?'
'*Benissimo, grazie*! Would you like me to teach you Italian?'
'I'd like you to teach me anything, anything at all. Now, I've
been for my run... how about breakfast? See you down here
in half an hour? I'll have a quick shower and find some
proper clothes.'

'*Benissimo, a presto!*' Lily blew Charlie a kiss and turned
away from the window. She felt a bubble of excitement at
the prospect of breakfast with Charlie. She looked down at
the table under the window and her work, the files that had

remained untouched since the moment she had seen Charlie on the balcony opposite. She considered opening her laptop to check her emails and then shrugged. Why? She was on holiday and work was only an option, after all.

Just over half an hour later, Lily ran down the winding staircase from her apartment, anxious not to keep Charlie waiting for his breakfast... anxious to be with him again. At the last turn of the stairs, she almost ran into him as he was in the hall, just coming up to find her.

'Sorry, Charlie, I'm late!' Lily stood and stared at Charlie. Even with the extra height of the stairs she was still no way near his level. She looked up at him and almost blinked. This was a different style Charlie. No longer wearing shorts and a t-shirt, but dressed immaculately in a dazzling white shirt and dark navy trousers.

'Oh, my! You look so different with clothes on!' The words slipped out before Lily could think, and they both laughed. Charlie held out his arms wide and turned in front of her,

'Why thank you, ma'am, I'm hoping that's a compliment.' Charlie bowed in front of her and then held his arms wide again. Lily jumped, from the stair above, straight at him, her legs encircling his waist and he held her easily and spun around the small hall until she was dizzy.

'Stop, stop, put me down now.' Lily laughed and something in her memory clicked. Could she recall her father carrying her like this and dancing? She closed her eyes for a moment and saw herself, as though in playback, carried by her father as they danced at a festival. Yes, that was it... a carnival night in some southern Italian village. Everyone dancing under the stars and her father picking her up to join the celebrations. The memory lasted less than a few seconds, but it was vivid and clear. Lily opened her eyes as Charlie lowered her to the floor. She stood for a moment, still giddy with the movement and the reeling memory. She felt a wave of happiness wash over her and a complete sense of childlike liberty. She took Charlie's large hand in her own and led the way out into the sunlight of the street.

'Let's find breakfast. I'm ravenous again and I know you must be.'

'You're always ravishing my dear, Lily Fairfax, knock-down ravishingly ravenous. I have to confess I had an early breakfast at six when I went for a run, I found this bar where market guys were eating. But that seems an age ago now. You're right, I am hungry. Somehow, it's not just for food... it's for you and everything in this beautiful life.'

'Likewise.' Lily said quietly, as they walked the length of the street, hand in hand. When they reached the piazza, they found the usual calm space bustling with activity. Market day had come to Pistoia. The large square was packed with stalls under blue and white striped canvas awnings. Lily and Charlie stood for a moment, on the edge of the activity, watching.

'Wow, the place has certainly filled up since I was running through early this morning. There were just a few vans and men unloading fruit and veg then, this is a huge market.'

'You must have been up really early... I can't believe I didn't hear you leave me.'

'I crept away at first light. It was a wrench, I can tell you, you looked so sweet curled up tight, your glorious hair spread over my pillow. But...' Charlie sighed, 'I have to keep running and building up my left leg muscles. Can't do that in a horizontal position, unfortunately!'

'How is your knee this morning?' Lily asked as they began to wander around the edge of the market, 'Is it painful?'

'Oh yeah, agony most of the time but it eases up a bit after half an hour of running and then starts to ache again as I get near an hour. Just have to keep going.'

'How awful, I'd never be able to do that.'

'Yeah, I bet you would if that was your field of work. I guess it's like ploughing on with more and more research if you are writing a thesis.'

'That's true, actually. Sometimes I do feel like giving up on a topic and then sort of force myself to read a bit more and then, suddenly, it gets interesting again. I try to explain that to my students. Maybe I'll use the analogy of your knee injury in the future. It sort of graphically spells it out. Yes, very good.' Lily was almost thinking aloud and then stayed silent for a moment while she considered the matter.

'Glad to be of any academic assistance, Doc. So tell me, do you have students then? Aren't you a bit young to be a university professor?'

'Oh, I'm the child prodigy of my college in Cambridge.'

'Really? I'm impressed but not surprised... you do have a quiet confidence... when you're not being a wild tigress, that is!' Charlie smiled down at her and then pointed across the square, 'I ran that way this morning, and I think I passed a good place for breakfast. Shall we see if we can find something to eat? Then I'd like to hear all about your life and work in Cambridge.'

The café that Charlie had noticed earlier was thronging with people, mostly drinking coffee.

'Do you think they'll serve a proper breakfast here?' Charlie stood in the doorway, filling the frame and looking around doubtfully.

'Well, I don't think you'll find bacon and eggs sunny side up or whatever... shall I go and ask what they have?' Lily threaded her way through the busy café, everyone turning to stare at her and across at the Charlie. It was obviously a very popular bar with the Pistoian locals. The barista turned from the espresso machine and looked at her enquiringly. He seemed surprised that she spoke fluent Italian and very soon he was smiling and offering to cook a breakfast, especially for Charlie.

'*Il campione di basket? No? Bravo, bravo …. piacere! Si accomodi, prego, è un grande onore!*'

In a moment, a table was cleared in the centre of the small café and Lily and Charlie were seated and surrounded by excited Italians, all asking questions at the same time. Lily began to translate, but Charlie just smiled and shook his head, and patted his stomach to demonstrate that he was hungry. This caused a gale of laughter and shouts to the barista to hurry up with the food.

Lily looked across the table to Charlie, 'It seems your reputation has gone ahead of you. Everyone seems to know who you are and what you're doing here. I even heard someone ask if your luggage had turned up.'

'I guess I'm a big fish in a small pool. My size makes it pretty obvious from the start, and that's before I open my mouth. I don't think this is going to be the place for a quiet chat... I wanted to hear more about your work.'

Before she could reply, a huge, oval plate was laid in front of Charlie. He looked down at the large folded omelette, grilled tomatoes, mushrooms and slices of prosciutto with great satisfaction. 'Excuse me, Lily, I may not talk for a while... this looks like a serious breakfast. Perfect! You just nibble your cake thingy and sip your cappuccino. This is man's work.'

Lily thanked the barista and roughly translated Charlie's words. There was more laughter and a round of applause when Charlie took his first mouthful, then the crowd around them dispersed and left them to eat

13

'I've just remembered, the receptionist at my hotel gave me this envelope this morning.' Charlie held up a white envelope. He was standing on the balcony of Lily's apartment, a towel draped around his hips and drinking from a bottle of water. The sun was sinking again behind the rooftops and the room was filled with a soft golden light. Lily was lying in bed, half asleep and half admiring Charlie's silhouette.

'What is it?' She asked sleepily and without much interest.

'I guess it's an invitation. It's in Italian, of course, perhaps you'd better read it later?'

He came back into the room and threw the envelope onto the bedside table. 'It's time you woke up, anyway, you've been asleep for hours.'

'I certainly have not!' Lily replied, yawning. 'I can remember perfectly well what we were doing less than an hour ago.'

'Me too, sweet Lily, no, come to think of it, I think you had better remind me.' He looked down at her with a wicked smile.

Lily rolled over onto her back and spread her arms above her head, 'Does this remind you?' Then she rolled over again and looked back at him over her shoulder, her long hair falling across her face. 'Or this?' Suddenly she sprang out of bed and pulled the towel away from his body, and she put her arms around his waist. 'Oh, it seems you do remember, Charlie.'

'Lily, you are such a wicked girl, whatever shall I do with you?'

'Whatever you like, whatever you like.' Lily pressed kisses onto the smooth skin of his chest, she felt him shudder and then he ran his hands down the length of her back. For a moment, they held each other close and then fell back on the bed.

Only a few days and nights together but already they sensed each other's needs, and there was now a strong rhythm to their love- making.
The sky was dark when Lily next woke and once again found that Charlie had disappeared.
'How does such a large man move so quietly?' She spoke the words aloud to the empty room and then went into the shower. The warm water ran over her body, easing the ache in her muscles from their love-making. She slowly massaged shampoo into her hair, all the time thinking of Charlie. Should she be worried about falling into this unlikely romance? Was it a romance, was it an affair or was it something more? The intelligent side of her brain reminded her that they had so little in common and that he did live on the other side of the Atlantic. He was in Italy to recover from an injury and, naturally, he would be returning to San Diego as soon as he was properly fit. Lily rinsed her hair, running the cold water to refresh herself. She massaged her aching shoulders and smiled at the idea of Charlie being fitter than he was now. How could that be possible? So, was this an archetypical holiday fling for them both? Her brain was telling her that was what it had to be... but her body was saying something quite different. She dried herself quickly and dressed in a short silk dress and put on her highest heels. At least she could try to be as tall as she could. She stopped in front of the long, cheval mirror that stood by the door. Her wet hair was pulled back into a tight knot, and her skin glowed with the beginning of a tan. She knew she looked good, and she was longing to be with Charlie again. Strange that she had no thought in her head that he would not be waiting for her, ready to spend the evening and night with her. That was it, she suddenly smiled at her reflection, yes, she trusted Charlie implicitly.

And Charlie was waiting, sitting on the bottom stair. He looked up as she ran down to him.

'Wow, you look so beautiful, Lily. I was just coming up to find you when I heard you close your front door. 'I read that invite again while you were still sleeping. It looks to me like an invitation to dinner. It's from a Paulo Marinotti... I know the name from my transfer contract. I think he's the president or something of a group of Italian basketball teams.' He passed the envelope to Lily and kissed her lightly on her forehead.

Lily took the gilt-edged card out of the envelope and read it through quickly and then looked at Charlie. 'But it's for tonight and this Paulo is sending a car to collect you at seven-thirty. That's now!'

Charlie stood up slowly, 'Well, do you want to go?'
'But I'm not invited, the invitation is to you.'
'Well, that doesn't matter... of course, you can come with me... but do you want to go?'
Lily hesitated for a moment, 'Well, actually by a strange coincidence it seems that Paulo Marinotti lives in Villa Riveno, just outside of Pistoia. I've been intending to write to ask to see some of their artwork... research for my book. There are a couple of important Renaissance portraits at the villa... but of course, it is privately owned so I was waiting to make the right approach. Do you think I could go along with you?'

Before Charlie could answer they heard the low throb of a car pulling to a halt outside the porch. They looked at each other and smiled.
'Sounds like a car outside right now!' Charlie held out his hand, 'Shall we accept?'
'Why not? Sounds like fun to me!'
They walked hand in hand out to the street and saw a large black limousine filling the narrow cobbled road. The

uniformed driver jumped out of the car when he saw them and held open the back door.

'Signor Woods?' The man touched his cap and gave a little bow as Charlie moved forward. '*Sono l'autista per Signor Marinotto. Benvenuto a Pistoia.*'

Charlie looked at Lily, 'It's the car to take us to the villa, right?'

'Just so.' Lily slipped into the back seat and moved across, '*Buona sera, grazie.*'

Charlie sat beside her and the car pulled quickly away, filling the small road with the noise of its large engine.

Lily looked at Charlie, 'Do you always get driven around in limos, then?'

Charlie grinned, 'When I'm not driving my Lamborghini, you mean? Well, being a basketball star, even an injured one, has to have some compensations.'

'I suppose it's like being a top footballer in England. Do you have lots of fans?'

'Sure thing, whole gangs of beautiful women chasing me from dawn to dusk.' Charlie laughed at Lily's shocked face. 'Just teasing, Lily Fairfax, just kidding. I live the life of a monk in San Diego. As far as the perks go... I try to trade as much as I can for real money. I'm saving hard for my retirement and just worried that this injury will put me back a year.'

'Your retirement? When would that be likely?'

'Hard to say, but I don't want to go on after my mid-thirties. I have a scheme to open my own gym and basketball training centre for kids in San Diego.'

'Really, that's quite an ambition. Of course, you said your father was a coach, didn't you. Is that what gave you the idea?'

'Not really, my Pa works as a coach in university and the kids there are generally fairly well-heeled. I want to be able to offer coaching to kids with talent who don't usually get noticed.'

'Did you get spotted when you were young?'

'Well, my Pa always pushed me, of course, and I scraped into university mainly on my sporting talent. I took a degree in sports science and just scraped through that too. I never really got into academic studies. Not like you. So you were a child genius then?'

'Absolutely!' Lily laughed and rested her head back on the soft leather head-rest of the car. She thought again about the differences between her and Charlie... but also the things they did have in common. 'I suppose my father pushed me, too, in his own way. And, of course, that neither of us had mothers around make us special to our fathers. I was, well, still am, everything to my father. I think I learnt more in the holidays than I did at school. Although he worked in wine-importing, he was always wrapped up in history. He read and read and I suppose I automatically did the same. By the time it came to taking exams I was just way ahead of my age group.'

'You make it sound so easy but for someone who takes a long while to read a single page... well, you just can't imagine. So, how did it all end up? What do you do in Cambridge now?'

'Well, I'm officially Dr Fairfax, I have what is called a chair, which just means a post at my college. I supervise a few research students... and I have just finished my first book and sent the final edit to my publishers. I have a two-book deal, but I thought I needed a break from academia. I was feeling bored and boring.'

'You could never be boring, sweet Lily, never. Uh-uh! Looks like we've arrived.'

Lily looked out the window as the car swept through grand wrought iron gates and up a straight drive leading to an impressive villa.
'So we have,' agreed Lily, 'Villa Riveno, a perfect example of Palladian architecture, symmetry, perspective... all the qualities of the formal classical temple architecture of the ancient Greeks and Romans... do you want to know more?'

'I don't think so.' Charlie grinned at Lily, 'You lost me after 'architecture'. But I hope they have those old paintings you're so keen to see.'

'I'm sure they're here, but anyway, Charlie, we'll have a good time.'

'It did say dinner invite, didn't it? I'm starving!' 'Oh Charlie, you're always starving.'
'And you're always ravishing, my sweet Lily!'

14

'That was a splendid evening! Thank you so much for taking me along, Charlie. It was just so lucky.'

Charlie passed Lily a cup of take-away coffee. 'Careful, it's very hot. Yeah, and Mrs Marinotti seemed pleased to show off her old paintings. Were they what you expected to find?'

Lily sipped her coffee and thought back to the evening at the Villa Riveno. Charlie had taken his coffee out onto the balcony and was sitting looking back into the room and at her. He had returned from his early morning run with coffee for them both. The paintings in the Villa library had, in fact, been more interesting than she had expected.

'Oh yes, more than I expected. They have a wonderful collection in the library... and what a room. You should have come to see.'
'I guess, but I was involved with Mr Marinotti and his friend.

They spoke good English, but I struggled to understand what they were saying.'

'What do you mean?'

'Well, I think they were making me an offer... trying to outbid Macerata.'

'Is that possible? Isn't it all fixed with Macerata already?'

'Fixed is probably the key word. Anyway, I called my agent, Sam, early this morning.' Charlie laughed, 'Sam was just about to have dinner in a beach restaurant. Must have been about nine in the evening there. Sam's sure worried now that there might be some more money floating around me.'

'It sounds like they're haggling over you.'

'That's about it, and I'm a risky commodity. Could go well or could go very wrong.' Charlie slapped his knee, 'All depending on my kneecap.'

'How was it this morning?'

'Maybe just a little better. Hard to say.' Charlie turned away from Lily and looked down at the street. She could sense that he didn't want to talk about it any further.

'Signora Marinotti, well, she asked me to call her Flavia, anyway, Flavia said we could go and swim in the pool at their Villa today... if we wanted. Maybe it would be good for your knee?'

'That was nice of her but... I don't know, I have to be careful, Lily. I can't be seen to take any favours until this business is settled. Better not, if you don't mind.'

'No, of course, I don't mind. But... I think it was just a friendly invitation.'

'Yeah, sure you're right, but I'd rather wait and hear back from my agent. I just play the game with the ball and my agent sorts out everything else. It's how it works best.'

'Of course, anyway, I only said I'd call Flavia if we were going there today. But I'll write a card thanking her for dinner.'

'Fine, but post it tomorrow when I know what's happening.'

'Really?' Lily was about to say that it would only be polite to thank the Marinottis when she decided to stay silent. Charlie seemed to be worried that there was some hidden agenda. She thought again about the evening. They had certainly been wined and dined in extravagant style.

'Do you know the best moment of the whole wonderful evening?' She looked at Charlie, smiling suddenly at the memory. 'You know when they poured the champagne, and you asked for water instead...'

'Well, I never drink alcohol, you know that.'

'I know, but then you held out your champagne glass of sparkling water and when they raised their glasses in a toast, you suddenly sprang into the air and dinged the glass of that amazing chandelier. I don't know how you did it? It's so high up and you just touched the bottom crystal drop with the rim of your glass. It was amazing!'

'Well, I guess I was showing off a bit. I didn't want them to think I couldn't jump with this knee... or maybe I just didn't think at all. I don't know, I saw you across the room looking so beautiful, somehow in your right frame. Surrounded by all the Italian stuff, you know, antiques and everything. You looked fabulous, and I suddenly felt so happy. I guess I was jumping with joy.'

'You do say the loveliest things, Charlie. I'm so glad you can still jump... especially if it is with joy. Let's not worry about the Marinottis today, then. Maybe we should go swimming anyway? I could ask around and find out where we could go?'

'Good idea. You know, I'm supposed to be staying at some five star joint on the outskirts of Pistoia. I have the name of the hotel on my iPad. I'll go and get it. We could go there for lunch and a swim.' Charle swallowed the last of his coffee and came in from the balcony. 'What do you think, my beautiful Lily?'

'Lily stretched, 'I think it sounds a grand idea, but I was just wondering why you're staying in a two-star pensione when you were booked in at a five-star hotel.'

'Don't worry about it! It's all part of my plan to save money. Sam came to some arrangement that worked well for everyone. The great thing about Italy is that anything can be fixed.'

'I'm sure you're right.' Lily snuggled down into the bed. 'By the way, if there is an auction going for your body, can I put in a bid?'
Charlie laughed and came over to the side of the bed and looked down at Lily, 'You're already the highest bidder, Lily Fairfax.' He sat down next to her and took her in his arms and began to kiss her neck and shoulders. 'Shall we swim later today?' His voice was muffled as he rested his head between her breasts and circled her waist with his hands. Lily wanted to answer but her heart was beating so fast and her breath uneven. Her body was on fire at his touch, and there was nothing in her world except desire for Charlie. Was this love? All her emotions were jangling and vibrating as they moved in rhythm together. Was it just his powerful physical strength that overtook her every thought?
Later, much later, they lay side by side on the bed their hands linked.

'What am I to do about you, Charlie? You have taken me over? I feel like a puppet and you are holding the strings.'

'Nonsense, Lily Fairfax. You are the one in control. I am lost every time I look at you. How will I ever be able to play basketball? You wreck me?'

'Now you really are talking nonsense. Wreck... you are joking. You will kill me with your love-making. I'm permanently exhausted and yet wanting more. Now, please, go back to your own little hotel and leave me to have a shower.'

'You don't really want to shower all on your own, do you? I could soap your back, shampoo your beautiful hair and...'

'Stop, Charlie, stop it!' Lily rolled away from Charlie, giggling helplessly. Suddenly Charlie scooped her off the bed and carried her into the shower. Still holding her in one arm, he turned on the water. Lily screamed and laughed as the cold water streamed down over them. Charlie let her slowly down onto her feet and she stood with her back to him, resting her head back against his chest.

He began to gently shampoo her hair and then, the lather running over her body, he began to massage her shoulders. Lily closed her eyes and let the water course through her hair as her hands reached for Charlie. It was true, what she had said before, she was always wanting more of him.

15

The pool stretched to a glorious infinity, clear turquoise under the brilliant Tuscan sun. Lily and Charlie were stretched out on sun-loungers under the shade of a large cream canvas parasol.

'I could get very used to this,' Lily said sleepily, 'it's so heavenly it's wicked.' At that moment, a waiter hovered, holding a silver tray laden with a jug of fruit juice and a platter of canapés. Lily sat up and cleared a space on the slatted table at her side.

'*Grazie*!' She managed the one word before the waiter discreetly disappeared again. 'Oh my, and I thought it couldn't get any better. Look, Charlie, such delicious little canapés... olives, salami and some sort of cheese pastry thingummys. Mmm, delicious.'

'Did they leave a menu?' Charlie looked at the tray with a sigh, 'I need a lot more than whatever these little fancies are?'

'Yes, there's a lunch menu, too. But won't it be frightfully expensive?'

'Frightfully! You make me die, Lily, Such a great word... frightfully. Anyways, I'm frightfully hungry so pass it over, please.'

'But what about your plan to save money? I thought that was why you didn't stay here in the first place.'

'True, but I have the feeling I won't be picking up any bills in Pistoia from now on. My agent sent text to say that new negotiations were well under way. Mr Marinotti is very keen, very keen indeed to hire me now.'

'Really? That's good news, isn't it? But I thought you were playing your first match for Macerata here on Saturday.'

'Yeah, I was... but it looks like I may be playing against them now.'

'Goodness, how complicated. I can't begin to understand how it all works.'

'Me neither, but I don't let it worry me. Sam, my agent, gets a cut and has to earn it. That's my angle. Surely there must be similar plots in the undercurrent of your academic life in Cambridge?'
Lily was silent for a moment, thinking about it.

'I suppose so, in a way,' she said hesitantly, still trying to form her thoughts on the matter, 'I mean, there is a definite hierarchy, of course. There are what you would call stars and minor stars. At the moment, my star is flying high as I have a lucrative publishing deal. Also, I write what are called 'opinion pieces' for newspapers like the Times and the Telegraph. I've been offered an art documentary slot on BBC 2... stuff like that makes me flavour of the month. Maybe flavour of the year, but I don't dare take it too seriously as I could well be a shooting star. Public opinion can be fickle. Next year, I've been invited to Yale, but I haven't made up my mind yet.'

'Our careers are strangely similar and yet totally different. I just know that I want to get out while I'm at the top and start my own business. But for you, I guess you can always write or teach... it's not like you risk injury or just get too old.'

'True, I suppose, but I think your idea of your own gym is a fantastic challenge. I'm not sure how long I shall want to teach. Frankly some of my students bore me to tears. I have one guy, he is the typical perennial Ph.D. student. I truly believe he doesn't want to finish his thesis and grow up and enter the real world. Then, there are some of my colleagues who hang onto their students as a reason to be alive and kicking in the department. I think I'd get jaded staying as a doctor in residence at my college. As for the writing... I've been very confused about that recently. Very recently, actually.'

'What do you mean?

'Well, I had the germ of an idea, something my father mentioned in a letter. I was going to continue my theme of bringing to life a person in a mediaeval portrait. My first title is 'The Florentine Virgin'... and then...'

'Wow, that's a hell of a title. Is it as racy as it sounds, Lily?'

'Quite... it's about a very young girl called Engeldruda. Of course, she's the one Boccaccio described as a famous beauty.'

Charlie laughed aloud and helped himself to a cheese pastry. 'Sweet Lily, I love the way you assume I'll even know who the Bocatchy guy is... never mind what... he wrote.'

'Sorry, sorry... I get carried away. Anyway, let's eat... you're hungry and I'm sure you haven't eaten nearly enough yet today.'

'True, but just tell me why you feel confused.'

'Well, I had it almost sorted in my mind. I was going to write about a man this time, based on a beautiful portrait by Moroni, called 'Il Sarto', it means 'The Tailor'. I was very drawn to the man in the portrait. The way he held his large scissors and looked out of the frame, sort of judging your size.'

'I feel quite jealous of the man. I'm glad he must have died several centuries ago.'

Lily laughed but at the same time had a flash of memory. The young barista in Cambridge, the man who had reminded her of the Moroni portrait. The way he had looked at her, summing her up. Then she jumped up and held out her hand to Charlie,

'Come on, Let's go and find something for you to eat. I'm hungry now too.'

16

Lily and Charlie were seated in a small café in a back street of Pistoia. They were both looking at their phones, their faces concerned and rather miserable.

'Well, it certainly looks as though I am going to play for Macerata after all.' Charlie sighed and looked across at Lily. She looked up and nodded, 'So after tomorrow's match you'll be going south to Le Marche?'

'If that's where this Macerata is to be found, then, yes, I guess so.'

'And my editor has asked me to attend a conference in Florence. She knows I am in Tuscany and I can hardly refuse. I've been invited to speak and the topic is completely within my realm of knowledge. With my book just coming out she is keen for me to be there.'

'Well, yes, of course, I see that.' Charlie nodded and then added, 'It's no good pretending I don't mind, Lily. I do. I just want to be with you. I don't want it to end.'

'Well, I don't either but it doesn't have to... we shall still both be in Italy... we just have to sort our dates out and get together again as soon as we can.'

'I guess so,' Charlie reached out for Lily's hand, 'but it sort of seems like the party's over.'

'Well, I shall be in Florence the week after your match here in Pistoia. Then, perhaps I can come down to Macerata. I've never been there but I know it's a university city and I think there's a small open-air opera arena. I'll check it out.'

'Opera! Oh my god, the things you know about, Lily. Do you like opera?'

'Well, yes, I do. Don't you?'

'Never been, I think I may have seen something on TV and turned it off. Sorry, Lily, but can't imagine it's my scene.'

'Well, I've never been to a basketball match but I'll come if you're playing. As long as you promise me to be very careful.'

Charlie laughed out loud, 'That's one promise I don't think I can make, Lily dear. Basketball is not a cautious game, but I think the level I shall be playing at... well, it will be quite easy to look after myself.'

'What about this Saturday?'

'No problem, I'll meet the team tomorrow and see how it goes, but it's all second league stuff. It'll be a doddle. I just need to keep playing and exercising for a few months until I can get back to my own team.'

'San Diego, then. I suppose you can't wait, really.' 'No, it will be great to get back to where I belong.' There was a long silence between them. Lily stirred her cappuccino vigorously and blinked back tears. 'That would be more like the party really being over, wouldn't it?'

'Sorry, Lily, that came out all wrong. Of course, I need to get back to my team but... I just can't imagine being without you.'

Lily stood up, leaving her coffee unfinished on the table, 'Let's not even think about it yet. It's all too miserable. We can't let it spoil the time we have together right now. Come on, you'd better get to the stadium and I'll go back to the apartment and sort out some notes for this lecture in Florence.'

They walked out into the sunshine, still rather subdued by the thought of parting. As they reached the door to the apartment, Lily reached up and gave Charlie a light kiss on his cheek. 'Go now, Charlie, get your head round your game and we'll meet again later. Just call me when you're finished.'

Charlie grinned, 'You're right, Lily Fairfax, I must try not to behave like a silly teenager. Of course, we'll meet later and anything can always be sorted, right?'

'Absolutely!' Lily smiled and gave Charlie a little push to send him on his way. He laughed and jumped high into the air, kicking his legs back and blowing her a kiss. In two strides, he was then across the road and she watched until he disappeared into his hotel. He was right, of course, anything and everything could always be sorted out. Lily, of all people, knew how to organise and arrange anything that came her way. Or rather, she had done in the past... but then nothing quite like the sweet and gentle giant, Charlie Woods, had ever come her way before. Lily climbed slowly up the steep winding staircase to her apartment. She unlocked the door and looked around. The place seemed very quiet and empty without Charlie. She sat at her table in the window and looked across at Charlie's balcony. It was such a short time since she had first seen him there, asking for her help. Now the shutters to his room were closed. She turned on her laptop and began to arrange some paper files. Then, she heard a taxi in the street below,the diesel engine chugging as it waited outside Charlie's *pensione*. Lily went out onto the balcony and peered down, just in time to see Charlie, dressed in shorts and a t-shirt, come out of the hotel entrance. He looked up at her balcony and waved, his handsome face breaking into a grin as he saw she was standing there.

'See you later, Lily. I'll call as soon as...' Then he was in the taxi and out of sight. Lily leaned over the balcony rail and waved. She thought she saw Charlie waving from the back window and then the taxi pulled round the corner and drew out of sight. Lily sighed and went back inside and sat once more at her table. This just wouldn't do, she thought to herself. She really would have to pull herself together, forget Charlie for an hour or so, and get on with her own work. But, it wouldn't be easy.

17

After a slow start, Lily managed to pick up speed and had soon drawn together enough material from her recent research to make an engaging enough lecture. She regained her own interest as she read back through her lists of primary sources and her analysis of secondary sources. Then, she began to think about her next book. She had told Charlie she was confused but now, thinking about it again, she saw a way forward. She would use the forthcoming lecture as a springboard. Lily wrote fast and furiously for nearly an hour and then came to an abrupt halt.

The room was more airless than usual. She stretched and looked out the window. The sky had changed from its usual deep blue to a threatening grey. A small breeze was blowing, but the air was still as hot as a fan heater. Lily saved her work and closed down her laptop. If there was to be a storm, then she knew that there could easily be a power cut. She went into the small kitchen and opened the fridge. She took out one of the bottles of water that Charlie kept stacked up. She rested the ice-cold bottle against her forehead as she felt the beginning of a headache. Then, with a tall glass of water, she lay down on the bed. She thought back through her work and was satisfied that she had made a good start. The lecture would be easy enough, she was confident talking about her own subject and sometimes, as she spoke, another idea came into her head. There would usually be a few heckling questions, but she was well accustomed to dealing with that and could often raise some laughter. Then there would be positive comments, too, and often inspiring ideas thrown in. Yes, although she would have to be apart from Charlie, she really looked forward to the Florence conference.

Then her thoughts turned to Charlie. What was he doing right now? She had no idea what his life was really like. Apparently he was well recognised in his field and, until his accident, had been at the top of his game. He had told her that he made money modelling for a Californian fashion house and was sponsored by an international sports company. Although he was saving hard for the future, he managed to live a high lifestyle. Now, here in Italy, it seemed that he was treated royally. The evening at the Villa had obviously been a bid to impress and win him over. Lily smiled at the memory. How glad she had been that she had worn her best silk dress and high-heeled Manolos. She thought about the paintings that Signora Mariotto had been so proud to show her. There was one in particular that interested Lily. Lily felt sleep creep over and she pushed the painting to the back of her mind, as though saving it to think about later. Then she remembered the moment that Charlie had jumped in the air, holding his champagne flute of sparkling water high and touching the crystal teardrop of the chandelier. The high- pitched ting that had stopped everyone talking as they had looked in amazement at the height he could jump and the accuracy of his hand and eye co-ordination. It had been a magic moment and Charlie had told her he was jumping for joy because of her. All in all, it was no wonder to Lily that he was such a good lover. Lily turned over in bed and fell into a deep, dreamless sleep.

More than an hour later she awoke with a start as lightning flashed through the room followed by a deafening crash of thunder. Lily jumped up and went to the window to close the shutters as the first large drops of rain began to fall. She was heavy with sleep and she looked hurriedly at the time on her phone. She felt she had been asleep for hours, but it was only five thirty. Charlie would be back soon. Lily went into the shower room and found the light didn't work. So there was a power cut and the shower room had no window. She left the door open to get some daylight through and stepped into the shower. The cold water ran over her and then didn't get any warmer. Of course, the electric heater would be down as well. Lily shampooed her hair as quickly as she could and then hurriedly wrapped herself in towels and went back to the bedroom, shivering with cold. She rubbed her hair dry, thinking that it must be the first time she had felt cold since she left England. Already her skin was drying and she felt warm again. Her headache had gone and she felt refreshed by the shower and her sleep. Certainly she had needed to sleep as there hadn't been too much time for that with Charlie in her bed. Lily gave a satisfied smile and caught her own reflection in the antique mirror over the marble fireplace. She moved nearer the mirror and looked into the dark, silvery depths. The mirror was edged with a heavy ormolu frame, the gilt dull with age. The glass was foxed around the edges, shadowy and mysterious. Lily tossed her head to throw her damp hair loosely over her bare shoulders. She unwrapped the towel to show one breast and then held her hand, with one finger pointing to her pink nipple. Then she smiled, Yes, that was exactly it... she was now exactly like the portrait painting in Signora Marinotti's library. A mediaeval courtesan who smiled down from the frame as though she knew the secrets of the universe. She had been fascinated to see the portrait as it was so similar to the famous portrait of Veronica Franco by Tintoretto, now the core of her research. Lily looked at herself critically. Was she behaving like a harlot? She frowned and her reflection frowned back at her. Just because she had enjoyed a brief fling with Quentin and then fallen so rapidly into this affair with Charlie... did she feel promiscuous? Maybe it was because she had been living like a nun while she had written her book. Lily laughed out loud and her reflection joined in the joke. Maybe she would show Charlie her mediaeval courtesan pose later?She dropped the towel to the floor and looked at her naked image. This is how Charlie saw her. She critically examined her body, her high pointed breasts and slim shoulders, her good curving waist and flat stomach. The frame of the mirror ended above the swell of her hips. Lily was satisfied with herself and she turned away from the mirror with one last look over her shoulder. Her hair flowed down her back, curling into a v shape between her shoulder blades. There was a slight change in skin colour where her bikini strap crossed her light tan. Tomorrow, she decided, if they swam again, she would wear her halter neck.

Then, there was another flash of lightning, reflected in the glass and another crash of thunder... and then her mobile buzzed. It was a text from Charlie.

'sorry, will be late.'
Lily frowned and tapped her reply,
'how late?' and the message returned immediately,
'have to eat dinner with team... can send taxi for you to join us.'
Lily looked at the phone for a moment. Have dinner with his basketball team... did he really mean that? She hesitated and then replied quickly.

'no thanks... have work to finish... see you later x.'

As soon as she had sent the message, she regretted her decision. With the power cut she wouldn't be able to work long, the battery in her laptop was already low... and soon it would get dark. She thought about sending another message but then Charlie's reply came back,

'probably right... you'd be bored with basketball talk... miss you x.'

So that was that. It didn't sound as though he really wanted her there and it was his work. She would only feel in the way. Lily sighed and pulled on her dressing gown and opened the shutters. The thunder was rumbling in the distance now and the sky was brightening over the hills. Lily took a deep breath of the air that was fresh after the rain. She looked at the narrow view of the Tuscan hills, the sun glancing across and casting deep shadows. Had she been looking at the same distant hills when she first seen Charlie? Now, as the sky began to lighten more she thought how like the faraway landscape looked to the background in so many of the portraits she had studied. Even the world famous Mona Lisa had a shadowy, mysterious landscape behind her dark form. The idea pleased Lily and her thoughts returned to her work. She moved back into the apartment and realised that the shower room light was on. The power was back and so was Lily's energy to work.

18

It was nearly midnight when Lily finally finished writing. She yawned and checked the time on her phone. Surely Charlie would be back soon? She went into the kitchen for another glass of water and looked at the empty fridge shelves. Back at her work she had forgotten to eat dinner. There was only a paper bag of apples that Charlie had bought at the market. She took one and began to munch it while she looked in the small larder to find if there was anything more to eat. Then she heard the low throb of a car outside in the street. She ran to the balcony and looked down. A red Ferrari was parked below, the engine still running, filling the night with the noise of its powerful engine. Lily leaned over the balcony and saw Charlie get out of the passenger seat. She was about to call out when she saw a woman's hand, small and white, rest on his arm, as though to persuade him not to leave. Lily gasped and drew back out of sight. Her heart was beating as she waited, hiding behind the shutters until the car pulled away and the engine noise died into silence. She stood quite still, uncertain of what she had seen and anger rising up in her. Was that why Charlie was so late back? A light tap on her front door brought her back to her senses. She ran across the apartment and stood by the locked front door. There was another light tap and then Charlie's voice, quiet and low,

'Lily, Lily it's me, are you still awake?'
Lily made no reply but stood quite still behind the locked door, her breath coming in shuddering gasps as she tried not to cry or make any sound.

'Lily?' Charlie called again and then she heard him begin to go back down the stairs. Suddenly she wrenched the door open and threw herself at him. He caught her in her arms as she started to pummel him with her closed fists.

'Lily... whatever is it? Lily?' Charlie was smiling and ducking her blows until he caught her wrists and held her firmly. She struggled and turned her cheek away from his attempt to kiss her. Charlie was looking worried now and, struggle as she might, he carried her easily into the apartment and kicked the door closed behind him.

'Lily, stop it... whatever is the matter? Talk to me.' He set her down on the floor and she sank to her knees, all her energy and anger depleted. She began to sob,

'How could you? I was waiting all evening for you and... and then, then...' Her words ended in a flood of tears. Charlie sat on the floor next to her and tried to put his arm around her shoulders, but she flinched away from him. 'Don't touch me, I hate you.'

'What have I done, Lily? I know I am late, but I asked you to join me... I would have sent a taxi. I thought you wanted to get on with some work. I know you have to prepare for the Florence thing.'

'Well, it didn't take you long to find someone else to be with, did it?' Lily was seething with anger again. Never in her quiet life had she felt such emotion sweep through her.

'What are you talking about?'

'I saw you, I saw you in the car outside with another woman. I saw her hand on your arm.' Lily turned away from Charlie, unable to look at him.

'Oh my god, is that what it's all about? Lily, Lily you have no idea what my life is like then. I don't want to brag but anywhere I go, any function or dinner, whatever, there are always a few girls I have to dodge. All basketball players have fans and groupies. The girl who gave me a lift here tonight was the sister of one of the Pistoia team. Just a kid, really, and very silly. Sure, she wanted me to go back to her place but I told her my girl was waiting for me up here. You are my girl, aren't you, Lily?' He reached out a hand and gently turned Lily's face to look at him. 'I guess we're both kinda afraid of saying it, but I am falling in love with you, Lily Fairfax. I'm the one that's running scared, knowing I am not good enough for you and not knowing how our future together will be.'

Lily looked into his dark eyes and began to feel relief wash over. She believed his every word and all her fears and doubts dissolved into happiness. She threw her arms around him and he drew her onto his lap as they stayed sitting on the floor. They kissed and then kissed again. Slowly his hands moved under her dressing gown and she began to unbutton his shirt and then unbuckle his belt. At last, wrapped naked in each other's arms they began to make love. Charlie reached up and pulled a quilt from the bed onto the floor and lifted Lily onto it. They rolled over together and Charlie pulled Lily on top of him. Her hair fell forward and she swung her head, brushing his skin with the soft curls of her hair. He gasped in pleasure and pulled her closer to him, holding his hands on her hips as they moved together. Lily forgot her jealous anger, the hot tears she had shed... she forgot everything except being at one with Charlie again.

19

The stadium was packed. Lily sat in the front row
completely amazed at the noise of the crowd and the
excitement buzzing in the air.
Early Saturday morning Charlie had arranged everything,
but nothing could have prepared her for the size and sheer
energy that filled the stadium.

'Are you sure you don't want to sit with my support team?'
Charlie had asked as he bounced up and down on his toes,
ready to leave the apartment.

'Absolutely certain, I don't want to be in the midst of all
your gropies.'

'I guess you mean groupies, really, Dr Lily Fairfax, your
command of the English language is appalling.'

Lily laughed, 'Well, you'd better watch they don't grope you
when I'm around.'

'I'll put out a warning. You are a wild tigress when you're
mad. Lily. And I thought you were such a sweet, gentle girl.'

'I think I was until I met you, Charlie. I led a quiet and
studious life, surrounded by my books and files.'

'I find that hard to believe. There is a fire always
smouldering in you, my sweet Lily.'

'Then you'd better get out that door and off to your training
or whatever it is you get up to when I'm not around.'

'Yeah, I'd better go before you lead me astray. So the taxi
will be here for you at seven. Just give them my card at the
gate. I'll make sure someone is looking out for you.'

'Good luck, then. Be careful!'

Charlie laughed, 'You'll see how careful I am when you watch me. After the match, do you want to join me in an ice-cold bath?'

'Are you serious? You really take a bath in iced water?'

'Yep, 'fraid so, Doc's orders. It's the best cure for muscle strain, especially with my injury.'

'Oh my, how awful. No, I'll get a taxi back here. Just the idea of an ice bath would put out any fire you might think I have smouldering inside me.'

'Oh God, Lily, just those words, 'inside you', and both my knees feel weak.'

Lily laughed, 'Go, Charlie, go... and go well!'

Now, sitting waiting for the match to begin, Lily gripped her hands tight together in excitement and fear. Supposing Charlie fell and injured himself again?

There was a huge surge of noise and applause as the teams ran out onto the court. Lily gripped the rail in front of her and shouted Charlie's name. For a moment it was as if he looked straight at her, he raised a hand and then turned and greeted the whole crowd. From the beginning until the last moment of the match it was evident, even to Lily, that he was the king of the court.

It was nearly two in the morning before Lily heard the light tap on her door. She ran to open it and threw her arms around Charlie.

'You were amazing! I've never seen anything like it. I've never screamed aloud and been so excited in all my life.'

Charlie picked Lily up and danced around the room with her, holding her high in the air.

'I was showing off to you, sweet Lily. Every ball in the net was for you.'

Lily clung to Charlie, her arms tight around his neck, 'You were magnificent.'

Charlie laid her gently on the bed and looked down at her, 'Well, it was an easy contest. I wouldn't show up or show off so well in my usual league back home. This was a walkover.'

'It did seem like you were dancing around them, almost teasing them with the ball and then twisting and turning amongst them and then scoring. Oh, Charlie, it was so great!'

'I can't believe you enjoyed it so much. I thought you'd be bored and hate all the noise and stuff. I was still thinking that when I was heating up.'

'Bored, are you joking? At first all I could think was that you might fall and hurt yourself. Some of the other side kept elbowing you... which I thought was very bad form.'

Charlie roared with laughter, 'Bad form, I love it, you crack me up, Lily.'

'I wish I'd had a whistle and could have told them off properly. We were never allowed to push and shove like that in netball when I played at school.'

'You played netball, how come you never told me that? 'Ah, there are lots of things you don't yet know about me.' Charlie laid down on the bed beside her, 'I want to know

everything about you.' He stroked her hair and then slipped his hand inside her nightdress.

His hand was cool on her skin and Lily shivered with pleasure, but she continued talking, 'And I heard lots of new vocabulary.'

'Vocabulary? What are you on about now my little academic... or do you mean the swearing?'

'No, I mean all the Italian words I'd never heard before, well, not in context.'

'You're beginning to lose me, Lily... in context? Is that like contest?'

'You know quite well it isn't. And you're not concentrating.'

'Oh, I am, completely focused, just not on your vocabularies.'

Lily giggled, ' My vocabularies are not what you're playing with...'
'I know lots of words in English that I bet you don't know the meaning of Doctor Fairfax.'
'Oh yes,' Lily was beginning to breathe faster as his gentle

hands caressed her skin, 'Like what?'
'Like an eight-second violation... I bet you don't know what that means?
'No, but don't stop, tell me more.'
'That would be when I was in possession and failed to advance out of the backcourt to pass the midpoint line in eight seconds.'

Lily was panting now, as she replied, 'You never fail, Charlie, never. Tell me more.'

'Do you even know my position. I'm power forward at home but tonight I played centre.'

'Did you?'
'I did... and did you realise I am renowned for my finger roll shots?'
'I think I guessed that... but tell me what you mean?'

'Well, it's a pretty special lay-up shot... I roll the rock, as I jump and achieve a high arc... just when you need it. And did you see that in-n-out shot that Fabrizio made?'

'In and out?'
'Then there are rim shots, of course...'
'Of course...' Lily sighed.
'And did you see Macerata get a penalty for palming?'
'Palming?' Lily's voice was almost a cry.
'Resting the palm of the hand at the apex of the bounce... like...'
'Ahh, Charlie, Charlie...'

'And not to forget the lay-in, that's a close-range shot using one hand to tip right, absolutely right over the rim.'

Charlie slid his hand under Lily as she cried out, a primeval sound that filled the small apartment. Then he pulled her on top of him and held her close. They lay for a while, quiet and still until Charlie began to move under her.

'Aren't you tired, Charlie?'

'Tired? Why would I be? But, you know, I have just come from an ice-cold bath, so now I want to feel that smouldering fire deep, deep inside you. I need you to warm me through and through.'

20

Charlie took her to the station in Pistoia, and they had little time for a fond farewell as the train had just pulled in. Lily threw her arms around Charlie to give him one last hug.

'Be careful, Charlie, not just on the court but in your monster new car.' Lily looked over her shoulder as she spoke and glanced at the shiny blue Alfa Romeo, parked on the double yellow band.

Charlie kissed the top of her head and smiled, 'It's not the first sports car I've had, you know, and anyway it's only on loan. I'm going to make sure I give it back in mint condition. Of course, I shall drive carefully, don't worry, I'm a big boy.'

'Oh, I know that perfectly well...' Lily gave Charlie a wicked smile. 'And I shall remember it all the time while I'm away.'

'That wicked green-eyed smile, you're a bad girl, Lily Fairfax. Now, you'd better go, or you'll miss your train. Are you sure you don't want me to drive you to Florence?'

'Of course not, you have a meeting this morning. You do your work, and I'll do mine. I'll be back by Thursday.'

Lily wrenched herself away from Charlie's arms and ran into the station. She quickly validated her ticket in the yellow box machine and a guard came forward and hurried her into the last open door of a carriage.

Lily made her way through the crowded train, carrying her heavy leather hold-all and with her laptop bag slung over her shoulder. Finally, she made it to her numbered seat and settled down, relieved to find there was a table to work at and an empty seat beside her. As the train gathered speed, Lily looked out of the window, lost in thought and barely aware of the luscious Tuscan landscape rolling past. Her thoughts were still with Charlie. How quickly he had become part of her life but... how could it possibly work out in the future? Each day and night she spent with Charlie made her feel more and more that she didn't want this to be just a holiday romance. She was sure he felt the same, but their lives ran on such different levels. It was not just the logistics of where they both lived and spent their working lives, there was the wide gulf between their interests. Lily caught a glimpse of her reflection in the smeared glass of the train window. She saw her worried frown and then began to take in the beauty of the landscape flashing past outside. The pale, ochre earth between the olive groves and vineyards, the lines of dark, cypress trees like exclamation marks punctuating the scene. Small red-roofed villages clung to the hill-tops and then, Lily caught a brief glimpse of an impressive villa set in a perfect forest. It was a landscape so eternal, so unchanged by time... a classic Italian background that she had just described in her lecture notes. Lily turned to her briefcase and pulled out her files. The neatly written notes were in order, her usual colour coding for different themes. She flicked through it and felt a familiar pleasure in returning to her old world. She opened a new file and began to write rapidly, the movement of the train making her hand-writing more uneven than usual. She felt a small shiver of excitement as she suddenly knew she had found the core subject for her next title.

She was still writing when the train slowed down and pulled into Santa Maria Novella station in Florence. She hastily packed away her work and made her way toward the door, feeling glad to have arrived, satisfied with her new work and very pleased that she would soon be meeting up with her father. Lily had invited him to hear her lecture and she was excited to be seeing him again. They saw very little of each other during the year, apart from holidays that they still often chose to spend together. Although he had spent his working life in the wine trade, he had a great love and sound knowledge of history and art. Maybe she would run the idea of her new book past him?

It would be good to have his opinion.

21

The taxi drove rapidly through the busy city traffic and around the block to the Palazzo dei Congressi. It was only a short journey from the station, and Lily would have enjoyed the walk through the park if she hadn't her luggage to carry. She had attended a similar conference here some time before but this was the first time she had been asked to speak. Her publishers had arranged everything in advance, and Lily was to meet Rachael West, her appointed PA, at the conference centre. She would give Lily the timetable of events and her hotel booking. Until now, Lily had been so involved with Charlie and the basketball match that she had not given any thought to the small detail of the weekend. Her own work was in order, and that was all that mattered. The taxi drew up outside the Villa Vittoria, the venue at the large conference centre. She checked in at the reception desk and left her overnight bag in the left luggage rack. She was asked to show her passport for an identity check and then given her name badge. Finally, she passed through the electronic security and was in the large, cool hall of the Palazzo dei Congressi. Lily stood for a moment enjoying the classic symmetry of the architecture. For a brief moment, she remembered arriving at the Villa Riveno with Charlie and how she had begun to talk about Palladian style architecture. She smiled to herself at his total lack of interest and then moved on, looking around to find any sign pointing to the Literary Conference. She was just about to make enquiries from a uniformed attendant when there was a voice behind her,

'Dr Fairfax, wonderful, you've arrived exactly on time. My name's Rachael West, I'm your personal assistant for the conference.'

'Pleased to meet you. Please, call me Lily, I very rarely use the doctor tag. I don't think we've met?'

'No, no... but, of course, I recognised you from the publicity photographs. Come on into the hospitality sala. Your father is already here.'

Lily followed the enthusiastic Rachael West, who walked ahead briskly, her high heels tapping on the marble floor. Then with a flourish of her hand, Rachael pointed to a life-size cut-out figure of Lily.

'Now you see why I could recognise you!'

Lily looked with shock at the shiny coated version of herself. She was wearing a pale lemon dress and holding a book. Did she really look as good as that? Lily walked closer to the figure and laughed. 'My goodness, you have been busy. I do seem to remember a photo of me at a college garden party. Did you create it from that?'

Before Rachael could answer, Lily walked on past and entered the long room furnished with sofas and tables for drinks and canapés. She had seen her father at the far end of the room, and he was watching the door. He raised his hand as he saw her and then nodded at the man talking to him. Lily stood quite still for a moment. The man talking to her father, waving his hands in the air and tossing his long, dark blonde hair was very familiar. No other than Quentin Howard.

22

'There's your father, over there talking to Quentin Howard.' Rachael was striding ahead again as Lily hesitated in the entrance to the room. 'Do you know Quentin?'

Lily tried to pull herself together and answered, 'Er, yes, I know Quentin Howard.' Her voice sounded unusually high, so she cleared her throat and tried again, 'Of course, everyone knows everyone in Cambridge. I'm surprised he's here. His subject is more straight history based.'

'He's not speaking... in fact he wasn't really on our invitation list, but, of course, when he asked to come we were delighted. He's a big name in the academic world and especially on the lecture tour scene.'

Lily followed in Rachael's footsteps, feeling an alarm bell ringing in her head but trying to concentrate on meeting her father. The long room seemed to stretch ahead, and they moved forward, weaving a path through the crowd of people drinking and talking loudly. Finally, her father moved forward to meet her and held her in his arms,

'My dear girl, you look marvellous! Tanned, of course, but something more about you. I've never seen you look so well.' Her father held her shoulders and stood back a pace, looking at her, 'You must be having a very good summer in Pistoia.'

Lily felt a blush rise to her cheeks as he looked at her closely, 'Yes, yes I have. You look well, too, father.' First exchanges had been made, but it was no good putting it off any longer. The tall figure of Quentin was looming just behind her father. 'Quentin what a surprise to meet you here. How are you?'

Quentin came forward, and Lily quickly held out her hand for him to shake, evading the double-cheek kisses that she knew he was about to give her. Somehow, he was looking less confident than his usual exuberant self, even smaller in stature. Lily thought for a moment that he might be unwell or was it just his size compared to the towering strength of Charlie? But Quentin was talking now, flicking his long mane of dark blonde hair back from his face and flashing his usual smile.

'Lily, good to see you... well, I was in the area and heard your name... you're a big name now. *Bravissima*!'

'I didn't mean to be a big name... I'm not even sure I want to be. You know I hate this scene. It's more your territory.'

Quentin looked down at the floor, once again seeming unusually troubled.

Lily's father spoke, 'I was wondering if Lily and I could snatch some time together now. We haven't seen each other for a while.'
Before Rachael could answer, Lily replied, 'Yes, of course,

I've left my bag in reception. Rachael, do you have my hotel booking? I need to freshen up.'

Rachael looked disconcerted. 'Well, I'd like to introduce you to a lot of people here but, of course if you insist,'

'I do,' Lily answered quietly but with a determined nod. 'I saw there was a dinner planned for tonight so I am sure I shall have a chance to meet everyone then.'

Rachael gave a resigned sigh and took an envelope out of her large handbag. 'This is your booking, everything's arranged.'

'Thank you so much! That's wonderful. I'll see you back here this evening.' Lily quickly took the envelope from

Rachael and turned to her father, 'Let's go. Good to see you again, Quentin. Bye.'

Quentin put a hand on Lily's arm to stop her, 'Lily, I really need to talk to you. Could you make some time, maybe later this afternoon?' Lily was already shaking her head, and he carried on with a desperate look, 'Or meet for a cocktail before the dinner, say, six?'

'Sorry, Quentin, I don't think so.' Lily replied curtly and then looked down at his hand on her arm. He quickly withdrew it, and Lily turned on her heel and walked away.

Her father caught up with her at the reception desk.

'I have to say, Lily, that was rather rude. I know you have ended the affair with Quentin, but he seems a nice enough chap and he is troubled about something, I think.'

'Well, he won't be troubled for long, that's not his style. And I had to be abrupt or the next thing you know he would be joining us for lunch and choosing the wine. Don't worry about Quentin Howard, he'll always be fine and dandy.'

They walked out of the cool Palazzo and into the mid-day heat of Florence. Her father was still worried,

'We had a very interesting chat... I still don't think you needed to be that rude to him.'

'Dad, if you want to have lunch with him and talk endlessly about wines, then go ahead. I'm going to find my hotel and have a long cold drink and then some lunch.'

Her father burst out laughing and took her arm, 'My dear Lily, how you make me laugh. Just like when you were a little girl. Once you make up your mind, there's no stopping you. Look, there's a taxi.' He raised his hand and the taxi pulled over. Lily quickly undid the envelope and pulled out the hotel details. She jumped into the taxi and said to the driver, 'Hotel Villa Medici, *per favore*.'

'My goodness, Lily, you must be very popular on the lecture scene yourself. That's a very grand and famous hotel. By the way, I notice you called me Dad, not Father just then... you always do that when you want your own way. But, I was thinking, now you're so very grown up... why don't you call me Richard? I notice several of my friends' children call their father by his first name. What do you think?'

Lily looked at her father as the taxi swerved around the park and into a stream of traffic, 'Hmm, not sure, also not sure I'm very grown up either. I do behave like a spoilt brat quite often. Sometimes I think it's like I've just left school, and I don't know anything about the world in general.'

'Well, that's not true, of course, I'm so proud of the way you are making your mark in the world. But you never had much chance for a real childhood. You were catapulted into classes of students always much older than yourself. Not surprising if sometimes you behave like a little child prodigy.'

'And there I was thinking you would disagree and say I was never spoilt or badly behaved... really Dad... Richard.'

Her father laughed, 'You'll always get the truth from me, Lily, you know that. And I shall always spoil you as long as I can. Now then, we're at your hotel already.'

'Where are you staying, Dad-Richard?'

'At the little *pensione* behind the Pitti Palace, where we have always stayed. *Il Ritrovo*.'

'Of course, I love that little hotel and its shady courtyard.' Lily looked out the taxi window as it drew up at the steps of a large hotel. 'In fact, I'd rather be staying there that this five-star job. I should have thought about this trip more. Charlie... I'll tell you about him later, he has some scheme where he takes expenses and stays in small hotels to save money.'

'Does he indeed... that doesn't sound very honest to me.'

Lily looked at her father in alarm, 'Oh, it's for the very best of reasons.' She wanted to explain further, anxious that her father should not get the wrong first impression of Charlie, but the taxi driver was holding open the door for her. Lily stepped out into the blazing sunlight and waited as her luggage was carried up the marble steps by a uniformed porter. Explanations would have to wait as now, taking her father's arm, she went into the cool foyer of the Villa Medici.

Richard Fairfax laughed as they stood at the reception desk waiting for her room key. 'I think you will find this place much more comfortable than our little *pensione*, Lily. Why don't you go up to your room and I'll check out where we can eat lunch? Food and wine are my business.'

'OK, Dad-Richard, see you back here in half an hour. I'm starving.' Lily smiled at her father and then followed the bellhop over to the lift. She looked back over her shoulder and caught a brief glimpse of her father walking quickly across the vast marbled foyer. Did he look smaller than usual? Was everyone going to seem smaller to her now that she had met Charlie?

23

'That was a perfect lunch, Dad-Richard.' Lily sat back contentedly and threw her napkin on the table. 'Thank you, you always do know the most excellent places to eat. I don't know how you do it, central Florence, mid-summer, and you find this peaceful oasis.'

'Glad you enjoyed it. But, I think you'd better give up on the Richard idea. It's obviously not going to come easily to you. Just forget I ever mentioned it. Yes, that was a truly great meal. You mentioned that courtyard at my *pensione* and then I remembered this place. I haven't been here for years, but it's exactly as I remember it. The *Pollo alla Fiorentina* was superb. Would you like coffee here or maybe back at your hotel?'

'I have a feeling the coffee here might be a lot better than the five-star stuff. Do you mind? I love it here in the shade amongst all the leafy plants and flowers.'

'Good, I can see the *signora* hovering in the archway.' Richard raised his arm and called out, '*Due espressi, per favore.*'

'Are you happy living full time in Italy, Father?'
'Oh yes, I don't miss anything about England, except you, of course.'
'Well, I suppose we see as much as we would if you did live in the UK. I mean most holidays we get together at some time or other.'
'True, I'm very lucky. I expect one day you'll meet some young man, and I shan't see so much of you, so I intend to make the most of it. Now then, tell me about this Charlie of yours, is it serious?'

Lily remained quiet for a moment, wondering where to begin. She was about to start when the coffee arrived. They both sipped the hot coffee, and the silence continued.

'You don't have to tell me, of course...' Lily's father finished his coffee and looked at her quizzically.

'No, I do want to tell you, but I just don't know where to begin.'

'And you're the star lecturing Don? Maybe just begin at the beginning?'

Lily laughed and relaxed then slowly she told her father the long, complicated story. He listened in complete silence until she ended,
'So you see, Father, I just don't know what will happen, or where it'll all end up.'
'Far be it from me to offer advice but I can't quite imagine you living in San Diego and helping to run a basketball club. I mean, it's simply beyond my scope to even try!'

Lily looked at her father and suddenly laughed out loud,

'You're so right, Father. It's just impossible! And anyway, we are so totally different. I mean, Charlie is the best company, and we have a great time together, but it's like a holiday at the moment. We go out to eat all the time and have fun but... well, I have a job imagining actually living with him. I mean he doesn't even have any books... I'm not sure he ever reads anything except the sports newspapers.'

'No, books!' Richard was laughing now, 'Well, I guess you both find something to do in your spare time. Which leads to the point that it may be more of a physical attraction than... well, intellectual harmony?' He raised his eyebrows and looked at Lily, waiting for her reply.

'OK, Dad, I get where you're coming from, and he certainly is the most amazing looking guy on this earth but it really is a whole lot more than that. He has a great sense of humour, and he makes me feel so...' Lily searched for a word to sum up all she felt when she was with Charlie, 'so... completely happy.'

There was nothing more to be said, and they paid the bill and decided to walk back to the hotel through the quiet back streets and into the *Piazza del Duomo*. They stood side by side in silent admiration of the facade of the cathedral soaring above them.

'Shall we go in?' Richard looked at Lily, 'It seems a crime to be here and not just have a quick peep.'

'I remember the first time you brought me here. It was so hot, then too. You carried me on your shoulders.'

'Fancy you remembering that... yes, yes... I showed you those statues of the architects.' He pointed up to two high niches, 'Do you remember that too?'

'Of course, Arnolfo de Cambio and Filippo Brunelleschi. I loved the sound of their Italian names. I still do.'

'What a dreadful little clever clogs you were. Always asking questions and writing in your little journals.'

'I suppose I was. The trouble is, I think I still am like that most of the time. But sometimes I just want to be sort of normal and not think and learn a thing.'

'I don't know if you'll be able to do that, Lily. You are what you are. You shouldn't try and change and be something you're not. Now then, I suggest we make our way back to the hotel, leave the magnificence of the *Duomo* to another day. Why don't you do just go back to your five-star luxury land, have a swim and rest up before tonight's dinner.'

'Good idea! Really good idea... what about you, will you come back you my hotel, too?

'I think I'll go back to my quiet little pensione and have a kip. If I'm to be your escort tonight, I'd better have a good rest. Anyway, it's too hot to think about sight-seeing, and the tourists are thronging everywhere. But I'll see you back to your hotel first.'

'No, absolutely not. You need to go in the opposite direction for the Pitti. Anyway, I think I'll give in to this decadent life I'm seduced into living... I'll jump in a taxi.'

'Good, then I'll see you at the Palazzo, *sta sera, verso le sette?'*

'*Si, si, va bene, ci vediamo dopo. Ciao, ciao!'* Lily gave her father a quick kiss and then ran over to the taxi rank.
Lily was suddenly pleased to have some time to herself and to catch up with her thoughts. As soon as she was in the taxi she checked her phone but there were no messages. Charlie would probably be in Macerata by now. She sent him a quick message to say that she had arrived safely. She waited for a moment, looking at the blank screen, hoping that Charlie might respond immediately. Nothing. She put her phone back in her bag and sighed. Of course, he would be busier than she had been, and she had, after all, only just found time to call him. It wasn't that she hadn't missed him but there just hadn't been a moment. The taxi pulled up at the hotel entrance, and Lily walked slowly into the foyer, looking forward to a few hours of pure and solitary luxurious pleasure.

But it was not to be. Waiting in the foyer, lounging on a cream leather sofa under a palm tree, was Quentin Howard.

24

Quentin saw Lily the moment she entered the foyer. He stood up quickly and strode toward her, his arms outstretched.
'There you are Lily, I've been waiting for you.'

For the second time that day, Lily dodged his kisses as she carried on walking to the reception desk to collect her key card.

'*Due cento tre, per favore.*' The receptionist handed her the key and then a letter. Lily opened the envelope, expecting it to be from the conference organisers, but it was a message from Charlie.

'I miss you, my sweet Tiger-Lily. Hurry up back from being Dr Fairfax.'

How had he found out where she was staying? Lily held the message close and thought about Charlie, wondering where he was at this moment. She certainly wouldn't be able to find him except by phone. She snapped on her phone and sent a text message, ignoring Quentin who was still standing by her side. But Quentin Howard was not a man who liked to be ignored.

'Lily, I really must talk to you, it's important.'

'I can't think why... there is nothing to talk about. Now, please excuse me, I'm going to my room.'

'Let me come with you, just half an hour. I need to talk to you in private.'

'Certainly not, Quentin, can't you understand that what we had together is over, completely over. I'm sorry.' Perhaps she shouldn't have added the last two words, it seemed as though she was softening the blow, and he jumped to the advantage.

'Nothing to be sorry about, Lily. I had a wonderful time with you. I wish it weren't over, but I respect you...it's not about us. Well, not really, it's about me.'

'Why does that not surprise me, Quentin?' Lily sighed, 'Everything is always about you.'

'I'm in trouble, Lily, serious trouble.'
Lily looked up at him and tried to suppress her laughter. Was he going to tell her he was pregnant with her child? She was just about to say something of the sort, trying to lighten the moment when she realised there were tears forming in his eyes. Certain that they would be tears of self-pity, nonetheless, Lily felt obliged to drop her facetious attitude.

'Right, let's go and sit on that sofa you found under the palm tree, and you can explain... just ten minutes, no longer. I have things I need to do.'

Quentin immediately looked happier and took her arm to lead her quickly to the sofa. He sat next to her and seemed to be peering through the green fronds of the palm tree as though checking for eavesdroppers. Once again, Lily struggled to treat the matter seriously. Had Quentin been recruited to the secret services? The situation was ridiculous.

'Do start, Quentin, the suspense is now killing me. Whatever is this all about.'

Quentin's handsome face was dark with worry, 'I've been foolish, Lily. I've been messing around at Cambridge. After you left me... well, I felt very low and lonely.'

'Oh no, is this about a new love affair?'
'Well, yes and yet no, not really. There was this young girl...'

'Please don't tell me she was one of your students.'
'Yes, but that's not ever been a problem. I mean they're all old enough to know what they're doing.'
'All... how many girls are you talking about.'
'Sorry, Lily, this is all coming out the wrong way. I'll start again. After you left me, I was in shock.'
'I do hope you're not trying to blame me for any stupid thing you did after we parted, Quentin.'
'Well, no, of course not but in a way, it was your fault. If we had still been together, none of this would ever have happened.' 'Oh please, just tell me the worst. Get on with it, Quentin.' 'Well, on the rebound, remember that... I had a fling with a girl called Julie. A lovely girl but I have no idea where she found the brains to get into Cambridge. She's reading Psychology at Homerton. We met in a bar and ...well, one thing led to another and... it seemed to be fine... we had a good time. She came with me to a lecture I was giving in Berlin. That's when I began to be seriously tired of her. She talked about nothing except her dreams... I don't mean aspirations, I mean her night time dreams... and when she wasn't analysing herself she just wanted to go shopping.'

'Hmm, pity you hadn't talked with her a while before you jumped into bed.'

'I know, I know. I hate myself now. I hadn't realised how important it is to have shared interests. You know, how we could talk about everything, Lily. Art, history, literature, films... we shared so many interests and exchanged ideas and knowledge. You finally made me realise that sex isn't everything.'

'Well, thanks! I thought we had a good time in bed, too!'

'You know we did, Lily. It was the best ever. I can't even bear to think about it, looking at you now, so beautiful with your lightly tanned skin and in that thin little dress...'

'Stop right there, Quentin. Your ten minutes is nearly up.'
Lily glared at Quentin and shifted further away from him on
the long sofa.
'Sorry, sorry,' Quentin held up his hands in apology, 'but I
can't help saying how beautiful you are and how sad I am to
have lost you.'

'Weren't you telling me about your young Julie? Can I go
now? Is that the end of your story. ' Lily began to stand up,
but Quentin looked at her in alarm, his face anxious again.

'I wish it were.' He exhaled heavily and seemed to shrink
into the sofa. 'Anyway, back in Cambridge, I told Julie that
the affair was over. She cried... I tried to explain our
differences. She threw my favourite ceramic jar from
Syracuse into my fireplace and ran off. I thought that was it.'
Quentin held his head in his hands and was silent.

'But it wasn't?' Lily looked at Quentin in despair, 'Don't tell
me, you found consolation in the arms of another girl?'

'No, no, nothing like that... well, there was another young
woman on the scene but that had nothing to do with it. The
dreadful part is that Julie has charged me with rape.'

The violent word fell between them like a stone thrown into
a deep well. Lily sat up straight with shock, 'Oh my God,
Quentin, that's dreadful.'
'I know,' Quentin was looking down at the floor, his long
hair now hiding his face. Lily was sure he was crying.

'Can she just do that? I mean, what is the procedure? What
happens next?'

'So far, it's being kept as a college matter, and the police are
not yet involved... the Master is very anxious that it doesn't
go any further. I have a college lawyer helping me. I have to
supply evidence that she had sex with me willingly. He is
using the fact that she willingly accompanied me in a double

room in Berlin as evidence that she obviously chose to be with me. But that was previous to the night she swears I attacked her.'

'Of course, that's the path you must follow. Anyone that knows you will confirm that you have never had to persuade a woman to go to bed with you. Surely they must be queuing in the corridors?'

'It's no joke, Lily, and you of all people must know that I have lonely times.'

'What do you mean? Lonely?'
'Well, I put that ad in the newspaper, didn't I? That's how we met.'
'Oh my, I see what you mean. That does look a bit desperate or sort of shady, I suppose. Makes you look like a predator.'
'Well, thanks, Lily. I don't need you to spell it out. And, of course, my lawyer thinks the same.' Quentin threw himself back on the sofa and stared at Lily, his handsome face lined with anxiety. 'And that's exactly why I came to you for help. You can attest how we just met by chance and had a good time. That I was always a perfect gentleman and...'

'Hold on, hold on... I can't lie about how we met and...'

'Before you go any further, Lily, there's something else... I told my lawyer that I was with you all night, the night that Julie is accusing me of rape.'

25

'I thought you were rather subdued and quiet last night. No sign of Quentin so I guessed it might be something to do with him... but this, this is monstrous!'

Lily's father looked at her in consternation. They were sitting at breakfast in the poolside restaurant of Lily's hotel.

'I know, I just couldn't believe he would ask me to lie.I know the Master at his college. He's a tremendously pompous man and lives for his college. That's good, of course, but he'd do anything to protect the reputation of the place. He'll certainly want to keep the whole matter under wraps. Quentin is one of the leading lights of the place. He appears on TV, roams around the world giving guest lectures... I mean, he's the virtual image for the college... he represents it in the world's eye.'

'That's all very well, but supposing this young woman is telling the truth.'

Lily looked at he father, her eyes wide with shock, 'Oh no, Dad. That's not a possibility. I know Quentin well enough to be sure of that. He really is a very gentle man. He'd never step out of line. He loves women, maybe too much, but I am sure he respects them in his way. He was always very sweet to me. It was more his lifestyle I couldn't cope with... all the parties and travelling. But, no, I'd be happy to swear to his gentleness any time. If it were only that.'

'But it's not, he's asking you to say that he was with you the night in question.'

'I know, I know. And, of course, I can't. I told him straightaway that it was out of order. There is no way I would commit perjury for Quentin Howard.'

'Exactly, you should never lie and neither should he. What a fool to tell his lawyer that anyway... and without even asking you first. Preposterous!'

'Well, at least he has only told his lawyer and so I told him that he had to go straight back to Cambridge and tell him the truth.'

'Which is?'

'Apparently he went to a concert that evening, on his own, although he saw people there who know him. Then went back to his flat, again alone, and worked on his next lecture. That was it. So he has no alibi from about ten thirty onwards.'

'Well, that just has to be his problem, Lily. You mustn't get involved.'

'I know, but I do feel just a bit sorry for him. He went off looking so miserable.'

'Maybe, but it seems to me he has made his own bed and now has to lie in it.'

'Good metaphor, Father, very apt.'

They both managed to laugh and continued to eat their breakfast in companionable silence.The waiter came up and refilled their coffee cups and gave Lily a message. She read it aloud to her father,

'*Pranzo Limonaia, Villa Vittoria, Palazzo dei Congressi a mezzogiorno*, and Rachael West has added a postscript reminder. What do you think? Shall we go to lunch in the Lemon House... or not?'

'Up to you, my dear. I don't mind either way. Do you have work to prepare for this afternoon's lecture?'

'Not really, I have it all ready to go but there is something I was going to ask your opinion on... my next book title.'

'Already? You don't stop, do you!'

'I know, I was going to take a break, but I have the spark of an idea... it makes a carry-on to my "Florentine Virgin" title. If you don't mind, we could talk it through now and then go to lunch as well.'

'That's my girl, always try to do everything... you were never one for compromise.'

Lily laughed, 'I blame my upbringing. Anyway, the thing is... I've become rather fascinated with the idea that we pre-judge people by appearances.'

'A very true thought, Lily '"Who makes the fairest show, means most deceit"?'

Lily smiled, 'Exactly on that basis. By the way, it's Pericles, Act I, Scene... probably IV?'

'Quite right. Can't catch you out there. I suppose your idea is rather more complicated though... it's one's judgement of people by their appearance...hmm, sort of summing up?'
 'Yes, it's as you said earlier, seeing a sportsman in shorts and a vest doesn't mean he's not interested in history of art... or something like that... but one assumes that he isn't. Anyway, do you remember you sent me that postcard of Moroni's portrait 'The Tailor'?'

'Yes, of course, I remember, *'Il Sarto'*, a seminal work... yes, ground-breaking.'

'Well, that led me to a week's research in Bergamo but there wasn't quite enough in it somehow. Then, with Charlie, I was lucky enough to be shown the portraits hanging in the library of a private villa near Pistoia. It was a wonderful evening...' Lily faltered to a halt as she thought about being with Charlie, his leap up to the crystal chandelier...

'So, Lily, concentrate... where did that lead you?'

Lily almost laughed as she thought how the evening had led to anything but academic study. 'Well, nothing straightaway. I didn't have a chance to think about it and, much as I love being with Charlie, there is no way I could discuss it with him.'

'Well, a point made, perhaps, I don't suppose you would expect a basketball star to be interested, I see that.'

'True enough. Strangely though, after I sent Quentin away, it occurred to me that I would have liked to talk to him about my work. We did share so many things in common and, whatever his weaknesses are, they are certainly not academic. He has sold himself out to a life in the media, but he does have an excellent brain. And he told me he was quickly bored with the conversation of the girl he is in trouble with... I don't know, it just made me think. There I was giving him advice and yet... well, there I am with my Charlie Woods.'

'So it has made you question whether you are with the right man? Surely you're not thinking of going back to Quentin?'

'Good God, no, never! And I love being with Charlie... I can't wait to see him again. No, it was just a momentary regret that I couldn't have a discussion about my work. Quentin does have a lot to offer in academic thought.'

'Hmm, maybe, but the man's obviously a charming charlatan. He had me fooled. We had such an interesting conversation about Tuscan red wine... and really he was just using me to get to you.'

'Oh no, Quentin loves talking wine... he would have quite genuinely been carried away on the subject. That's the thing, he is interested in all the finest things in life... he is charismatic, certainly, but I don't think he's a charlatan. Good word though, Father.'

'Yes, well, I still think it may sum him up. Be very careful, Lily. Your Charlie may not have the abstract cerebral side to him, but he sounds a good guy.'

'Oh, I'm sure he is, absolutely. He had a very hard childhood. Similar and yet so different to mine. His mother died when he was very young, and he is an only child, just like me. He wasn't as lucky with his father, though. After his mother died, his father took to drink but he finally came out of it and took Charlie back to live with him. He had been sent to live with his mother's sister in Mexico.'

'So Charlie is half Mexican?'

'Yes, he calls himself a coconut!' Lily laughed at the memory, seeing in her mind's eye Charlie stretched out beside her in bed, the sun glinting on his dark golden body, highlighting every contour of his muscles.

'You're dreaming again, Lily. No wonder you can't concentrate on your work. I've never seen you like this.'

'I know, I feel different. It's as though my feelings have suddenly awoken... I can't really describe it. It's as though I am in the real world at last.'

'For better or worse then, I suppose. So when Charlie's father came back to his senses, was he good to Charlie?'

'Oh yes, I think they mean a lot to each other. That's what I meant... we have a lot in common in that way. He is close to his father as I am to you. His father is a basketball coach and trained Charlie from a young age. Just like you teaching me so much when I was young.

'Yes, I suppose I understand that in a way, even though your lives are so different... but that still leaves you unable to talk about your work with Charlie.'

'Yes,' Lily sighed, 'I know, and I don't understand a thing about basketball either. There are loads of young girls following teams around who seem to live for the game.'

'Do you mind that?'

'I don't know. I suppose I do, but I trust Charlie. That's what he's like... he's so honest and dependable. I love that feeling of being able to trust him.'

'Certainly one of the most important features in any partnership, that's for sure. Well, time will tell.'

'You're right and I keep telling myself to enjoy the moment. Carpe momentum... why not?'

'In the meantime, do you think you'll be able to write your next book with your love life zooming around you?'

Lily laughed, 'I think so, I only have to be alone for more than half an hour, and I find myself scribbling away.'

'So, tell me, have you got your next title in mind?'

'Yes, I have now. I thought I would make my next book about a mediaeval Italian courtesan. I'm thinking about a title... 'The Tuscan Strumpet'... or perhaps, 'The Tuscan Harlot'... what do you think?

'And there I was happily thinking you led such a quiet, sheltered life in the hallowed halls of Cambridge University.' Lily's father sighed and then smiled,

'I think either title would make you another very best seller, Lily.'

26

Lily's lecture went down well, very well. She had started confidently, suddenly ditching her carefully prepared notes and speaking directly to the audience with a clear, confident voice. Her decision to change her opening was brought on by seeing Quentin in the front row, sitting next to Rachael West. Quentin most decidedly had his hand resting lightly on Rachael's thigh.

'Portraits, good portraits, tell us a story. The person in the frame looks at us, and we look back. There is a communication between the sitter and the viewer. Every gesture of the person in the portrait helps us to understand the character, whether it is in the eyes or perhaps the gesture of a hand or where the hand is placed.' Lily looked directly at Quentin with these last words and was gratified to see that he quickly withdrew his hand from Rachael's silk clad thigh.

Lily smiled around at the whole audience and felt a surge of confidence. The *sala verdi* was packed full, and an anticipatory hush fell over the crowded seats. Lily was an accomplished speaker, and she knew she would easily have this audience in her thrall. She caught a glimpse of her father in the front row, nodded at him briefly and flashed him a quick smile. He sat forward in his seat and she realised he was more nervous than she was at the long speech ahead. Lily took a small sip from the glass of water on the lectern and continued to speak without reference to her notes.

When she drew to a halt, satisfyingly exactly on the time allotted to her, Rachael West stood up and led the applause. Then, to Lily's considerable surprise, the whole audience rose from their seats to give her a standing ovation. She blushed with pleasure and gave a small bow with her head, her long red-gold hair shining in the spotlight, then held up her hands for silence.

'Are there any questions? I think we have a few minutes if anyone would like to ask about any points I have made?'

Several hands were raised, and Lily fielded all the questions efficiently. Her knowledge extended well outside the narrow topic of her lecture, and she was accustomed to answering difficult questions raised by her students. This audience was lightweight, people with a general interest in history of art and a definite interest in a pleasurable weekend in Florence. Lily decided enough time had been given and asked for one last question. A man seated in the back called out quickly,

'Can we hope for another book to follow your "*Florentine Virgin*" triumph?'

'Thank you for asking. This is as good a time as any to announce that I do have my next work in progress... even my publishers don't know this yet... but the title will most probably be "*The Tuscan Strumpet*". That's my working title at the moment. Thank you.'

There was a strange intake of breath from the audience and then some laughter and a round of loud applause. Lily gave an exaggerated mocking curtsey, switched off the microphone and walked quickly off the podium.

There was a small anteroom behind the stage and Lily sat down, suddenly exhausted. She enjoyed a moment of silence before Rachael came bustling into the room.

'That was fantastic, Lily, the audience loved it and announcing your next book title was so exciting, I am absolutely thrilled to bits. Can I get you anything? You look quite exhausted.'

'Thanks, I'd love a fresh glass of water and then could you see if you can find my father?'

'Of course,' Rachael hurriedly poured Lily a glass of water and then went off again. Lily ran her fingers through her hair, refreshed by the cold water and now feeling pleased with herself. She pushed the notes that she had hardly glanced at into her briefcase and stayed quietly thinking through the lecture. There was nothing in particular that she had omitted... maybe she could have elaborated on... Lily's thoughts were interrupted by Rachael returning, followed by Lily's father.

'Hi Dad-Richard, what did you think?'

'I knew you'd be good, but I had no idea how good. You have a lucid way of talking, most effective. It was excellent.'

Before Lily could reply, Rachael interrupted,

'Lily, I have Quentin Howard asking if he can speak with you. He's waiting in the auditorium. What shall I tell him? I know you're tired now.'

'Yes, I am, very tired of Quentin Howard. Tell him I just don't have the time. He's all yours. Now then, is that fire exit working? I'd like to leave now and get some fresh air.' Before Rachael could say another word, Lily jumped up and pushed the bars on the fire exit. The double doors opened easily, letting in a stream of late afternoon sunlight. 'Come on, Richard, what are you waiting for... Florence awaits!'

Her father hurried across the room, politely nodding at Rachael as he edged past her and followed Lily outside. They stood for a moment, side by side, blinking in the bright light.

'Shall we walk across the park, Father? There's some shade under the trees.'

'Good idea... what I need is a cup of tea. I think I know just the place.'

'Why am I not surprised? Of course, you would know just the place, Dad.'

'This is getting out of hand, Dad-Richard, Father, Dad and even Richard just now. I fear I may lose my identity.'

'Well, it was all your idea, what can I say? I'm just trying to please you.'

'Hmm, what you mean is you're just attempting to bait me. You always do that when you're a bit bored or tired.'

'Bait you, what an idea and what a great word. I love your vocabulary. Here, carry this a moment, Father.'

Lily thrust her briefcase at her father and ran ahead on the stretch of grass in front of the Villa Vittoria. Suddenly, exhilarated the formality of the lecture was over, she felt free as a bird and turned a quick and perfect somersault. She heard her father laugh, and she carried on running. No longer Dr. Fairfax but a young woman, running on the grass in the sunshine and looking forward to getting back to her lover. The word 'vocabulary' had slipped off her tongue, and suddenly she was back with Charlie... remembering the way he had taught her the vocabulary of basketball. She came to a halt under the shade of a line of trees and waited for her father to catch up. She panted slightly with the effort of her run, and she closed her eyes to better recall being with Charlie. How she longed for him, his arms holding her close. Her whole body ached with yearning. Was this burning desire what love was all about? If not, whatever was it called? Was there a special vocabulary that Lily had yet to learn?

27

It was late evening by the time Lily arrived back at her
apartment in Pistoia. The sun was low in the sky, but the
heat of the day was still lingering. Lily looked up warily at
the cloudless sky, wondering if the heavy heat would bring
another storm. As she pulled her bag into the dark, narrow
hallway, Signora Marelli popped out from her rooms on the
ground floor.

*'Buona sera, Professoressa Farefazzi, entra, entra per
favore!'*
Lily put down her case in the hall and reluctantly followed

Signora Marelli into her rooms. All she wanted was to get
upstairs to her own apartment and take a cool shower. But
her landlady was a kindly woman who seldom interfered, in
fact, Lily rarely saw her at all and had never been in her
rooms before. She looked around the dark living room. The
shutters were closed, and a large fan was circulating the
stifling air.

'Prego, si accommodi, si sieda!'

Signora Marelli directed Lily to sit in a small armchair and
then, holding her hands in the air, said excitedly, *'Aspetta un
attimo, un attimo!'*

Lily waited in the small and rather uncomfortable chair, still
wishing she could escape and climb the stairs to her own
place. Signora Marelli returned carrying a very large
bouquet of flowers, so large that she could hardly be seen
behind them. Her excited voice said, *'Un mazzo di fiori, e
guarda, anche un messagio.'*

Lily stood up and took the small envelope that Signora
Marelli held out to her. The perfume of the flowers, a huge
bunch of orange lilies, now filled the heavy air of the room.

Signora Marelli looked over Lily's shoulder as she opened the envelope and read the words,

'Missing you, dear Lily... I hope these tiger lilies arrive before I do. See you Monday. Charlie.'

'Allora?' Signora Marelli was watching Lily's face and waiting for her to speak.

'Grazie, Signora!' Obviously this was not enough information and so, Lily explained that the flowers were from her boyfriend and that he was away at the moment.

Signora Marelli sighed with satisfaction and laid the flowers carefully on the table in the centre of the room. She continued to look at them for a moment.
'Un mazzo grandissimo, certo, certo. Il signor fa le cose in grande... certo! Un giocatore di basket, giacotore prima grandezza, professionista di basket, si, si!'

Lily smiled, realising that Signora Marelli may have seemed invisible but she was well aware of Charlie Woods coming and going. Lily stood up, but Signora Marelli almost pushed her back down in the chair.

'No, no, un'altra cosa, aspetta, aspetta! La rete per le zanzare, sopra il letto matrimoniale?' Signora Marelli winked at Lily and nudged her in the ribs.

Lily searched her memory for the word *'zanzare'*. Of course, Signora Marelli was offering her a mosquito net to hang over the bed. Lily blushed as Signora Marelli continued to wink and chuckle and mutter about being only young once. Lily decided it was time to leave and, thanking Signora Marelli again, she picked up the huge bouquet and made for the door. Signora Marelli hurried forward, holding the bundle of white netting under her arm and, reaching the hall before Lily, she then picked up Lily's holdall. Before Lily could protest, Signora Marelli was already half way up the stairs. On the top landing, she produced a bunch of keys and let herself in before Lily.

The apartment was airless and hot. Lily took the flowers into the little kitchen, and Signora Marelli put down the bag and opened the shutters and turned on the fan. Lily could hear from the kitchen that she was muttering about the infernal heat of the summer. Carefully removing the cellophane from around the delicate flowers, Lily smiled as she thought of Charlie. So he would be back tomorrow. She found the largest jug in the cupboard, a tall galvanised watering jug that she used for watering the few plants on the balcony. She carefully arranged the flowers and then stood back to admire the effect. The bright orange petals, speckled with dark violet stood out against the spiky foliage and reflected dully in the aluminium pitcher.

'Perfetto!' Signora Marelli was standing close behind her. '*Quasi artistica, anche!'* Signora Marelli tapped the metal pitcher and nodded her approval. *'Si, si, giglio tigrato… un simbolo femminile… gentilezza, ma… la pietà la ferirebbe ancora di più, si, si…veniamo al mondo a cercare l'amore incondizionato… oppure… il giglio arancione … il simbolo rappresenta il veleno che è la rabbia.'*

Lily turned to Signora Marelli as she continued to mutter and then walked past her into the bedroom, translating in her mind, the strange Italian words. The tiger lily seemed to be symbolic of so many female emotions... kindness, unconditional love and then... the poison of jealous anger. Lily suddenly stopped still as she saw that Signora Marelli had managed to hook a voluminous white mosquito net from the beam over the bed. She turned and found Signora Marelli behind her again, carrying the large pitcher of flowers. *'Grazie, mille grazie, Signora Marelli… e magnifico!'* It was true, the room was now magnificently transformed... cool, and with the draft from the overhead fan wafting the white net over the bed.

Signora Marelli gave a satisfied smile and set the flowers down on the table in the window. *'Che profumo, bellissimo!'* Signora Marelli touched the stalk of one of the lilies lightly between her finger and thumb and showed Lily the yellow pollen. *'Il polline! È un simbolo di fertilità.'* She rubbed her thumb and finger together and laughed at Lily's look of shock.

Lily decided that it was definitely time for Signora Marelli to depart. There was quite enough now said about the symbolic meaning of the delicate tiger lily, especially now that it included fertility. But Signora Marelli was already making for the door, still muttering and chuckling.

Lily followed her, *'Grazie per tutti, Signora. Molto gentile!'*

'Niente, niente! Lei è giovane ed è giusto che si diverta! Ciao, ciao!'

The door closed after her and Lily looked around the apartment, lost in translated thoughts about youth and enjoyment.

28

It was nearly midnight and Lily sat at her little table in the
window, writing page after page, her mind full of ideas for
her new book. She had moved the huge bouquet of flowers
away from the table in the window to make room for her
laptop and files. The sweet perfume still filled the air, wafted
in the movement of air from the ceiling fan. Finally, she
drew to a halt, her fingers held in suspense over the
keyboard as though waiting for another idea. Then, she
stretched her hands above her head and yawned. She was
satisfied that she had noted down all that she needed, and
before she could do much more, she would need to research.
Lily stood up and stretched again and then walked over to
admire the flowers. She had cleared a space on the mirrored
dressing table, and now it was as though she had two huge
bunches of tiger lilies. She looked at her reflection, her face
nearly obscured by the bright orange petals. She thought
again about Signora Marelli's muttered words about the
symbolism of the flowers. Strangely it had carried on from
the theme of her lecture. Symbolism in art was something
that fascinated her, and it seemed quite remarkable that it
was part of her landlady's everyday knowledge. She yawned
again and saw herself, tired and pale in the mirror. Time for
bed, she told herself sternly. Charlie will be back tomorrow,
so I had better sleep tonight. She smiled at herself in the
mirror. Never mind all this talk about symbolism, she knew
very well why Charlie had chosen to send her tiger lilies.

Lily turned to look at the bed, now under the billowing
white mosquito net. She raised a corner and looked at the
empty bed. She would lie down for a while and see what it
was like under the net. She lay flat on her back, looking up
at the whiteness and the hazy view of the room. Listening to
the whirring sound of the fan she fell fast asleep. She dreamt
she was running, running but not moving. She wanted to cry
out, but she could make no sound. Quentin was running after
her, catching up with her as she tried to reach a long winding
staircase ahead of her. The scene changed to a darkened

room, and she was leaning against a tall door, her breath coming in short gasps, desperately trying to keep the door closed. She fumbled with the key, trying to turn it, but her fingers were numb. Now there was a soft tapping on the other side of the door. Still she tried to turn the key in the lock but... the tapping came again, and a soft voice called her name. Lily awoke with a start and sat up in bed, confused by the terror of her dream and the white net shrouding the bed. Had she really heard her name... could it be Charlie? She pushed aside the netting and scrambled off the bed and ran to the door. There it was again, the soft tapping and her voice,

'Lily, sweet Lily, are you awake?' It was Charlie. She hurried to unlock the door, now, in reality, her fingers turned the key easily and the door swung open. Lily threw herself into Charlie's open arms.

'You said you'd be back Monday.'

'It is Monday, am I too early? Do you want me to come back later?' Charlie laughed as Lily pulled him into the room and took his bag from him.

'This is so wonderful... I can't believe you're here! I was in the middle of the most terrifying nightmare, and the knocking on the door seemed to be in my dream and then I awoke.'

'Sorry to wake you, but I just couldn't wait to see you. I drove back straight after the match finished.'

'All the way from Macerata? That's miles.'

'No, the match was in Perugia last night, only two hours on the A1 highway.'

'But you must be shattered, what can I get you? Are you hungry?'

'Not for food...' Charlie looked at her and smiled, his dark eyes shining. 'I'll just get some water and you go back to bed. By the way, what exactly is that enormous cloud thing hanging over it? Is the bed turning into a bride?'

'Signora Marelli put it up for us, now we can have the windows wide open and not get bitten by mosquitos. Oh, and she took in my beautiful flowers, thank you, Charlie, They're so beautiful... can you smell them?'

'Yeah, sort of cheap barber shop smell in here, if that's what you mean.' Charlie laughed at Lily and dodged as she threw a pillow at him. 'Lily, you don't really expect ever to hit me with a moving target, do you?'

'How was your match then?' Lily watched as Charlie went into the kitchen and then suddenly called out, 'Charlie, you're limping!' She jumped out of bed and ran into the kitchen where he was drinking from a large bottle of iced water. He turned to her and nodded, 'Yeah, some guy managed to kick my knee... but it'll be fine. It just seized up a bit in the car.'

'Did you have it checked out?'
'The physio had a quick look, but there's nothing to see.'
'Take your trousers off and let me see.'
'Now there's an offer I can't refuse. Do you mind if I lie down on the bed, too, Dr. Fairfax. I don't want to faint or anything. And maybe you should lie beside me?'

'Charlie be serious for one minute. All right, go on, get undressed and lie on the bed.'

'Your wish is my command, Doc.' Charlie limped over to the bed and pulled aside the net and stretched out on the bed. Lily laid her hand gently on his knee. 'It's very swollen, Charlie, you should go to have it x-rayed or something... it looks livid.'
'You are talking about my knee, aren't you, Doc?'

Lily slapped her hand on Charlie's arm, 'I told you to behave yourself, Charlie Woods. Surely your poor knee hurts?'

'Well, as soon as I finished driving I took a couple of painkillers, and they're kicking in now. It'll be fine. Come to bed, Lily. Come on.'

'I'm going to put some ice on it right now. I have one of those freezy wine bottle wraps in the freezer, which might be good.'

'If you insist, I guess that would be a good idea although I've already sat in my ice bath tonight. God, I hate that... I'm a coconut, a gringo who likes the heat.'

'Well, you're going to get some ice on that knee. Don't move.'
'I have no intention of moving without you, Doc.'
Lily went into the kitchen and wrapped some ice cubes in a clean kitchen towel and then found the bottle wrap.
'Now, stay still, I'm going to lay the bottle wrap gently on you, OK.'
'Why does everything you say sound so sexy, Lily?'
'It doesn't, it's your interpretation, it's all in your mind.'
'You have no idea what's in my mind... Ouch, that's really cold, Lily.'
'Don't make a fuss, now I'm going just to rest the ice cubes in the tea-towel on your leg above the knee.'

'You're enjoying this, aren't you? I had no idea my wild tigress was a sadist. You're scary, Lily, that's what you are... very scary. You'd have made a good medical doctor, calm and ruthless.'

'Oh yes? Do you see me as a dominatrix, all black leather and whips?' Lily sat astride Charlie and threw her hair back as she looked down at him.

Charlie laughed aloud, 'Absolutely not, you're my sweet Lily tigress and that's all I want.' He put his arms on her hips and held her close to him. 'Hmm, your skin is so soft... and so hot!' Suddenly he slid his hand down and reached for the ice cubes. He held a few in his hand, the melting water running down his muscled forearm, and then put his hand between her breasts. Lily gasped and screamed as the icy cold water ran down her body. She wriggled to escape, but Charlie was holding her too tightly on top of him. Then, as the ice melted over their bodies, she didn't want to escape at all.

When Lily next awoke, the moonlight was streaming through the open shutters and casting a white light through the billowing net. The air was still warm, and she lay, for a moment, thinking about Charlie and his new injury. She turned to look at him and saw that he was wide awake, staring at the ceiling.

'You're awake, Charlie? Is your knee hurting?'

'I'm OK, I was just considering taking some more painkillers, though.'

'I'll get them, they're in the bathroom, I saw the bottle.' Lily jumped off the bed and fetched the pills and a glass of cold water. Charlie was still lying on his back, staring at the ceiling. As she came back to the bed, he pulled himself up and winced with pain.

'You don't seem very OK, here take the pills.'

'Thanks, sweet Lily, I have been trying to summon up the energy to move at all.'

'Oh dear, do you think you should go to hospital and have an x-ray or scan or something?'

'Nah, I'll be fine in a day or so. The bruising will come out, and it'll get better.'

'It's so unlucky to get kicked on that knee.'

Charlie laughed as he passed her back the empty glass, 'I'm angry with myself, I should have watched out more. The guy was jumping, and he managed to flick his foot back and rap my kneecap.'

'You don't mean he did it purposely... that's so nasty.'

'Nasty... another one of your cute little words, Lily. You can't afford to be vulnerable on the sports field. Someone will always be ready to take advantage. If you have a weak spot, then you're a target. Especially as they were losing badly, and I'd been shooting the ball through the hoop from behind the three-point line. It happened in a bundle in the D, near the end of game... I guess that was unlucky.'

'Well, it just doesn't seem sporting... I mean it is supposed to be a game, isn't it?

'Hmm, well I guess it's gone way past that. There's so much money involved. I shall have to keep a low profile for a few days. I don't want to be seen hobbling around Pistoia.'

'Well, you can just rest up in bed.'

'Do you think we will be able to think of something to do?' Charlie laughed.

'You know, we could do nothing, just relax.'

'You might be able to do nothing, but I know, I couldn't... especially when the moonlight shines on your hair, turning it to liquid gold... and your little white nightie is just slipping off your shoulder... but you're right. We could try talking.

You haven't told me about your trip yet.' Charlie lay back in bed, holding her hand in his.

'Well, not that much to tell. My lecture went very well, and Rachael West, my publicist or whatever she likes to call herself, is quite pleased with me. She would have liked me to hang around the various functions and meet more people, but I wanted time with my father.'

'So you met up all right?'

'Oh yes, we had a great time, we had a few good meals together and I told him about my next book.'

'That's good... what's it going to be about?'

'Well, it's about image... not exactly imagery. The significance of outward appearance and the pre-conceived values and judgements. Of course, it will basically be a study of mediaeval portraiture. I'm calling it 'The Tuscan Strumpet'.'

Lily turned to Charlie, to see what effect the title of her book had on him, expecting him to laugh. Charlie was sound asleep. Lily pulled the thin cotton sheet gently over him and curled up close to his side. She continued to think about her work and then her mind wandered to all that Charlie had said about the game of basketball. It seemed a vicious world and not one that she could begin to understand. His world was so far removed from the quiet life she led in Cambridge. Certainly, there was corruption in the background of academia. Favouritism, nepotism... words that fitted the devious way some colleges were run. Quentin Howard would doubtless be protected from scandal to preserve the image of the college. He would continue to rocket around the world, giving his flamboyant lectures and carrying on his dubious love life. That was bad enough, but purposeful physical harm seemed so much worse. Lily sighed and rested her arm over Charlie as he slept. How she would like to protect him from more pain... keep him safe and happy, here with her under the white cloud of the mosquito net. With this thought, she slipped into sleep and didn't wake until the early morning.

29

The sun was streaming through the open shutters, brighter than the silver moonlight. So bright that Lily blinked and shaded her eyes. Charlie was already up, and she heard him in the kitchen. She pulled back the mosquito net and went to the window. It was going to be another searing hot day. She pulled the shutters half closed to cast the room into shadow. The fan still whined above her head and stirred the warm air.

'Are you hungry, Charlie?' Lily went through to the little kitchen and found Charlie staring into the fridge. 'There's not much to eat because I was away. I was going to buy supplies this morning.'

'I'm starving... there are only two apples in the fridge.'
'How's your knee?'
'I think it's much better, but all I can think about is my empty stomach.'
'Charlie Woods, you are hopeless. Go and sit on the balcony while it's still a bit cool out there, and I'll see what I can find.' Lily watched Charlie go through to the balcony and saw he was definitely trying not to limp. 'You're also a hopeless liar, Charlie, your knee still hurts, doesn't it? Have you taken more pain-killers?'

'Yes, just took two. I'll be fine. I'm just hungry, Lily.'

Lily remembered a large slab of Pecorino cheese in the larder and put it on a plate with some crackers and a bowl of olives. That, with the two apples, was all she could find. She took the plate out to Charlie, who was sitting on the balcony with his leg resting on another chair.

'Cheese... fantastic!' Charlie cut a very large slice and ate it happily. 'A breakfast fit for a king, that's what my Pa would say.'

'Do you miss him?

Charlie looked at her in surprise, 'I haven't thought about it... yeah, I suppose I do. I just hadn't noticed. Here!' Charlie cut another large slice of cheese and speared it on the end of his knife and held it out to Lily.

'Oh, I couldn't... I'm not hungry yet. I'll just have an apple.'
'Can I eat all the cheese, then?'
Lily looked at the large slab of mature cheese and then quickly nodded, 'Of course, eat as much as you like.'

'And the olives? They're very good. Very garlicky... you'd better have one or you won't want to kiss me.'

Lily laughed and took one olive. 'I think we can go out for breakfast about eight. The cafe's start to open then.'

'Oh, the cafe I go to when I run is open at six... but I can't go there this morning.'

'Why not?'

'I told you last night, I have to keep a low profile. I don't want it all over the media that I'm laid up with injury.'

'But you are!'

'That's really not the point. I'll speak with my agent this morning, and a news story will be put out. I'm not playing again for a week so I'll take time out.'

'Really? What... like a holiday?'

'Well, that will be difficult... I mean, being six foot eight and a recognisable coconut makes it kinda hard.'

'You mean your gropies will find you?'

'My gropies, I mean my groupies, are the least of the problem. And, by the way, there's no way I let any of them near enough to grope... they're just silly young girls, believe me. But, I have to protect my position in the ratings. It's like war between top players. I'm already losing ground having my operation, and now everyone is watching, waiting to see if I'll recover. There's shedloads of money involved. Don't worry, I'll speak to my agent later.'

'What you need to do is swim. Maybe we could spend time at that lovely hotel where you were supposed to stay?'

'Are you mad? The press would be out there taking photos of me limping around the pool before I even got in the water. No, that's not possible.'

'I know what we could do... we could go and stay with my father. His villa is in the back of beyond, in the hills near Montepulciano, and he has a lovely little swimming pool.'

Charlie looked at her, nodding and smiling, 'That would be perfect... but would he mind?'

'Mind? No, of course not, he'd love to meet you! He's already said so.'

'You told him about me then?
'Yes, of course, I tell him everything.'
'I hope not. I won't be able to look him in the eye.'

Lily laughed 'Well, all right, I didn't tell him everything, of course. I'll ring him later. He's never up before nine.'

'Sensible man.'

'Now, why don't you go back to bed and I'll go out and get some fresh milk and coffee and stuff.'

'I'm not that sort of hungry any more, Lily. Will you carry me to bed?'

Lily stood up, laughing, 'I would do most things you asked, Charlie Woods, but carry you I can't.' She went to go past him into the room when Charlie jumped up and swept her up in his arms.

'Then this poor old cripple will just have to carry you.'

'Put me down, Charlie, you're always doing this... and your knee, be careful of your knee.'

'Knee? What knee? It's not my knee I'm thinking about right now.'

30

'Do you call your agent, Sam, to arrange everything in your life, Charlie?' They were driving south from Pistoia, the hood of the Alfa down and the wind in their hair.

'Pretty much so... I reckon Sam has to work for the percentage of everything I earn. Anyway, the car insurance is fixed to cover you, that was no trouble?'

'I suppose not. I can't imagine being able to get my publishers or my newly appointed publicist, Rachael West, to fix anything like that.'

'You should try. You may be surprised what hoops they would jump through to keep you on their books. You're just not used to the ways of the world, Dr. Fairfax.'

'I'm not used to driving an open Alfa Romeo, but I'm loving it. It's such a beautiful car, Charlie. But you know, in the films, when the heroine is driving like this, her hair always streams backwards, not like mine, flying all over the place. I may have to stop and find a hair band.'

'Just move your car seat forward a little... there's a button on your right, it's electric so just press it a little.'

Lily did as he said, and the car seat slid forward a little and her hair immediately blew back from her face. 'That's fantastic, Charlie, how did you know?'

'Must be all the gropies that drive me around the whole time. Of course they are all fabulous beauties with streaming long hair and...'
'Shut up, Charlie, you shouldn't tease me. I am a very jealous woman.'
'I know, you're a scary, green-eyed, savage tigress. Believe me, you have zero need to be so! Any man lucky enough to

persuade you to go out with him would never look further afield.'

'You really didn't need to persuade me to go out with you, Charlie. But, seriously, I suppose you do have a romantic past.'

'Doesn't anyone with red blood?'

'That's a very clever and evasive answer. Rhetorical questions are so annoying and final.'

'If you say so.'

'There you go again. Now you're making me mad. Tell me, Charlie, who were you with before you met me?'

'Are you going to tell me the same thing?'

'Hmm, well at least that's a direct question.' Lily was silent for a moment as she thought about Quentin Howard and that she hadn't mentioned to Charlie that she had met him at the conference. 'I suppose that would be only fair... but...'

'No buts, either yes or no... tell or not tell? I don't have any idea what sort of question that is but it seems clear enough.'

'OK, fine. You tell first.'

'I knew you'd say that, you're so clever, Lily. But OK, I have nothing to hide. Yes, I was living with a girl called Jeanette... it lasted about six months.'

Lily felt a pang of such jealousy that she almost stopped the car, but she managed to ask calmly, 'What did she look like?'

'Oh, she was fat and spotty, of course.'
'Charlie, don't be horrid. Tell me the truth.'

'OK, she's in a women's basketball team in San Diego. She models for a sportswear fashion house in Los Angeles... she's got dark hair and...'

'OK, changed my mind, don't want to hear any more.'

'But you haven't heard the best bit... yes, I thought she was very cute and beautiful until I ended up in a hospital bed, and she didn't visit once. Just sent a message to my agent to say to tell me that she was moving on and moving out.'

'No! She dumped you when you damaged your knee? That's so mean and horrid.'

Charlie laughed, 'You said it... she's mean and horrid. I realised she wasn't cute and beautiful just scheming and money- grabbing, wanting to swim along with my success. As soon as the chips were down she vamoosed to live in LA.'

'Well, I just hope she stays there... it's a long way from San Diego, isn't it?'

Charlie laughed, 'Down the street would be far enough for me. I don't ever want to see the vixen again.'

'I'm glad to hear it.'
'Your turn now.'
'Oh, nothing to tell, really. My life was so boring.'
'Lily Fairfax, now who is being evasive? Tell me or I shall never trust you again.'

'Well,' Lily heaved a sigh, 'I did have a fling with a guy called Quentin Howard, he's a fellow Don.'

'A fellow Don... is that like another professor or is he a man called Don? Anyway, I hate him already... so he's clever then?'

'Well, yes, he is... I suppose.'

'So is he weedy and bald, wearing a tweed jacket and horn-rimmed spectacles? I do hope so.'

'Afraid not, he's tall and well-built, he works out all the time as he's rather vain and he has long blonde hair.'

'I really hate him now, but he's a sissy, right? Very arty girlish type?'

Lily thought for a moment, 'No, not really that either. He's masculine enough... maybe that's his trouble. He loves women too much... and too many.'

'Are you saying he was unfaithful to you? Was he deranged?'

'Well, fortunately for me I left him before he could be unfaithful, though I am sure it would have happened. He must have some fatal flaw that makes him unable to have a real relationship. I didn't realise that at the time, but I was suddenly tired of the way he lived. All parties and rushing around Europe giving superficial lectures... it just wasn't for me, I suppose.'

'But isn't that what you're going to be doing. Lily? You just gave a lecture in Florence...' Suddenly he slapped his forehead, 'Oh my God, Lily, I fell asleep last night when you were telling me about your book. I'm so sorry!'

Lily laughed, 'Don't worry, I was just droning on, talking to myself really, trying to get to grip with my new subject matter. I think your painkillers began to work, and you drifted off. I had a lovely time just cuddling you.'

'And I missed it all, damned pills, I want to stop taking them. I do feel a bit fuzzy on them... that's why I didn't want to drive. It's luxury sitting here next to you, my sweet, good, kind, Lily.'

'My pleasure, entirely... anyway, we're nearly there now.'

31

Lily parked alongside her father's battered Lancia and had a sudden moment of doubt. Was this a good idea? She looked at Charlie who looked back at her and grinned.

'This is a first for me, a meet-the-father moment. Just my luck we probably have nothing in common except loving you.'

Lily smiled with relief, 'Charlie, that's just the most perfect thing to say. Of course, you'll get on very well together.'

'Yeah, right, dumb injured athlete meets intellectual, sophisticated wine expert. Sounds like a good match.'

'Why do you think you're dumb? You're just fishing for compliments, Charlie Woods.'

'Maybe, maybe not ... but there is an elegant old guy coming out to meet us right now... this is it, Lily, ready or not.'

Lily jumped out of the car and ran to meet her father on the steps leading to the villa.

'Hi, Father, it's so good to be here.'

'Lovely to see you. What a fantastic Alfa! And this must be Charlie.'

Charlie had unfolded himself from the low-slung car and was standing, watching Lily and her father with a broad smile. He moved forward and Lily could tell he was trying to disguise his limp. She ran back down the steps and stood between her father and Charlie. 'Father, this is Charlie Woods. Charlie this is Richard, my father.'

Her father was standing on the second step, and as the men shook hands, Lily was amused to see that Charlie was still the taller.

Her father spoke first, 'Pleased to meet you, Charlie, I see I shall have to stay on the steps to look you in the eye as a stern father should.' He laughed as he spoke. Charlie smiled and looked a little more relaxed.

'It's very good of you to invite me, Mr Fairfax.'

'Oh, Richard, please, call me Richard. Lily has been trying to lately, but old habits die hard. Come in, come in!'

'I was just admiring your Lancia Zagato, sir. What a car!'

'My old Zagato... not many people recognise it. She's old like me, but she keeps going.'

'An absolute classic. I've only ever seen one before.'

'Well, most of them gave in to rust, I believe. I've spent much too much money on keeping this one on the road. I know I should move on and sell her, but I'm actually thinking about having a spray job.'

'Oh, I definitely think you should. Does the rear window have that neat little catch?'

The two men walked over to the car and Richard showed Charlie how the rear window flipped open.

'So, you can drive with that lifted open a little... it's such a cool idea! And the lines of the side windows... sheer poetry.'

'I'll take you out for a spin later if you want?'
'Absolutely, I'd love that!'
Lily called out, 'Dad, are you going to offer us a cold drink?'
Richard looked at Charlie with a confiding nod, 'She always

calls me Dad and not Father when she's cross with me.'
Charlie laughed and nodded back, 'Your daughter is the

sweetest girl on earth, but she can get in a bit of a bait
sometimes.' Richard laughed aloud, 'Bit of a bait... yes, I
like that. It describes her mood perfectly.'
Lily called over to them again. 'I am still here, you know.

Waiting in the heat... and why did I wonder if you two were
going to get on. I'm the one who feels the odd one out.'

'Well, Lily, you never did appreciate my poor old Lancia
Zagato.'

'That rust bucket... no, I never did.'

'How can you say that?' Charlie looked at Lily in
amazement. 'It's a beauty, an absolute classic.'

'Hmm, really, well then give me my Mini or better still your
spanking brand new Alfa sports any day. You have no idea
how often I have been in that thing when it starts to
overheat. Two minutes in traffic and it starts to smoke... not
to mention how many times Father has had to have it de-
rusted or de-coked or de something or other.'

'But that's all part of its character.' Charlie turned to
Richard, 'My Pa has the same trouble with his old Chevy.'

'Your father has a Chevrolet?'

'Yeh, a 1963 Impala. He's hung on to it through thick and
thin... always lavishing money on it.'

'An amazing car, classic American beauty. I'd like to see it...
and meet your father, of course.' Richard laughed,
embarrassed that he had put it in the wrong order.

Charlie laughed, too. 'You know that's a somewhat bizarre thought... you and my Pa talking cars.' Lily laughed at them and thought, too, how strange it would be. Could there be a more unlikely idea?

'Yeh,' Charlie grinned, 'Sophisticated wine wizard meets worn out basketball coach!'

'Brain meets brawn' Lily added, still laughing.

'Are you saying my old man doesn't have a brain?' Charlie looked at Lily in mock anger.

Richard added quickly, 'More likely she is inferring I don't have any muscles!'

'Well, it's not very likely our fathers will ever meet, anyway, is it?' Lily said, immediately regretting her words, spoken in jest but falling into an awkward silence between them all.

Charlie walked back to his car and opened the boot, 'Anyway, I'd better rescue the flowers you insisted on packing, Lily.'

Lily and her father stood beside Charlie as he opened the Alfa boot. The huge bouquet of tiger lilies lay on top of their luggage.

'My goodness, what an enormous bouquet! Better put them in a large pail of cold water to refresh them, Lily.'

Lily carefully lifted out the flowers and the perfume filled the air. 'Yes,' she turned to her father, 'Charlie sent them to me the day before yesterday... they were still so fresh that I couldn't bear to leave them to die in the heat of my apartment in Pistoia. They're so beautiful and so fragile.'

Her father sniffed the perfume appreciatively, 'Ahh, *"beauty is a fragile gift"*, Lily.'

'Is that Ovid or Horace.' Lily looked at her father, smiling, 'Yes, Ovid, of course.'

'Well done, Lily, I thought I might have caught you out there.' Richard turned to Charlie, 'I used to play the quotation game with Lily when she was little. Now she can usually catch me out.' Charlie nodded, 'I get the picture, talk about brain versus brawn... it seems right enough. My Pa used to test me all the time with running speeds and personal best times for everything.'

'Really? I think you were very lucky. I was a hopeless case as a father on the sports' field. Much too old, really when we were lucky enough to have our baby Lily. No, I was never one to throw a ball or wield a tennis racket. I was very proud and surprised when Lily played netball for her first team at school.'

Charlie hugged Lily, 'Now wouldn't that be just too damn much if your beautiful daughter has brain and muscle. Lily, I shall test you out later... maybe water polo? Your father must be an unbiased ref.'

'Oh, I could never manage that, I'm afraid I have always been heavily prejudiced in Lily's favour.'

'Then I shall have to cheat and deceive.'

'Father, can you believe how Charlie was injured last week? Someone on the other team knew his knee was in recovery and actually kicked him ... purposely!' Lily's face was pink with anger as she told her father.

Charlie took the flowers from Lily and held them over his head like a trophy, 'Well, *"It's not whether you get knocked down, it's whether you get up"*... now I bet neither of you knows who said that... I'll give you ten seconds to answer!'

Lily and her father looked at each other and laughed, shrugging hopelessly.

'Time up! That was by the famous football coach, Vince Lombardi. It was written over the sports academy where I trained as a kid. Well, I have to say, I'm disappointed in you both.'

'You win, Charlie.'
'Yeah, I have to admit I do like to win.'

32

Lily and Charlie were sitting by the pool as the sun went down.

'Do you see the swifts dipping and diving over the pool surface. Last time, I stayed with Father, he told me they all fly in as the evening insects start up.'

'Shall we have a last swim and then go and help your Dad in the kitchen. I feel bad lolling around here as he cooks for us.'

'Oh, don't worry about that, he loves cooking and will be happy on his own in there. I could stay right here looking at the view over the olive groves forever but, OK, one last swim then.'

Lily dived into the pool and surfaced to find that Charlie was already ahead of her in the water. 'How do you do that? You swim so fast.'

'I played a lot of water polo when I was a kid, and our bungalow is right on the beach, so I guess I'm at home in the water.' 'Sounds wonderful. Imagine having a Californian beach as a front garden.'

'Yeh, I guess, but it's probably not how you're imagining.

The place is just a two bedroom shack up the rough end of Mission Beach, way past the end of the boardwalk. The beach was a great training ground, of course, you can run for miles, and the sand is a good, forgiving surface.'

'So did you surf? Were you a typical Californian beach boy?'

'I can surf, of course, but I never much cared for the ocean... I prefer dry land and a ball to bounce.'

They were swimming and floating idly in the cool water when Richard called out from the kitchen,

'Dinner ready in ten minutes.'

'That means he wants me to lay the table,' Lily swam to the edge and pulled herself out of the pool. Charlie was behind her and gave her a helping push, 'Now that's a view I could look at forever.'

Lily stood at the edge of the pool and looked down at Charlie, who was treading water and looking up at her with a wicked smile.
'Charlie Woods, you're a bad boy. I'll tell you off correctly, later tonight.'

'Is that a promise?' Charlie dived under the water and emerged at the far end. 'I'm looking forward to that then!' He pulled himself out of the water and stood at the far end, the rosy sunlight lighting on the water trickling over his muscular body. Lily took in a deep breath. Would she ever get used to the sheer size and beauty of Charlie?

An hour later they were all three sitting under the long pergola, finishing the main course.

'You're a fine cook, Mr. Fairfax, very fine.'
'I told you, Charlie, call me Richard.
'Sorry, I mean Richard. How did you learn to cook like that? 'Oh, very much self-taught, all from recipe books at first and then over the years I began to experiment, I suppose. My wife died shortly after Lily was born, so I took to cooking then. Matter of survival, I think. Lily was always a very fussy eater.'

'I can imagine that... she just picks at her food now.' Charlie looked at Lily's plate, 'Lily, you're not leaving that potato salad, are you?'
'Yes, I'm so full. You're going to eat it for me, aren't you?'

Lily looked at her father, 'You have no idea how much Charlie can eat. It's like sitting beside a human hoover... he's always got one eye on my plate to see what he might be able to clean up.'

Richard laughed, 'Well, it's a great pleasure to cook for someone with a good appetite.'

'It must have been very hard for you, bringing up Lily on your own.' Charlie took a sip from his water glass, then added, 'If you allow me to say, sir, I think you made a very fine job of it.'

'Why that's a very kind thing to say, thank you, Charlie. I should say the same thing to your father.'

'I hope you'll get the chance, sir. I really do.'

The rest of the evening passed pleasantly and by ten o'clock, when the heat finally died down, they all decided to go to bed early.

'Good night, Father, thank you for a lovely evening.' Lily kissed her father goodnight and wanted to say more but Charlie was waiting for her at the bottom of the stairs. She wanted to say how glad she was that her father seemed to approve of Charlie and how grateful she was that he had made them so welcome. She looked into her father's eyes for a moment, and he smiled and nodded, then patted her on the head. It was as though he had understood her silent thoughts. Lily gave him a quick extra kiss on the cheek and followed

Charlie up the stairs. The bedroom was cool and dark; the polished terracotta tiled floor was refreshingly cold under her bare feet. She walked to the window and pulled the fine white voile curtain closed.

'Maybe the curtain will keep the mosquitos out.' She called over her shoulder to Charlie who was sitting on the bed, watching her.

'I won't turn on the bedside light. It should be fine.'

His voice was low, and Lily went over to him, 'Are you all right, Charlie? Is your knee hurting?'

'Do you know, I had forgotten about my knee. I think that arnica lotion your Father gave me is excellent stuff.' He looked down at his knee, but it was still as though he was thinking about something else, something that seemed to be making him sad.

Lily rested her hand gently on his knee, 'It's amazing, it's not swollen at all now. The ointment and maybe the swimming has helped.'

'Yeah, all that...and my body is very fast at recovery. Most injuries take me four days to get over.'

'Good, that's so good. But what is it then, Charlie, you seem quiet or something.'

'My body's fine, but my heart is sad, Lily, my sweet Lily.'

'What do you mean?' Lily looked at Charlie in confusion,

'Your heart is sad?'

Charlie threw himself back on the bed, 'Just something you said earlier when we arrived. It keeps going through my head.' 'Something I said? What, whatever did I say that could make you sad?'

'Oh, forget it, it doesn't matter.'

'I will not forget it, Charlie Woods!' Lily threw herself on top of Charlie and attempted to shake his shoulders. He held her away from him and smiled at her, but his dark eyes were still sad. Lily wriggled free from his grasp and sat on the side of the bed, turning her back to him. 'Please tell me, Charlie, I have to know what I said that was wrong.'

'Come here, my little Lily Tiger, you didn't say anything wrong, of course not. It was just sad when you said that you thought it wasn't likely our fathers would ever meet.'

Lily snuggled into Charlie's arms, pushing her cheek again his chest, feeling his heart beating against her skin. 'I'm sorry,

Charlie, I just said it without thinking. It's just that the future, our future, is so hard to imagine. I'm sorry.'

'No, I'm sorry, Lily. The last thing I want is to upset you. I guess I'm just scared you'll get tired of me, and I'm sort of preparing myself to be dumped.'

'Don't Charlie, don't even say it. Kiss me, let's forget all about it.'

'You're right, my sweet, clever Lily, there's nothing to be done now and it's best to forget it. I know the best way to do that.'

'You do?'
'I do, but it does involve you taking all your clothes off.' 'I thought it might.' Lily stretched as Charlie slipped her thin, cotton dress over her head and began to kiss her. 'Doesn't it involve you taking all your clothes off, too, Charlie?'

'Yes, it does seem to call for that.'

Soon, all sad thoughts and fears for their future together were lost as, wrapped in each other's arms, they began quietly and slowly, very slowly, to make love.

When Lily awoke, several hours later, she looked at Charlie and saw he was wide awake, staring at the ceiling.

'I knew you'd be awake and staring at the ceiling, Charlie, you're always doing that. Why aren't you asleep now?'

'I don't need much sleep. Usually, I'd go for a run but I want to give my knee another day or so rest. Don't worry, go back to sleep. I love lying next to you, hearing you breathing so softly.'

'I'm wide awake now. What time is it?'
'About four am... it will start to get light soon.'
Lily switched on the bedside lamp and immediately a moth fluttered around the shade. Charlie jumped up and turned off the light, then carefully caught the moth in his hands and carried it over to the window. Lily watched as Charlie opened his hands and let the moth fly out into the night. He turned back to her, 'I can't stand to see the way moths fly into their death.'

'I know, it's so fatalistic and at the same time annoyingly stupid.'

Charlie laughed, 'Exactly! That's what I've always thought too, but I'd never have found such good words to explain it... but then you are Doctor Fairfax.'

'Oh shut up, Charlie and come back to bed.'

'Just a minute, I've had an idea.' Charlie went into the little shower room that led off the bedroom and Lily could hear him rummaging through his sponge bag.

'What are you looking for Charlie, do you need your painkillers?'

'No, no, my knee feels just fine. This is what I was looking for.' He came back into the bedroom holding a small bottle. The silver lid glinted in the moonlight. 'Lavender scented massage oil.'

'Charlie? What are you up to now?'

'Just roll over onto your beautiful tummy and relax. Did you know that part of my university course was the study of kinesiology?'

'Kinesiology?'

'Yes, my clever little Doc Fairfax, now what do you know about that?' Charlie sat on the bed beside Lily and began to smooth the sweet scented oil into her shoulders.
'Kinesis, er, a Greek word,' Lily sighed as Charlie's hands moulded the muscles on her shoulders, 'Yes, Greek ... er, meaning an undirected or involuntary movement to... oh Charlie, that feels so good... er... yes, involuntary movement to an external stimulus.'
Lily exhaled as Charlie moved to kneel astride her, moving his hands down the length of her back, pressing firmly into her spine.

'Quite right, my dear little smart-ass. I am expert at body movements. Particularly yours and mine.'

Lily quietly moaned with pleasure as the perfumed oil slid between their bodies and they began to move together, in a familiar and yet new way.

33

The next time Lily awoke she reached out to touch Charlie and found the bed next to her empty. Lily took a deep intake of breath... was there no end to the vital energy of this man? She curled into a ball, determined to go back to sleep, but she could hear quiet voices outside. She screwed her eyes tight closed and pulled the linen sheet over her head. The scent of lavender wafted around her and she began to think about the night... and Charlie, her passionate lover, larger than life and yet so sweet and gentle. Lily yawned and pushed back the sheet again and blinked at the bright sunlight filtering through the louvred shutters. There could be no doubt that it was morning, maybe late morning and Charlie and her father were talking together. Lily stretched, smiling to herself as she wondered how the conversation would be going. She took a quick, cool shower to refresh herself from sleepiness and then quickly slipped on her bikini and went out onto the terrace that surrounded the villa.

Charlie and her father were down at the pool, not swimming but sitting close together on the edge surrounded by motor parts.

'*Buon Giorno!* Whatever are you two doing?'

Charlie looked up at Lily as she came down the steps to the pool, '*Buonas dias, senorita...* your father and I are working. Only princesses like you are allowed to sleep until mid-morning.'

'I checked the clock in the hall, it's only nine-thirty, actually, my man, and I should still like to know what on earth you are doing.'

Her father stood up and stretched, 'Charlie thinks he can mend the power jet stream fitted at the end of the pool. It hasn't worked for months now... but look, he's taken it apart.'

'Ah yes, I can see that now.' Lily looked down doubtfully at the number of parts spread out across the terracotta tiles, 'but Charlie, what do you know about jet streams?'

'Well, it's quite a simple motor with a pump and filter... I worked on cars and motorbikes with my father since I was a kid. It began with working on his old Chevy which was always breaking down and then I worked my way through college working in a motor boatyard and in their dry dock. This should be simple enough. Just got to clean it down a bit.'

Lily picked up a small cog and inspected it, 'My, it looks complicated to me.'

'Don't move anything, Lily, I want it left laid out exactly as I had it. Please don't touch.'

'Sorry, sorry! Can this little woman make some coffee perhaps?' Lily asked, replacing the cog carefully back on the tiles, 'I'd hate to disturb man work.'

Neither Richard or Charlie answered as they returned to cleaning the motor parts, both absorbed in the work. Lily shrugged and walked back to the villa. Why was it that men couldn't talk at the same time as using their hands? Then she thought about Charlie's sensitive hands massaging her body in the night. She looked back over her shoulder and saw that he was now firmly pushing the nozzle of a hose into a round fan-shaped part. Certainly, he was good with his hands. Smiling at her own thoughts, Lily went into the kitchen to brew a large pot of coffee. Soon the rich aroma of the coffee filled the small kitchen and wafted outside. Her father called out,

'Do I smell coffee, Lily? Will you bring a tray down here... and there's some fresh *cornetti al cioccolato* in a white paper bag on the worktop.'

Lily moved around the small kitchen, thinking how well her father had organised the space. He obviously enjoyed cooking even though he lived alone. The window ledge was covered with a wooden rack of green tomatoes ripening in the sunshine and pots of herbs stood each side of the door. Lily laid the breakfast tray carefully and thought about the empty fridges of her own domestic life. In Cambridge, she would usually have a pot of lemon or mint tea first thing in the morning and then... well then, she would throw herself into work and forget about food altogether. Very soon now, she would be starting her next book and the routine would have to return. She stared out of the window, not seeing the view that stretched to the blue Tuscan hills, but wondering how it could all possibly work out with Charlie. Could he be part of her future? Her heart lurched at the idea of life without Charlie. She sighed and picked up the tray, once again pushing the problem to the very back of her mind.

Arriving at the top of the steps to the pool, Lily squinted into the sunshine, amazed to see that the motor parts were no longer spread out on the tiles. In fact, Charlie and her father were stretched out on two sun-loungers, looking suspiciously relaxed.

'Ah, breakfast at last!' Richard sat up and clapped his hands, 'Well, second breakfast for you, Charlie.'

'Have you already eaten then, Charlie?' Lily placed the tray on a low table set between the sun-loungers.

'Why yes, your father cooked me an amazing breakfast earlier this morning.'

'How much earlier, how long have you been up then?' 'I was up about six... was it six, Richard?'
'Yes, about then, I'd only been up a short while myself.' Lily yawned, 'Buy why? This is supposed to be a rest,

Charlie. And as for you, Dad, you're supposed to be retired.'
'Hmm, well, retirement can take many forms, Lily. By the way, I have been meaning to tell you. I've been offered a new job. I was going to tell you when we were in Florence.'

'Really? Oh, Dad, so sorry, I never listen to you do I?' Lily was suddenly aware that she had spent all the time they had together in Florence talking about her own life.

Her Father laughed, 'That's just as it should be... I'm glad you do still tell me about your work and your life.'

'Yes, but... anyway, I'm sorry. Tell us now... what is this new work?'

'I've been asked to write another wine book. Another in my 'Tasting Notes' series. Apparently they still sell well.'

'Of course they do, Father. You know that... will this be on Italian wines then?'

'Well, that's the thing I need to think about. The new title is on New World wines.'

Charlie sat up, suddenly showing interest, 'Then you should begin in California, sir. I believe you Brits call our local wines New World. Although, from what I've seen in local wineries, there seems to be a long history.'

'You're absolutely right, Charlie... but then, the vineyards you can see covering that slope just over there,' Richard pointed to the sloping land that stretched away from the villa, 'those vines have been around since the Romans.

Anyway, as I said, I have had the proposal for this new title and I am just thinking about it.'

'But Dad, you must do it, it would be such a great opportunity to use all your knowledge... and to travel and see a new side to the wine trade.'

'True enough, although I've travelled so much already in my career and I've become settled in my ways here in Tuscany. Anyway, I'll think about it.'

Lily sat quietly, drinking her coffee as they all finished their breakfast. She wondered whether her father enjoyed his lonely life and if she, too, would be happy on her own again. There was an order and a rhythm to a solitary life that made it easy to work. Then, realising she was heading back to the same troubled thoughts of earlier she said quickly, 'So what happened with the repair work? I see you've put it all back together again. No luck?'

Richard and Charlie looked at each other and both sighed, 'I'm going into town to get some motor oil. I'll be back for late lunch. You two can at least have a swim. Charlie said it improved his knee.'

'Sure thing, I found I could actually kneel on it again.' He looked at Lily as he spoke and she flushed, remembering how he had knelt over her in bed. She felt her body respond to his dark-eyed gaze and she stood up quickly, trying to regain her composure.

'Shall I come with you, Father?'

'No, it will just be a food shopping trip, very hot... and it's market day. I love to wander around. I'll find something for lunch. You stay and swim.'

Charlie stood up, 'Are you sure, sir? I could drive you in if you want. I'm sure my knee will be fine for driving today.'

'Very good of you... but no thanks. I'm used to my routine market day and I'll meet up with a few chums. By the way, Charlie, you really don't have to call me, sir, you know. On the other hand... I can't help but admit I do rather like it!' They all laughed and Richard went back to the house.

'I can't believe how well you get on with my father, Charlie. He can be quite difficult with some people.'

'What did you expect then, Lily? That I would behave like a sporting lout and your Dad would be a stuffy old snob? Really, your imagination runs riot sometimes. Of course, we get on... he's a great guy and I respect him. Especially for the way he has brought you up.' Charlie suddenly grinned, 'Although you are a spoilt little princess, aren't you?'

Lily turned and pushed Charlie, who was standing on the side of the pool. Even though she threw all her weight against him, he stood rock firm and caught her up in his arms and swung her over the water. 'One, two...'

'Don't you dare throw me in, Charlie Woods!'

'Three!' Charlie threw Lily high in the air and she landed with a large splash in the water. When she surfaced Charlie was already in the water beside her, water streaming over his head as he laughed at her. Still spluttering, Lily swam toward him and put her arms round his neck,

'You are a big bully, Charlie. I wish I didn't love you.'

'Do you love me, truly, Lily?' Suddenly Charlie's face was serious, 'Because I do love you so much, my sweet Lily Tiger.' There was a moment of silence between them, only the lapping of the water and the sound of the birds in the trees until Lily finally replied.

'I think I do, Charlie, I feel I do... but I don't know what to do about it.'

'Then give me time, sweet Lily, give me more time to win you. Remember I like to win.'

'I know that, I know...' Lily kissed him and he began to swim with her. They glided through the water until they reached the end of the pool. Charlie reached up and turned the switch to the whirlpool, 'Surprise!' The water swirled around them, foaming and bubbling as Lily clung on to Charlie.

'You have mended it! Charlie, you're a wonder! Father's been waiting to get it repaired for months.'

'All part of the service, Princess Lily, do you like it? I told your father it would give you a surprise.' He turned his back into the jet stream and the water swirled and frothed over his broad shoulders as he still held Lily in front of him.

'I love it! It feels so wonderful. It makes such a difference to a small pool and...' Lily gave a small gasp as one of Charlie's hand slipped inside her bikini. Slowly they let the strong current of water glide them down to the far end of the pool. Charlie untied Lily's bikini top and she pulled off his swimming trunks, hurrying now to be with him again, her body aching with desire as she circled his waist with her legs.

'Oh Lily, my beautiful water lily, I shall make you love me, I shall win you over with my love, with my body.'

Lily arched her back and looked up at the blue sky as the cool water lapped around them. What more was there in the world than being loved by Charlie?

34

'You know, Lily, you have to be careful how you treat Charlie?'

Lily looked at her father in alarm. They were sitting on a swing seat on the veranda of the villa. Charlie had gone for a run, testing the strength of his knee.

'Whatever do you mean, Father?'

'I mean that Charlie is in love with you. It's obvious in the way he looks at you. He is completely devoted to you. Have you thought about how this affair can work out?'

'Oh Dad, I don't seem to think about much else the minute I have a moment to think of anything. I have such strong feelings for him and I know he is in love with me. But... but I just can't think how we can ever live together in a real world. Now, he is in a state of recovery and I am really on holiday. Both our real working lives are not only thousands of miles apart but... well, so different.'

'Exactly, that's exactly what I have been thinking about. You say you have strong feelings... not that you are in love with him. What does that mean?'

'I have no idea. In fact, I'm not sure if I know what love is all about. I mean, it's such a complicated thing, isn't it?'

'It shouldn't be, of course, but I can see the problem. But what I wanted to say... what I started to try to say is... more, that you must be careful not to hurt Charlie. I know he's a giant of physical strength, but it seems to me that he is a very gentle and tender-hearted young man. Very vulnerable.'

'I don't want to hurt him, Dad, of course, I don't.'

'You know we were talking recently about your precocious childhood. When we were in Florence, we talked about it. Being a child prodigy forced you to grow up quickly. I just wondered whether you are going through some sort of teenage crush. How can I explain myself?' Richard stopped talking and rested his hand on Lily's shoulder as she began to stand up, 'Don't get mad, Lily, hear me out. I know I'm making a mess of this, but it needs to be said. I just think perhaps your fascination with Charlie is something like a first-former falling in love with the head boy at school. Obviously he is a muscular, handsome young man and very charming, too. But, it has to be said, what do you have in common apart from the obvious?'

Lily pulled her long hair back from her face and looked at her father, 'To be quite honest, Father, I truly don't know how to answer you. I understand everything you are saying... I even agree with it, if I am truthful. I can't talk about my work with him and I have absolutely no interest in basketball. I went to watch a match and it was exciting but I felt I'd landed in some alien environment.' Lily let go of her hair and it fell across her shoulders again, 'All I do know is that I can't let him go. I love being with him. He makes me feel so happy and relaxed. I miss him when he's not there. I miss him now, even though he's only gone for a short run.'

'Well, I can see him pounding down the path at the side of the vineyard right now so you won't need to miss him much longer. Now, I'm going to open a bottle of cold wine and make a fruit drink for your Goliath. Good God, Lily, your young man doesn't even drink wine!' Richard patted Lily on her head and smoothed her hair, then went into the villa.

Lily remained sitting on the swing seat, waiting for Charlie to return. The seat swung slowly back and forth and she closed her eyes, wondering how long she could avoid further thoughts of her future.Then, hearing approaching footsteps, she opened her eyes and saw Charlie running up the drive to the villa. How could she doubt her feelings when at the sight of him she just wanted to throw her arms around him. As he drew near he raised a hand in greeting,

'Hi, honey, I'm home. My sweet Lily, you look cute on that swing... are you happy?'

Lily drew in her breath sharply before she answered, 'Yes, that's exactly what I am, never happier.' The truth in her own words made her senses reel as the seat continued to swing gently back and forward. She pushed her foot on the ground and kicked, moving the seat to swing high. 'I'm so happy, Charlie, so happy.'

'Me too, Lily, me too... I'm going to take a cold shower at the poolside and then I'll be right back.'

'Hurry Charlie, I miss you!'
'Shucks, honey, I've had a hard day at work.' Charlie ran down the steps to the poolside shower.

Lily laughed and her father came out onto the veranda with a tray of drinks. He sat in an old wicker chair beside her,

'I don't know what you're going to do, my dear. He really is a very winning young man.'

35

As it happened, there was little time after that quiet day at the villa for Lily and Charlie to think about any plans for a future together. There was no doubt that Charlie's knee was completely healed and he was eager to return to his new team.

'Much as I'd love to stay on a few days, I just can't risk it.' Charlie looked across the breakfast table at Lily and her father, his handsome face creased with regret. 'News flies fast in the basketball world and I can't afford for anyone to know I've had another injury. I'm so grateful, sir, for you allowing me to hang out here. It's been the perfect hideaway.'

'Don't mention it, young man, it's been a pleasure to get to know you. Any time you need a rest and escape, you are always very welcome here. Anyway, you will have to return if my jet-stream packs up again. I can't tell you how grateful I am.'

'That was nothing... any time! I'll go and throw things in my bag if you'll excuse me now.' Charlie was about to stand up when his mobile beeped. In the last few hours, it seemed to have done little else. 'Sorry, another message from Sam. She's getting really anxious now.'

'She? Your agent is a woman?' Lily looked at Charlie, her green eyes stretched wide.

'Sam? Yeah, Sam's a woman... I guess she's called Samantha, I never thought about it.'

Lily felt an illogical rush of jealousy. 'So is she a motherly type, the way she manages your life for you?'

'God no! Sam's a high-rolling agent. Probably the best in California. She only has a very few high profile clients and I'm lucky to be her favourite.'

'Her favourite? How does that work?'

'Oh, I don't know, she just goes the extra mile for me. She's been fantastic sticking with me since my accident. Now she did visit me every day in the hospital. She was working on the idea of getting sponsorship from my sports insurance company or something. I really have no idea what she was up to.' Charlie checked his phone again. 'I really have to beat it. My next match seems to be in Brindisi... I have to have a medical there and then meet with the team for training.'

'Brindisi! That's miles away.'
'Is it? Well, we can just put it in the sat nav and hit the road.'
'I'm not coming with you!' Lily stood up from the table and looked at Charlie, her eyes now glinting with a new determination, 'You can't dream that I would come with you?'

Charlie looked suddenly crestfallen, 'Sorry, Lily, I didn't think you wouldn't want to come too. We can find a good hotel wherever this Brindisi is... I'll get Sam on to it now... she's probably already booked somewhere.'

'Sorry, Charlie, but there's no way I'm going all the way south to Brindisi. It's a port on the Adriatic coast. About the only reason to go there would be to take a boat to Greece, as far as I'm concerned.'

'Or to go to a basketball match?' Charlie looked across the table hopefully at Lily.

'No, sorry, Charlie, definitely not. I'll stay on here with Father and get some of my work done. Don't worry about me.'

'I do, though, Lily, I do.' Charlie looked at Richard, who had been keeping silent, reading, or at least pretending to read, his newspaper. 'Richard, can you persuade your daughter to come for a trip south?'

'Great Scott, no, Charlie. I haven't been able to persuade Lily to do anything she didn't want to do since she was two years old... maybe younger, come to think of it. No, no... you'll never get her to change her mind. But she does understand the importance of work, that's for sure.'

Charlie shook his head, 'I'm sorry, I just have to go now.'

There was an awkward silence around the table. Richard opened his newspaper again and Lily began to clear the breakfast table. Charlie stood a moment longer and then left the kitchen.

Richard folded his newspaper, 'You were a bit hard on Charlie, don't you think?'

'Dad, how can you say that? I can't traipse around Italy following a basketball team. I mean, really, would I?'
'Well, why don't you go and help him pack?'

'No, he hardly has anything to pack and he is very used to doing it all himself. Anything he can't do he just asks his agent to do for him. He has his life perfectly well planned out. By the time he gets to Brindisi, the efficient, amazing Sam will have booked him into some five-star hotel and he'll meet up with his team. He'll be just fine.'

'What about you? Will you be just fine, too?'

'Absolutely, of course, I will. I need to get started on an outline for my 'Tuscan Strumpet'. I can do with a few days to think quietly and then I shall need to research. As long as you don't mind me hanging around here?'

'Mind? Now, you're being silly. You know quite well there is nothing I should like more. I'll go along with whatever makes you happy, my dear.'

Lily smiled at her father and then finished clearing the table. She stood by the kitchen door for a moment, admiring the view across the vineyard and wondering if she could be happy without Charlie. She had a sudden desire to run upstairs and pack her bag, ready to fly off with Charlie... Brindisi or anywhere in the world. Her blood raced as she tried to decide what to do. She looked again at the vineyard where only yesterday Charlie had been running, running back to her. Would she be able to look out into the bright Tuscan sunshine and not long to see him there. And the sunlight was only part of it... how would she be able to bear the loneliness of the moonlit nights? Standing in confusion, she heard Charlie come back into the kitchen. She turned and saw he already held his suitcase in his hand.

'I'll call you tonight, Lily, as soon as I arrive.'

'It's a long journey, Charlie, I've no idea how long but I can't imagine you getting to Brindisi tonight.'

'Sam's sent me the route... it takes about eight hours so it will be late, but she's booked the hotel. I'll be fine.'

36

But if Charlie was going to be fine in Brindisi it didn't seem as if Lily would fare so well at her father's villa. She had waved goodbye to the Alfa until it disappeared out of sight then walked slowly back into the villa. Her father had already gone to the village for his morning shopping, and Lily wandered round the verandah, wondering how to start on her work. The temperature was soaring toward the zenith of the day and she decided to take a swim. The pool was shimmering in the heat as she walked slowly down the steps and immersed herself in the water. She lay on her back and floated, trying not to think about swimming with Charlie... swimming, laughing and making love in the cool blue water. Lily flipped over and swam underwater to the far end of the pool, angry with herself for allowing her thoughts to stray back to Charlie. She needed to think about her work. She pulled herself out of the pool and ran into the villa, determined to find her files and organise a work schedule before the heat overcame her again. Hardly bothering to dry herself, she pulled on a loose cotton kimono and began to flip through her written files and then fired up her laptop. Ignoring the long list of unread emails she opened her files of new work. She nodded with satisfaction... yes, it was an impressive beginning and something she could work on now. She pushed everything she needed into a wide basket and grabbed her sunglasses. Fine, she would set up an *al fresco* study area on the verandah. She hurried downstairs and had soon found a table and comfortable chair. She set them in a shady corner of the verandah and placed her work on the table. Then she found a fan and stretched the cable through the window so that she could work in its breeze.

Did she think for a brief moment of her bedroom in Pistoia? How the ceiling fan had wafted the white mosquito net around the large bed? How Charlie had run his hands over her breasts, the ice cubes melting fast? Yes, there was no doubt that Lily struggled to forget Charlie and their time together. But it was a struggle that she was determined to win. Until she had met Charlie, she had devoted her entire life to her work. Now, when she was on the brink of success and recognition, she could not let herself down. Her publishers awaited another book and she must and would deliver it to them. Charlie had rushed off to fulfil his own commitments and now she would do the same.

When her father returned just before mid-day, he found Lily fast asleep in the chair on the verandah. The fan was lifting the pages of her notebook and her pen had dropped from her hand. Trying not to wake her he moved passed, carrying the shopping into the kitchen. Lily stirred and then sat up quickly,

'Oh my, I fell sound asleep. Dad, why didn't you wake me?'

Richard came out of the kitchen and handed Lily a glass of cold water. 'Because I have just this minute come home. Anyway, you looked very comfortable and peaceful. Why wake you?'

'But I wanted to get some work done this morning. What's the time?'

'It's gone one o'clock. I stayed in the village a while longer than usual. I met a friend and we played three games of chess. Longer than usual. I thought you'd be waiting for lunch.'

'One o'clock, it can't be. I've been asleep over an hour. Whatever is the matter with me?'

'Why do you always push yourself, Lily? Remember you are supposed to be on holiday this month. Now go and put on a pretty frock. I've asked my chess-playing friend back to lunch.'

Lily jumped up, 'Goodness, Dad, you should have warned me. I look a complete mess.'

'I did just warn you... now don't get in a state. You go and wash and brush up. I'm going to grill some fish on the barbecue by the pool. It will be a very casual lunch. And I am chilling a decent bottle of Vernaccia di San Gimignano, come along, chop chop!'

Lily hurriedly put her paperwork together and closed down her laptop. She turned off the fan and handed it back through the kitchen window to her father. He was busy chopping tomatoes and whistling as he worked. Then, hearing a car coming down the drive she ran up to her room. She showered quickly, letting the cold water run through her long hair. Closing her eyes for a brief moment, she thought of Charlie... how she wished she could lean against him and feel his arms around her again. Then, angry with herself for letting her thoughts stray yet again, she twisted the tap off with a violent twist. She grabbed a large towel and wrapped it around herself and went back into the bedroom. She sighed with annoyance as she realised there was still a faint aroma of lavender in the air... how could she get Charlie out of her brain? Just for a second she looked at the empty rumpled bed. She gave another, heavier sigh and turned to her wardrobe to find what her father would consider to be a pretty frock to wear for lunch. She pulled a pale yellow cotton dress over her head and looked at herself in the mirror. It was the dress she had worn for the photo used in her publicity. Now, she looked very different. Her skin was tanned and shining with health, her hair wet but more golden from the sunshine, and curling loose across her shoulders. She pulled a face at herself and stuck out her tongue. Somehow she didn't feel in the mood to be polite to one of her father's friends. She wrapped a small towel around her head and then, hearing her father's voice she moved to the window. She peeped out between the slats of the shutter and saw her father walking down the steps to the pool, carrying a tray of food. Behind him, carrying a bowl of salad, was a tall and elegant, dark-haired woman. Lily drew in her breath sharply. So her father's chess- playing friend was a woman. Why had she assumed it would be a man? Was she making assumptions about identity without even seeing people? How did that fit in with her work on... Lily abruptly stopped her line of thinking and returned to the scene in the garden. She watched as her father set down the tray and then took the bowl from the woman. Did their hands touch? They were laughing now and Richard was placing a chair by the pool. The woman sat in it and looked up at Richard. Now Lily could see her face, a beautiful, laughing face. Not a young woman, probably younger than her father, but a woman full of the joy of life. It was obvious, even from a distance, that the woman had a magic vitality. Lily turned back to the mirror and examined herself again. Did she exude this same vibrant delight in everyday life? When she was with Charlie, she knew that feeling of happiness. Alone she was not so sure. She pulled back her wet hair and tied it with a neat band. Her father would be waiting for her to join them for lunch. Had he thought it necessary to tell Lily that his friend was a woman... had he even thought about it? Her thoughts were disturbed by her mobile beeping. She quickly pulled it from her bag and read the message.

'Sweetlily - have stopped for big lunch - miss you so x'

Lily hastily tapped a return text, her heart beating fast as she thought about Charlie missing her as much as she missed him. Another message came back immediately,

'Agent arranged hotel 3 nights Brin... can you join me?'

Lily looked at the small screen for a minute, trying to make up her mind how to reply. This wonderful agent of Charlie's was back to annoy her. Just as she had assumed her father's friend would be a man, so had she mistakenly thought Charlie's agent would be too. Sam, indeed! Lily pursed her lips in irritation at the idea of this other woman organising

every move Charlie made. So, to go to Brindisi or not?
Then, with a long sigh, she tapped her reply.

'Must work here... miss you x'
'OK call you later x'
The few words had been exchanged. Lily threw her mobile
back into her bag and went out of the bedroom. As she went
out into the bright sunshine, she straightened her shoulders,
determined to be very nice to her father's glamorous chess-
playing friend and then... then, tomorrow she would go back
to her own apartment in Pistoia and really get down to work.

37

The apartment in Pistoia was peaceful and cool when she
arrived the next evening. Signora Marelli had cleaned and
polished every inch of it and left a small bunch of flowers
where the huge bouquet of tiger lilies had stood. Lily, tired
from the hot train journey back from her father's, was
relieved to be there. She went to the fridge and found that
Signora Marelli had left a bottle of sparkling water and some
basic foods. She had been in the hall when Lily had arrived
in the taxi from the station. She had welcomed Lily
enthusiastically. Now, looking at the food in the fridge, Lily
felt guilty that she had so hurriedly rushed up to her
apartment. Signora Marelli had wanted to know where
Charlie was, or, as she called him, *il giacotore prima
grandezza*. Lily had begun to explain that Charlie was
playing in Brindisi, but it was obvious that Signora Marelli
could not understand why Lily had returned to Pistoia on her
own. Somehow, it made no sense to Lily either, now that she
was back alone in the apartment. She poured herself a large
glass of water and took it out onto the balcony. She looked
across the street to where she had first seen Charlie. Now the
shutters were closed and Lily tried to push the memory of
first seeing Charlie to the back of her mind. She went back
into the apartment and pulled her laptop out of her bag.
Opening it up she decided it really was time to tackle the
growing number of unanswered emails. She sighed as she
saw no less than eleven emails from her agent, Rachael
West. As Lily opened the latest one, she smiled,
remembering how she had last seen Rachael with Quentin
Howard. There were a few emails from Quentin, too. She
propped herself against a pile of pillows on the bed and
settled down to reply to Rachael first. To her dismay, she
found that Rachael had been trying to get in touch about
another conference appointment. She was eager to hear back
from Lily and to know whether to accept or not? Lily looked
at the date and saw the last email from Rachael was only
that morning and that the conference, to be held in Siena,

was for the following Saturday. Lily yawned and typed a quick refusal. She knew it would annoy, or at least disappoint, Rachael and her publishers, but it was just too bad. She had no inclination to go to Siena... or Brindisi for that matter. She scrolled on down through the emails, deleting and answering briefly to messages from her department. Finally, she was left with three messages from Quentin. She opened the most recent one first,

'Dearest Lily, I know you will be pleased to know that my troubles are over. The student has dropped all her trumped up charges - well, of course, I knew she would but it has been a stressful time. I have decided to forgive you for not offering to help me. I hope we will be able to get together again soon. I see you are listed to speak in Siena and I shall definitely be there. I am sure we are intended to be together, we have everything in common. All my love, Quentin Howard.'

Lily deleted the message and the other two without even reading them. She had no intention of replying and was glad she had already turned down Siena. She could hardly stop from giving a small smile. The arrogant cheek of the man! Everything in common, indeed. The man was so conceited that he couldn't see that he was a cheating womaniser. Maybe, intellectually, they did share knowledge and a way of life in the world of academia... but what did that add up to? Lily thought about her father's warning words. It was true that Charlie was immersed in his sporting life and that she could never share it with him... nor would he ever understand her work... but... how she missed Charlie now. She thought then about the lunch she had shared with her father and his new friend, Gabriella Vincenza. She seemed to be the perfect companion for her father. A widow for over fifteen years, she managed her own vineyards and produced an excellent red Tuscan wine. Cultured and sophisticated, with a quirky sense of humour, Lily had found her to be excellent company. Richard had cooked and Lily had the opportunity to talk with Gabriella. It seemed that she already knew quite a good deal about Lily's life. Lily smiled now and closed her eyes as she lay on the bed and thought back to the scene by the pool.

'Your father is extremely proud of you, I am sure you know that.' Gabriella raised her glass of cold white wine and gazed at Lily, her beautiful brown eyes almost mocking.

'Oh dear, has Father been very boring telling you all about his precious only daughter?'

'Not at all, your Father is never boring. We talk of nothing and everything, which is very relaxing. I never thought to meet a man with whom I could share everything. We are at the same wavelength. Isn't that what you say in English?'

'Yes, that's right, on the same wavelength. Your English is remarkably good. Where did you learn to speak so fluently.'

'Strangely enough, I spent three years in Cambridge, your city, when I was a student... oh my, so many years ago now. But speaking with your father has certainly brushed up... you do say that, too, don't you? I love to use your idioms. I know that foreigners tend to overuse idiomatic language... sort of showing off, isn't it? And idioms can be very out-dated so I try to be in touch with your living language. But, I think my English language skills have definitely been brushed up by being with Richard and I think I have improved his Italian.'

'How did you meet?'

'I was giving a wine tasting at my villa and, of course, I was delighted when the famous wine writer, Richard Fairfax, accepted my invitation. Then we began to meet to play chess in the village café. I remember the first time we played, he let me win. I was so very furious.' Gabriella laughed, throwing her head back and showing her long, elegant neck.

Lily saw Richard glance across from where he was cooking on the barbecue.

'Are you girls gossiping about me, by any chance? What are you laughing about?'

Lily looked at her father and suddenly saw him as Gabriella would... a handsome man, not young... but not so old, either. She looked then at Gabriella, who was still laughing, her eyes flashing and her hands fanning the air, fluttering, pretending that she couldn't stop laughing. Lily waited for her emotions to catch up with the obvious fact that Gabriella and her father were in love. Did she feel jealousy? This was a very new situation. Her father never had, as far as Lily knew anyway, loved any other woman than her mother. Lily looked at Gabriella again, now she had gone over to help Richard at the barbecue. The blue smoke from the fire circled around them as they both deftly moved the plates and served the fish. It looked as though they were very accustomed to cooking together.

Lily opened her eyes and looked up at the ceiling. The mosquito net was bunched up and tied to the side of the bed. The scene at the pool disappeared from her mind's eye, but she was still thinking about this new development in her life. Her father and Gabriella Vincenza, an item? Brushing up language skills together and being on the same wavelength. Lily got up from the bed and went back to the balcony and stared unseeingly at the closed shutters opposite. She was glad and not a little proud that she felt no green- eyed jealousy toward Gabriella. Charlie had laughed at her for having green eyes and being illogically jealous. No, she was delighted that her father had found such a good companion, so well- matched. On the same wavelength... now, what did that mean exactly?

She would have to think about that.

38

The days Lily spent alone in her apartment in Pistoia began to form a routine. She awoke early, usually after a restless night, and began immediately on her work. Sitting at the table in the window with a pot of lemon tea and her files spread out around her, she would work for the first few cool hours of the morning. Then, finally feeling the need for breakfast she would walk to the nearest café for a coffee and pastry. Here she would be greeted enthusiastically as the owner was a basketball fan. In fact, it seemed to Lily that the whole town was following the Pistoia team with fervour. She would relate any scraps of news that she had heard from Charlie the day before. Charlie phoned every day, always finding time between training and matches. His tour continued across the length and breadth of Italy and it was a great success. His knee was fully healed and he was covering himself with glory at every game. Lily was glad of his recovery and could hear the excitement in his voice as he related each match. She tried to show intelligent interest, but her responses on the phone were mostly monosyllabic. Every time another match was announced Charlie tried to persuade her to join him. Still Lily refused and she knew he tried not to sound disappointed. Her own work was flowing rapidly into the formation of a serious book and Charlie struggled to ask her about it. After the first few calls, they managed to laugh at each other's inability to understand. They usually ended with a few reminiscences of their happy time together and then a sad exchange of regret at now being apart.

'I don't know when I shall be back in Pistoia, Lily. I miss you so much. Listen, I have a match next weekend in Macerata. Sam has arranged the hotel as usual and she had difficulty finding a good room as the town is full of opera fans. She thought you might like to go to the opera... you said once you liked opera stuff... I mean, is that your sort of thing?'

Lily was quite for a moment, reluctant to admit that the ever-efficient Sam was completely correct.

'The opera in Macerata is an international event... like Verona but on a smaller scale of course.'

'Verona? I don't think we have a match there...' The phone line crackled as he answered.

'No, I didn't mean that... sorry, you're breaking up... it's a bad line.'

'Sorry, is that better? I've moved outside the *palestra*. *Scusami, momento, devo telefonare*.'

'Charlie! You're speaking Italian!'

'Sorry, Lily...it's mad here at the moment... everyone's waiting on me to work out a new strategy. Er, yes, I guess I am picking up a few words in Italian.'

'Goodness, you sound busy... I was just trying to say that I really would love to come to Macerata for the opera, but I doubt I'll get tickets. It's an international event. I tried last year with my father, but we had left it too late.'

'Oh don't worry about tickets... you mean you'll really come to join me?'

Lily paused again, she could hardly say that she would come if they could go to the opera. Before she could reply, Charlie was speaking again,

'Leave it to me, sweet Lily, I'll sort it out and call you later. I've really gotta go now.'

The phone line crackled again and then went dead. Lily looked at the blank screen and wondered if she had done the right thing. Of course, it would be wonderful to be with Charlie again and Macerata wasn't so very far to travel. She still felt the remnant of annoyance that it was Sam who had contrived the weekend. Of course, Charlie would be straight on to Sam to arrange everything. She opened her laptop and searched for the opera programme. Saturday's performance was Madame Butterfly with a famous Japanese soprano in the lead part. Lily flicked through to the ticket booking page and saw, not to her great surprise, that it was fully booked. She sighed, and closed her laptop and returned to her work of the day. Less than an hour later, Charlie phoned again,

'It's all booked, Lily. I can hardly believe you'll be with me again on Saturday.' He spoke rapidly, his voice buzzing with excitement.

'That's great... text me the hotel details and I'll be there. Pity about the opera, I looked, but it's fully booked.'

'No, it's fine, Sam has two tickets for us on the Saturday evening. I know it sounds mad, but I'll only have time to shower and change after the match and get to the opera place in time for the performance start. Sam's told me that we should meet in our seats as

I'll only just make it. Your ticket will be held at the box office under your name and she's arranged a taxi from the hotel for you.'

'I see,' Lily said slowly, although, in fact, she couldn't actually see how Sam had arranged it at all, let alone in under an hour. 'Er, that's great! It will be fantastic to meet there. It's an open- air arena called the Sferisterio... I went there once with my father when I was a teenager. It's magical.'

'I'll have to take your word for it, my sweet Lily. I have to admit I never thought I would go to hear a lot of overweight people sing in a foreign language, but I would do anything to be with you.'

'Oh, but you'll love it! It's Puccini's Madame Butterfly... a very sweet and sad story about a shameful American naval officer who deserts his true love.'

'Well, this shameful American is no deserter and anyway... whatever, I couldn't care a rap! I shall just sit right close to you and watch you all the way through and dream about what we can do after the fat lady sings.'

And so, it was arranged.

39

The full moon hung over the open air arena, like a glowing lantern amongst the stars. Lily sat alone, excitedly waiting for Charlie to arrive. She had collected her ticket from the booking office and then been escorted to her seat in the middle of the ranked seating. Decidedly one of the best seats in the entire arena.

'*Ecco signorina, due belle poltrone accanto… in una posizione migliore, le poltronissime*.' The usher had left her sitting, rather dazed, and wondering how many strings this agent, Sam, had to pull. She anxiously scanned the milling crowds of people who were beginning to take their seats. The air was full of excited anticipation... noisy Italians greeting each other, laughing and calling. Everyone was here, ready to enjoy the night of music under the moon and stars. Everyone except Charlie. She sat, looking at her programme and trying not to worry. He had said it would be a race to get there on time. Then, there was a quiet English voice at her side.

'I hope you haven't been stood up!' The young woman sitting beside Lily looked at her with a friendly smile, 'Only joking, do excuse me. You are English, aren't you? My name's Zoe and this is my husband, Alexander. I thought you looked anxious and I just said the first thing that came into my head. It's a failing of mine, sorry!'

The man on the woman's other side, leant forward and shook Lily's hand, 'Pleased to meet you, sorry about my wife, I really can't take her anywhere!' They were both laughing now and Lily relaxed, pleased to have someone to talk to,

'My boyfriend is supposed to be meeting me here, but he said he might be late. Pleased to meet you, too. My name's Lily Fairfax.'

'Of course, you're Doctor Fairfax, we went to your lecture in Florence recently. It was so interesting.'

'Thank you, I'm glad you enjoyed it. There's a similar lecture in Siena this weekend, but I came here instead.'

Alexander leaned forward, 'Same here. We live near Siena, but we were lucky enough to get tickets for tonight. It should be a grand event with the Japanese soprano flown in specially. We just couldn't miss it.'

Zoe sat back in her seat, 'Well, it looks as though your boyfriend may miss the first act anyway, it's about to start now.'

Alex sat back too, 'He must be a rich man to miss sitting in a *poltrona*... they cost a small fortune.'

'Now you're behaving badly, Alex, you shouldn't talk about the price of the seats... Lily, here, may be unaware.'

Lily was about to reply when a shushing noise spread through the arena as the orchestra began to warm up. She had one last searching look for Charlie but now everyone was seated and she could see the attendants standing by the entrances. It was too late now. She could only hope that Charlie would arrive in time for the second act.

Soon she forgot all about Charlie's absence as the music swelled up and across the arena. The plaintive overture soared up to the sky and her thoughts turned to the sad story that was about to begin. The scene was magically set with a Japanese garden and the perfume of almond blossom wafted across the arena. The soprano lived up to her reputation and when the first act came to an end, there was a moment of awed silence and then a storm of applause. Zoe turned to Lily,

'Wasn't it superb! Words fail me and I need a drink... will you join us? We've pre-ordered in the little opera café outside. Or maybe an ice-cream...it's so hot, isn't it?'

Lily considered for a moment, now that the crowd were out of their seats it would be difficult to find Charlie, even though he would probably be the tallest man in the arena.

'I think I'll wait in my seat, thanks. Otherwise, I might miss Charlie.'

Alex stood up and stretched. Well, they might call this an armchair but I need to stretch my legs, I'm too tall for these Italian so-called *poltrone* armchairs.' He laughed and Lily smiled up at him. Alex was certainly very tall, very handsome in an English way, with dark grey hair and a surprisingly young face. Zoe stood up, too, and said,

'Oh, do come with us. You need refreshment on such a hot night and it's fun in the opera bar... some of the cast are there sometimes.'

'You could be back well before the end of the interval... or leave a note on your seat perhaps?' Alex felt in his pockets and brought out a small silver notepad and pencil.

Lily took it from him and quickly wrote a note to Charlie and left it on his seat with her programme.

'Thanks, I really would love a drink and an ice-cream... it's too tempting and very kind of you.'

'Come on then, let's go.' Zoe took Lily's arm and they made their way down the steps and out of the arena into the crowded piazza. The café was packed with people all trying to catch the barman's attention.

'Leave it to Alex, it's the sort of thing he's really good at!' Zoe laughed and took Lily over to sit on a low wall to wait. 'Alex is a very organised man and I let him get on with it. What's your boyfriend like?'

Lily hesitated, then laughed, 'Well, he would be hard to miss here, even in this crowd. He's a basketball champion, six foot eight, dark skinned and ... well, handsome!'

'Goodness, how astonishing... I imagined you would be with some very arty intellectual type. Sorry, I'm speaking out of line again!'
'What are you saying now, Zoe? Can't I leave you for a minute?' Alex returned carrying a small enamel tray. 'Here you are, *signorine*, A bottle of iced bubbly and three ice-creams... I hope you like pistachio, Lily, it was like a rugger scrum in there and I just took the first flavour they offered.'

'Oh, thank you. Pistachio is perfect.' Lily took one of the small silver goblets of green ice-creams and began to eat it with relish. Then Alex passed her a flute of chilled champagne.

'Here's to new friendships!' Alex raised his glass and Lily and Zoe clinked theirs against his. For a flashing moment, Lily remembered Charlie clinking his champagne glass of water against the chandelier in the Villa Riveno. Would that scene be burnt into her memory forever, replaying every time she clinked a champagne flute? It seemed so long ago now and so much had happened. Zoe was talking again and Lily came back to the present,

'Guess what, Alex... Doctor Fairfax has a basketball player boyfriend. Don't you think that's extraordinary?'

'Really, Zoe, why on earth should it be? Basketball players can be opera fans, surely?'

'I suppose so,' Zoe spoke doubtfully and waited for Lily to comment.

'Well,' Lily smiled, 'actually I don't think he is so interested in opera... but he knew I would love it... or rather his agent thought so.' Lily couldn't decide how to end her sentence. 'I mean, he wouldn't be interested in one of my lectures and I don't enjoy basketball matches... it's just... well, it's just how it is, I suppose.' She ended rather lamely and took another sip from her champagne. 'He doesn't drink alcohol, either... and my father is a wine expert. It's all ridiculous, really!'

'Oh, my goodness, is your father Richard Fairfax, the wine writer? I've read all of his series 'Tasting Notes'. When we came out to live full time in Tuscany, I read everything I could about wine as we have our own small vineyard. His books and articles were undoubtedly the best.'

'Yes, that's my father!' Lily answered proudly and relieved that the conversation had moved on. 'He's supposed to be retired, but he's been asked to write another book... and he seems to be re- energised since coming to live in Italy.'

'That's good, I'll look out for it on Amazon. The way of life here is revitalising, we love it here.'

Lily smiled and nodded, thinking to herself that her father's rejuvenation might be more to do with the charming company of Gabriella Vincenza than day to day Italian life. 'Thank you so much for the refreshment. I think I'll make my way back now as Charlie must be here by now.'

'We'll come with you, as Alex said, there's a crowd of people to get through. Let Alex go first, he may not be a basketball hunk but he's a fairly effective outside half.'

Lily laughed and followed Zoe and Alex through the throng of people and back into the arena. They climbed up the steep staircase between the tiers of seats until they reached the end of their small central row. Lily was surprised to see one of the ushers waiting, holding a neat posy of flowers and a letter.

'*Professoressa Fairfax? Questo messagio per voi*' The young man gave a small bow and passed the flowers and the envelope to Lily. Alex and Zoe returned to their seats and Lily stood for a moment, holding the unopened letter and looking down at the hand- tied posy of very beautiful miniature tiger lilies. She took her seat and opened the letter. Zoe, sitting beside her, was obviously trying not to appear inquisitive. Lily scanned the words anxiously and then sighed and read it through again. Charlie's handwriting was difficult to read and it had evidently been written in a hurry.

'My sweetest Lily, I have heard that my Pa has had a heart attack. I must go to him straight away. You know how I long to be with you tonight, but I have to get to the airport in Rome. I will call you as soon as I can. All my love, Charlie.'

Lily folded the letter and placed it back in the envelope, then became aware that Zoe, sitting beside her, was eager to hear the news. They had been so kind to her that Lily felt she owed them an explanation.

'Well, you were right, Zoe, I have been stood up!'
Then the second act began, the soprano's voice soared up into the moonlit night sky as she pined for her lost American lover.

40

'I'm glad you phoned, Lily. I was going to call you today. I'm so sorry to hear about Charlie's father having a heart attack. Do you have any more news yet?'

'Yes, Charlie called last night. His father is recovering fairly well, but Charlie is so upset. I think he is a lot closer to his father than he realised.'

'Well, he doesn't really have anyone else, does he?'

'No, I know. I feel dreadful. He's asked me if I can go to San Diego... but Father, I really can't.'

'Why not? You're still on holiday officially.'

'I know, that sort of makes it harder. I suppose the truth is that I just don't want to go. My work on my book is going so well and I'm worried about dropping it.'

'Well, you must make up your own mind, of course.'

'I know, Dad. It's hard, though. I do long to be with Charlie but, on the other hand, I feel I've worked all my life to get where I am right now. This second book could make or break my reputation in the art history world. I need to write it now while I have the whole structure in my mind and the energy to write it. And I've been asked to speak at a conference in Rome. I turned down that Siena gig so my agent is really pushing for me to take it up. Then, soon I shall be back in Cambridge and the whole academic routine will surround me again. My Ph.D. students can be demanding, I have to give them a certain number of contact hours and... oh, I don't know.'

'Why don't you think on't?'

Lily laughed, 'OK, Dad, *"Let me not think on't - frailty thy name is woman."* I get it.'

'Yes, Hamlet, Act I, Scene III.'
'No, Father, Scene II, I'm sure.'
'You're probably right. Maybe the name of frailty should be man.'
Lily laughed again, 'Anyway, Father, if I do go to Rome I wondered if you and Gabriella might be able to attend?'
'That's a lovely idea. Very good of you to ask. I'm glad you like her, you know. We didn't have much time to talk before you left for Pistoia, but you were very understanding and sweet.'
'I think she's a lovely, interesting woman and almost good

enough for you, Dad. Of course, I'm glad you have good company. If you can make Rome, it would be another chance to meet her. The conference is next weekend, though. They have been waiting on my decision.

'Next weekend! I'll ask Gabriella right away, but I think it would be possible. I was going to phone you about dates anyway.'

'Yes, sorry, Father. I've been going on about my troubles as usual. Why were you going to ring me?'

'Well, you know I told you about this new 'Tasting Notes' plan. I've decided to take it up, Gabriella has encouraged me to do it and we're going to Australia for a while.'

'Australia! Wow, how fantastic. When do you plan to go?'

'Well, the Northern Hemisphere wine harvest is just starting so we plan to go as soon as possible. We shall fly from Rome so maybe we shall be able to work that out.'

'Fantastic... sounds like you need an agent like Charlie's to plan your trip.'

'Your eyes get a little greener when Charlie talks about her... is there any reason?'

Lily hesitated a moment, 'No, I don't think logically that there is. I think she's just super efficient and Charlie just leaves her to organise his life in every detail. I suppose I think that's a bit strange. I mean, my agent Rachael does try to run my working life, but I don't let her.'

'Maybe, you should... that's her job, isn't it?'

'I suppose so, but I resent any intrusion like that. Still, I shall get to Rome... all roads lead to Rome.'

'That's an idiom, not a quotation, or is it a metaphor?'

'An idiomatic metaphor I would say... if I was trying to dig myself out of a hole. I like it, though ... the image of the Roman Empire's incredible road system radiating from the capital like the spokes of a wheel. It always amuses me driving around Italy, however far from the capital, you always happen on a road sign that points to Rome.'

'Yes, I've noticed that, too. So, it rather seems you have made up your mind already. Poor Charlie!'

'Yes, true,' Lily's voice was quiet with sadness, 'I won't be going to San Diego. I have made up my mind talking to you. Poor Charlie.'

They ended the conversation and Lily sat at her table in the window of her apartment in Pistoia. It was the wrong time of the day to call Charlie. It was strange to think of him in San Diego, nine hours behind Italian time. Lily looked at the time on her mobile. It would be one in the morning in San Diego. Would Charlie be wide awake, looking at the ceiling, thinking of her, missing her? Any alternative was too painful to think about.

41

The rest of the week passed quickly, Lily worked through the days and often into the night. The only interruptions were her conversations with Charlie. The more he said that he understood that Lily couldn't get away from her work and join him in San Diego, the worse she felt. By Friday, she was exhausted and drained, more from emotion than her long hours of writing. She had reached a difficult stage in the compilation of notes for her book and had finished her preparation of notes for the lecture in Rome. Now, she was packing a small bag to take to the station and the train to Rome. She carefully folded her favourite silk dress that she had collected from the cleaners. She sighed as she remembered the last time she had worn it was to the dinner party at the Villa Riveno. She thought about the paintings that hung in the long galleried room of the villa. It would be interesting to see them again when she returned to Pistoia next week... but would she still receive a warm welcome from Signora Marinotti? She had been so cordially received that night and Signora Marinotti had even asked her to call her Flavia... Lily knew this was a good sign of friendship in the formal world of Italy ... but... how would it be now? Charlie was no longer with the Pistoia team and it could all be so different if she went there on her own? Well, Lily finished packing and closed her case, no time to worry about that now as she heard the heavy diesel engine of a taxi outside the apartment. It was time to go to the station.

It was a long five-hour train journey but, after changing trains in Florence, Lily spent the time checking her lecture notes and editing the work she had done that week. All roads might indeed lead to Rome but time spent driving on them was, to Lily, time wasted. As the train passed through the suburbs of Rome, Lily closed her laptop and checked her phone. There was a message from Charlie.

'Good luck in Rome. Call me when you can, any time.'

Lily checked the time and realised it would be early morning and that Charlie was certain to be awake. She still had another twenty minutes before the train reached Termini station so she quickly called Charlie's number. He answered immediately sounding slightly out of breath,

'Lily, I'm so glad you called. Where are you?'

'I'm on the train, just about to arrive in Rome. It's not a very good line... shall I call again later?'

'Lily, I need to talk to you. My father is coming out of hospital today and I'm taking him home.'

'Why, that's good news, I'm so glad.'

'Yeah, he's doing real well, but he's very weak. It seems he won't ever be able to seriously coach again.'

'I'm so sorry, Charlie. How will he manage?'

'Well, that's it... I'm going to look after him. He's always been there for me and now, I guess, it's payback time.'

There was short silence between them and then Lily said, trying to keep her voice calm, 'So does that mean you won't be coming back to Pistoia?'

'Exactly, the thing is...I've had a medical here and after some compassionate leave it's been decided I can play for my team here again.'

'Oh... that's good, isn't it?' Lily felt her heart racing as she tried to say the right things to Charlie. 'But...what about Pistoia?'

'Sam has sorted everything... getting me drafted back and with time off to look after Pa. Also, she's found a big apartment with a lift. I'm going to move into it with Pa.'

'But how can you do that full time if you're going to be playing again?' Lily asked the practical question, but there were a hundred things she would rather have asked.

'Well, the new apartment has a small studio flat on the side and Sam has found a full-time nurse... at least for the immediate future. Pa will be well looked after.'

'I see,' Lily searched again for the right words, 'er, won't it be dreadfully expensive?' Again it was not the question she wanted to ask.
'Yeah, but that's no problem. Hold on a minute, Lily, Sam's saying something now.' Lily heard a woman's voice in the background, a soft low voice with a strong American accent. Then, Charlie was talking again, 'Sorry, Lily, Sam was just telling me that I'm running late.'

'Are you out running right now? How's your knee? The line is breaking up again, I can hardly hear you.'

'No, I'm in the new apartment. Anyway, I was saying, do you remember that I told you that Sam was working on a new contract for sponsorship with my health insurers. Well, now that I am back playing again, Sam has signed me up as a great success story. The insurers are going for it big time... ads on TV, everything and that means shedloads of dollars.'

'Goodness, that's amazing... Sam certainly does her job.' Lily tried to sound generous in her approval of this unknown entity, the super-efficient and capable Sam. In fact, she found she was gripping her mobile in an iron grip, trying to control her emotions. The phone line was getting worse, but Charlie was still talking,

'The thing is Lily, can you think about coming out here?'

'Oh, Charlie I'd love to but...' Lily was about to try to explain when the line went dead. The train was moving slowly into the station. Lily drew in a long breath and

looked at the blank phone. How would she have continued if the line had not broken? Was everything to be broken between her and Charlie? Most of all... why was he in his apartment with Sam... and breathing hard?
Her eyes filled with tears and she angrily brushed them away as she grabbed her bag and made her way between the train seats to the nearest door. Before she had time to think any more about the distance that was growing between herself and Charlie she saw her father and Gabriella standing at the ticket barrier, waving to her. Lily straightened her shoulders, smiled resolutely and waved back.

'Did you have a good journey?' Her father hugged her and took her bag. 'It's so hot, shall we go straight to the hotel?'

Lily felt her father's arms around her and struggled not to burst into tears, but Gabriella was talking,

'My goodness, are you all right, Lily? You look exhausted... was the air-conditioning not working. Here, have a sip of this cold water. I bought a bottle for you in the machine here.'

Lily turned to Gabriella and kissed her on both cheeks, 'Hi, Gabriella, thank you so much, that's just what I need. It wasn't too bad on the train but...'

Fortunately without needing to finish Lily found herself being escorted out of the crowded station and into a taxi. It was strangely comforting to be looked after and Lily's strangled sobs began to die within her. It was good to see her father looking so well and happy in the company of the dazzling Gabriella.

'You look so well, Father, is that a new suit? The navy linen is so great.'

'So it should be...it cost far too much, but Gabriella insisted. She said that I have a famous daughter and that I mustn't let you down in my usual old cream linen jacket.'

'Absolutely, Dad... anyway, you will need it for your trip to Aussie. Did you manage to get flights?'

'Well, Gabriella did... she is complete dynamite. My life is no longer my own.' Richard laughed and took Gabriella's hand. 'I'm only too glad to put myself in her charge.'

Gabriella leaned forward in the taxi seat to speak to Lily directly, 'Your father has quite enough work on his hands with writing his next book. You must know how that feels, I am sure.'

'I certainly do... my work is so important to me that it seems to take prime position.' Lily felt tears welling up again and she turned to look out of the window. The taxi was now zig-zagging through the chaotic traffic from the Piazza dei Cinquecento through to the Piazza della Repubblica. Lily eyes swam with unshed teardrops as she looked at the busy Roman scene and felt herself lost in the chaos.

42

By the time they had booked into their rooms and met again in the foyer, Lily was more in control of her emotions. Gabriella had wanted to talk to her and Lily sensed that she would be a sympathetic listener but, still, she seemed something of a stranger. She was relieved when Gabriella had tactfully suggested that Lily might want time with her father before the formal dinner arranged for that evening.

'I must go to the hairdresser's,' Gabriella flicked her hair back from her face, 'I see there is one in the hotel. If you two would excuse me, I'll go and see if I can persuade them to fit me in right away.'

Lily looked at Gabriella gratefully, 'Well, your hair looks immaculate to me, but, if you're sure, then I thought I might go for a walk around. What about you, Father?'

'Oh yes, that would be grand. I'm ashamed of you, Gabi, wasting time at the hairdresser's when all of Rome awaits your approval.'

Gabriella laughed and again flicked her already perfectly smooth hair back from her face, 'Well, I have to live up to your navy suit, don't I? Shall we meet again in the foyer... maybe about six?'

Gabriella strolled over to the reception desk. Richard watched her go and then turned to Lily with a smile, 'I have a feeling that Gabriella will manage to get an appointment without much trouble. She is a very determined woman.'

Lily laughed then looked at the time on her phone, 'We have about two hours, then... shall we join the tourists?' She continued to stare at her phone... there was a text message from Charlie. Her heart almost stopped as she waited for it to open.

'Sorry, sweet Lily, but this is not going to work, is it? My heart is broken.'

Lily snapped the phone off and looked at her father. It was no good trying to hide her feelings any longer. The colour drained from her face and she held on to her father's arm as she led him from the hotel and out into the fresh air. She took a deep breath, feeling suffocated by an overwhelming sense of loss. Then she said, quite simply and quietly,

'Charlie and I are breaking up, Dad.'

'Oh no, I am sorry, Lily. Is he still in San Diego? How is his father doing?'

They walked slowly arm in arm down the steps of the hotel and toward the Trevi fountain.

'His father is coming out of hospital today, well, I suppose right now... the time difference is so confusing. Well, to be honest, everything is confusing. Charlie is going to stay out there to look after him.'

'Well, I can imagine Charlie wanting to do that. He's a very kind, gentle soul and would feel responsible, I'm sure.'

'I know, I know... of course, I understand that and he has repeatedly asked me to go out there... but, Dad, I just can't do that.'

'You could easily go for a few weeks, surely?'
'But what if I did? How would I leave him again?' 'Maybe you could arrange a sabbatical leave or even an exchange year with San Diego University. There must be some options open?'

Lily shook her head sadly and clung on to her father's arm as they made their way through the crowd of tourists throwing their coins into the gushing waters of the fountain.

The swamping feeling of uncontrollable chaos surged over her again, but she continued resolutely,

'I couldn't possibly leave my work in Cambridge just like that... I have students half way through their PhDs, all depending on contact hours with me... and others wading through research... I couldn't abandon them mid-stream. Sabbaticals and university exchanges are always arranged a few years in advance... it wouldn't be possible for this year. And then there is my own work.'

'Ah, I see. Wait a minute, Lily, I know a small café behind the Piazza Navona. I think we need a cold drink and somewhere to sit quietly. Come along.'

Lily gave a sigh, partly of relief, and followed her father through the cobbled back streets. How often she had done this before when her father had taken her on holidays. From when she was only just old enough to walk, she had followed in her father's footsteps around Europe. He always knew his way to a small café or restaurant away from the tourist trail. Now there was some comfort in letting him take over again. But Lily also sighed because she knew there was nothing her father could do about the distance between Charlie and herself.

They were back in the hotel foyer at exactly six o'clock and found Gabriella already waiting for them. She was sitting in a group of people, talking and laughing. Lily's fragile state of recovery, after a long, consoling conversation with her father took another blow as she saw that Quentin Howard was amongst the people in Gabriella's group.

'I'm going to dash up and change, Father, I'll meet you for dinner at eight.'

'Of course, good idea, you'll feel better if you have a cool shower and some peace and quiet. Off you go, trot trot!'

Lily walked quickly to the lift and was relieved to see her father intercept Quentin as he stood up. Even though her spirits were low, she gave a small smile as she saw her father place an arm around Quentin's shoulder and determinedly turned him away from the lift. She just caught the first words of the conversation before the lift doors swished closed.

'Hello, Quentin. I wondered if you would be here. Lily will be down later. I wanted to tell you about a wine that I have just discovered, it's a big red wine...'

As the lift soared upwards, Lily felt a sudden exhaustion and when she reached her room, she threw herself on the bed and began to cry. If Charlie's heart was broken, then she felt hers to be in small jagged pieces. Shuddering sobs wracked her body as she thought of Charlie so far away. Worst of all was that she knew it was all her fault. It was obvious that Charlie had to stay in San Diego and care for his father. On top of that, he had the chance to play with his own team again, make his fortune, save for his dream of opening a basketball training school for underprivileged kids. Everything, absolutely everything, led to the fact that his life was in California and always would be. But not hers. Lily sat up in bed and began to dry her eyes as her sobs subsided. How could she possibly leave everything she loved in Cambridge, all her hard-earned and early academic success... abandon it all to go to live in San Diego? If she felt like an alien at a basketball match then how would she feel living in a beach apartment in California. It was impossible to imagine. Simply impossible. Equally impossible, it now seemed, to answer Charlie's last message. Lily turned off her phone and threw it onto the bedside table. Her head was thudding as though her heart was beating in her forehead. Lily pulled off her clothes and looked at herself in the mirror. Pale lines from her bikini showed on her tanned skin and her face was swollen and pink from crying. Suddenly she felt angry with herself and with the rest of the world. She pulled her hair back from her face and spoke into the mirror.

'What a fine mess! Pull yourself together, Doctor Fairfax and let your brain rule your body. The other way round just doesn't work.'

43

Lily was on her way back to Pistoia. She leant back in her seat and closed her eyes. The conference weekend had been utterly exhausting. Then, her eyes flashed open as she realised something. The weekend had also been an outstanding success and a great deal of fun. After her outburst of sobbing, she had managed to pull herself together and go down to dinner. She had not been at all surprised to find that Quentin Howard was already there, cocktail in hand, standing and talking animatedly in the midst of a group of people.

'Lily, you're looking as beautiful as ever.' Quentin greeted her the minute she walked into the long dining room. His voice, trained for giving lectures, was smooth and friendly.

'Hi, Quentin, this is no surprise. How are you?' Lily managed to dodge his welcoming kiss and held her hand out to shake his firmly. 'You know my father and perhaps you have already met Gabriella Vincenza?'

'Yes, we chatted in the foyer.'

Everyone took their seats and Lily turned to the man on her left. 'I don't think we've met? I'm Lily Fairfax.'

'Pleased to meet you at last, Doctor Fairfax. I know a lot about you and Rachael arranged for me to be here tonight. A great pleasure.' The man, thickset and immaculately groomed, smiled at Lily. 'I'm Vince Wright, I work for a media company.' He looked at Lily through thick, black-rimmed glasses, his eyes bright with humour. 'I'm here to try to persuade you to run a TV series on the history of Italian art.'

'Goodness, and I thought I was just here to eat dinner!' Lily laughed and opened her napkin, 'Rachael works in mysterious ways... she certainly makes the most of these conferences. She gets to know everyone.'

Rachael looked across the table at Lily, blushing as she replied, 'It's my job to be social... to bring people together.'

'Of course, and you are very good at it, Rachael. You already know Quentin very well, I believe.'

Quentin interrupted, 'We only met at the Florence conference, but we did get together briefly.'

'I thought I saw you two together.' Lily was enjoying making Quentin squirm and she continued, 'But then, you know just about

everyone on the lecture circuit, Quentin, don't you?' She turned to Quentin and smiled sweetly, raising her eyebrows.

'Well, I...' for once, he seemed lost for words, 'yes, of course, I'm well-known but I intend to take next year seriously and get down to some writing. Also, take on this BBC project if you're going with it, too. I've just turned down an offer to go to the States. I want to spend more time in Cambridge.'

Lily was quiet then. So, the TV series would be working alongside Quentin. She thought about it for a moment and came reluctantly to the decision that they would, in fact, make a good working partnership. He was so extrovert and always a fluent talker whereas she would be happy to provide a more serious background. But then she guessed that Quentin was hoping to rekindle their relationship. She gave a long sigh,

'Strange coincidence,' she said and turned to her father, 'I've just decided to turn down that offer to go to California.'

'I thought you would, Lily.' her father answered quietly, 'I thought you would.'

The conversation then turned to a more general discussion on the subject of the conference the following day. Gabriella was in her element, talking about Italian history of art with knowledge and sparkling wit. Lily's father listened more than he talked but occasionally said a few words which were so to the point that everyone would look at him and wait for him to finish.

'I can see why you were an early child prodigy, Lily. Your father always sees through to the heart of a matter, doesn't he. Not just about wine, either.' Quentin looked at Lily, 'I hope I may be able to spend more time with him, pick his brain about some wines I'm interested in.' Then he turned to Richard, 'You live in Tuscany, now, don't you? Perhaps I could drop by some time?'

Lily caught her father's eye across the table and frowned at him as he answered,

'Good idea, Quentin, but Gabriella and I are going to Australia for some time.'

'Richard is writing a new book.' Gabriella added, looking proudly at Richard.

'Oh, I didn't realise you were both...' Quentin faltered to a halt and Richard answered quickly into the pause,

'Oh yes, we are most definitely an item... I think that is the modern day vernacular.'

Quentin raised his glass to Richard, 'My congratulations, Richard, you're a lucky man to have two such beautiful and clever women in your life.'

The ticket inspector came through the train, interrupting Lily's train of thought. She searched for her ticket and then saw there was a new message on her mobile. A message from Charlie.

'We need to talk - please call - you are always on voicemail.'

Lily's head began to throb as she replied and heard the ringing sound far away in San Diego. Why was she hoping that Charlie wouldn't answer? But he did,

'Lily, at last, I've been trying to get through to you. I know you've had your conference and probably had your phone off but...'

'Sorry, Charlie. I just didn't know what to say to your last message. At first I cried and then ... somehow I had to get through the weekend's work. How is your father?'

'It's hard, Lily, he's very weak. I can hardly recognise the man I left when I came to Italy.'

'I'm so sorry, Charlie. This is all so difficult and you having to cope all on your own.'

'That's the thing, Lily... that's why I needed to talk to you. I guess with all the high emotion around me and all... I'm sorry, Lily but, well, there's no good way to say this. I'm seeking comfort with Sam. She's been like an angel and my Pa loves her. My heart is broken by you, Lily. I know you'll never come out here and I shall never be back in Pistoia. I don't know what more to say.'

'I understand, Charlie, I do... I'm crying now, but I know I can never be what you need.'

'I shall never forget you, my sweetest Lily. I think you are the best thing that ever happened in my life, but there was always part of me that knew it couldn't last.'

'I know, I know...' Lily was sobbing now and then the train rushed into a long tunnel and the connection broke.

44

The last few days of Lily's lease on the apartment in Pistoia passed by quietly. Signora Marelli was hoping that Lily would extend the lease and asked daily about Charlie. Lily routinely explained that Charlie was now playing again for his team in San Diego, but her words seemed to be wasted. It was hard, repeating again and again that Charlie would not be returning to Pistoia. Lily stayed long hours in her room, working rather fruitlessly on her manuscript. She had not been surprised when, hoping for another viewing of the portraits at Villa Riveno, Flavia Marinotti had replied, rather coldly, that it would not be convenient. Nor had there been an offer of an invitation in the future. It seemed that without Charlie playing for Pistoia, Lily was not so welcome at the Villa. Now, she had reached a point where she needed to carry out more research and she looked forward to getting back to Cambridge and moving forward. Before she left Rome she had discussed at length with Quentin about their work and, again, she reluctantly admitted to herself that they did share many academic opinions and relevant knowledge.

'What do you think about this TV series offer, Lily? Are you interested?'

'I'm still thinking it over. I need to know more about the length of the series and how the time schedule would run. I don't know...' Lily hesitated and looked away from Quentin as she continued, 'I know we could work well together... I mean, I think it would be a success in many ways but...'

'Why any buts, Lily. I think it would be great and it would give us a chance to be together again.'

'Yes, well, that's where the 'but' comes into play.'

'Come on, Lily, you know we are good together, you pretty much just said so. I want to be back with you, Lily. I have never felt this way for anyone before... it's as though you are enough for me.'

'Really, well, that's just typical Quentin-talk. Does it ever occur to you that you are not enough for me?'

There was a long silence, if a silence could be loud then this was how it would be. Quentin's handsome face went through a range of expressions from astonishment to pain. So that was that. A crestfallen Quentin had turned away from Lily and nothing more was said on the matter. Now, as she moved around the apartment packing

the last of her possessions, she decided to postpone the whole matter of the TV series until she was back in Cambridge and on top of her work.
Signora Marelli gave Lily a tearful leave-taking, asking Lily to send her fond wishes to Charlie, *il giacotore prima grandezza*. Lily nodded and smiled, embraced Signora Marelli and jumped quickly into the waiting taxi. She waved farewell until the taxi rounded the corner and Signora Marelli was lost to sight. Lily heaved a deep sigh of relief and rested her head back on the car head rest. She was exhausted from controlling her emotions. Every day she thought about Charlie and fought a battle to subdue her tears. Sometimes she won the battle and threw herself into her work. Other times she had let the tears fall and felt choked by feelings of mixed grief and anger. As the taxi drew up at Pistoia Station and she began her journey back to England, she resolved that she would not spill another tear over Charlie Woods. He had already found consolation with Sam. How could love pass away so quickly? Was he just like Quentin, able to make love and then forget? Had they really loved each other? Why had she been able to put her work before her love for Charlie?

Half an hour later she was sitting on the train, travelling north. The train was crowded, but she felt dreadfully alone amongst the throng of passengers. She looked around the train. Opposite, was a mother with two children, already serving a packed lunch. Beside her, two women talked excitedly about their planned shopping trip in Milan. Families and friends, even lovers across the aisle, everyone seemed to be with someone... and to be so happy. Was she to be alone now, back to her secluded life, moving back and forth from her rooms in college to the dark panelled libraries. Work, work and more work? Lily pulled out her mobile and saw she had a good signal. She quickly dialled her father's number. It rang a few times and then Gabriella answered,

'*Pronto*, Lily is that you? Your father left his phone on the terrace and I thought I should answer it. I saw your name on the screen and he wouldn't want to miss you. Hold on, he's in the pool. I'll run down with his phone.'

'Hi, Gabriella, how are you? You're flying tomorrow, now, aren't you?'

'Yes, we're flying to Paris and then staying a few days ... then the long haul to fly Sydney. We decided to come back here for a week to get more sorted. I had some troubles with the vineyard. Now we are quite ready.'

Lily listened as Gabriella talked, getting accustomed to hearing a woman talking about her father and using the 'we this' and 'we that'. It was new and somewhat strange, but Lily was pleased for her father. How long must he have felt the sort of loneliness she suffered now?

'Your father is just drying himself, he'll be with you in a minute. Are you all right to hang on?'

'Oh yes, I'm on the train to Milan. I'm staying two days there for some research I need and then flying to Stansted. The line is good at the moment... unless we lose connection in a tunnel... it's fine.' Lily hesitated for a moment, her heart beating faster as she remembered the phone line breaking the last time she had spoken to Charlie. She sat straighter in the seat and continued, 'It's a good time to talk.'

'*Allora*, I am so pleased to have time to thank you for the wonderful conference weekend. Your lecture was definitely the highlight of the whole event. Everyone was talking about you... we felt so proud. I heard several people say that you were pushing Quentin Howard off his high pedestal. Apparently he has been on top of the lecture circuit for a few years now. Of course, his lecture was very exciting, but I was left feeling that not much had been said... even though it was so amusing.' Gabriella chatted on, her usual vitality much in evidence. Lily wondered whether she was always so ebullient and full of life. How did that work with her father's usual quiet, even sombre, lifestyle? '*Ah, eccolo qui! Tuo padre... finalmente.* But one last thing, Lily... talking of Quentin Howard... and I know it is absolutely none of my business, of course, but... well, *non ho peli sulla lingua...* I have a habit of saying what I think... especially to another woman. I don't know what there is between you and Quentin, but I think you should be very careful, *si, si... stare ben attenti* ... he is, I think you say now in English, he is a player? Yes?'

'Yes, thanks, Gabriella, you're quite right and I'm glad you do make it your business. Believe me, I need all the help I can get from a woman of the world. I seem to be permanently in a whirl of confusion as far as understanding love.'

'Dear, Lily, you are young and so far your life has been devoted to academia. You're a beautiful woman, *bellissima*, you are certain to break many hearts before you find the right one.'

'But I don't want to break anyone's heart, or my own. I just hate how I broke up with Charlie. It's been horrid.'

'Poor Lily, that was bad luck but maybe... all for the best, *non*? From what your father said he was a wonderful young man, but you didn't exactly share interests... I know, it's an odious expression, but one has to think perhaps it was all for the best... *cadere a piedi*?'

'Maybe?' Lily answered doubtfully, 'But I know Father liked him and they got on surprisingly well together. Charlie even mended the jet stream pump in the pool.'

'Well, my dear, if you really want some worldly woman's advice... it's one thing to have one's pipes fixed and quite another to make a life decision. I think Quentin has all the shared intellect and Charlie was your perfect lover but somewhere out there in this beautiful world, you will find the man who has everything you desire. Now, your father is getting quite jealous that we are chatting for so long, so now I really will pass you to him. *Buon viaggio, in bocca al lupo! Ciao, ciao!*'

'*Crepi il lupo*, Gabriella and have a great time over in Aussie! *Ciao*!'

'I'm on the phone now, Lily, I'm impressed with your idiomatic Italian. I thought you and Gabi were never going to stop gossiping. I'm not used to this, you know.'

'Sorry, Dad... but do you know, Gabriella said so many things I needed to hear. I think she's just lovely, Dad.'

'Well, it's good to hear you say that, Lily. I was quite worried about you meeting her at first. Now, I can see, I shall have to start worrying about getting a word in edgeways. Anyway, how are you?'

'I'm fine, Father, quite fine... you know, I think it's called moving on or something.'

'Are you on the train now?'

'Yes, on my way back to England via Milan. I'm recovering my equilibrium and Gabriella has talked some sense into me. I feel so much better. And, I suppose I'll work out this love thing one day.'

'Of course you will, just hang on to your own self... that's all I would say. Read some D.H. Lawrence in your spare time... his poetry ... all about the kernel of yourself.'

'Hmm, sounds too sort of free spirit hippie for me. I prefer Shakespeare's take on the subject...'

'I know exactly what you're going to quote.'

'This is taking our quotations game to the next level, Father. You're going to guess the quote before I recite it?'

'How about... "*Ay, me! For aught that I could ever read, could ever hear by tale or history...*' finish for me, Lily!'

Lily laughed and said in a mock, melodramatic voice, '*The course of true love never did run smooth*.'

Her father laughed too, 'Lysander in A Midsummer's Night Dream, Act I, Scene II'

'Act I, Scene I, Dad, not Scene II!' 'Just testing, Lily dear, just testing.'

45

Lily pulled her large wheeled bag across the wide marbled expanse of Milan Centrale. The station was one of Lily's favourites and she walked slowly, looking up at the huge steel canopied roof and the majestic domed roof. The station also housed one of Lily's favourite Italian cafés and she made her way through the crowds and found an empty table and ordered a citron pressé. She stood her large suitcase upright and slid her laptop bag off her shoulder, pleased to have arrived and to be off the crowded train. Just as the waiter was bringing her drink, there was a movement to her left and she suddenly felt her bag being dragged from her shoulder. Lily jumped up and clung desperately to the strap of the bag. The man facing her was hooded, his eyes dark but frightened as they looked at each other for a brief second. Suddenly, a terrible anger rose up within Lily. She kicked out at the man, her high heeled shoe making hard contact with his shin. She saw the flash of pain across the man's face but still he was pulling at the laptop bag. Lily hung on as long as she could but then, as the man gave a violent tug, it slipped from her grasp and the man turned to run. Lily was now in a wild temper, thinking of all her work in the bag. She grabbed the handle of her large suitcase and rolled it hard into the man's legs. He went down heavily as the bag made hard contact with his knees. Lily reached down and grabbed her bag, easily pulling it away from the man who was now scrambling awkwardly to his feet. Lily clutched her laptop bag close to her chest and gave a final kick to the man as he struggled to run to the door. Lily watched, panting and hot, as two men now grappled with the thief and held him between them. Her breathing began to slow down but Lily still kept her bag close as she began to be surrounded by a group of people. The waiter picked up her suitcase from where it had rolled across the marble floor. Lily sat down and, to her surprise, felt quite calm. It was over... apart from the crowd now milling excitedly around her, talking and asking questions. She stood up quickly and took her suitcase from the waiter. She pretended not to understand their questions and spoke in broken Italian.

'Taxi, please! *Aeroporto*!' Lily tapped her non-existent watch to show she was late. The waiter nodded and replied in English.

'You have a plane to catch? *Aspett' un' attimo, signorina*!' He dashed out onto the pavement to the taxi queue. Lily followed, escorted by the crowd that had gathered around her. The waiter held open the door of the first taxi and Lily slid inside quickly, still clasping tightly to her laptop as the waiter pushed her heavy suitcase in after her. The crowd now broke into a round of applause, clapping and calling after her, *'Brava, bravissima, bravissima signorina!'*
As soon as the taxi had pulled away from the piazza in front of the station, Lily leaned forward and gave the name of her hotel.

'All'aeroporto, signorina, no? Linate… no?'
'No, ho cambiato idea, grazie, all'hotel Cavour, per favore.'
'Va bene, signorina, prego, prego.'
Lily sat back in her seat and smiled with satisfaction. She had avoided the excited crowd at the café and possibly a lengthy round of questions from the police. Maybe she was not fulfilling a civic duty but, right now, she was not too worried about that. There were plenty of witnesses and the man had been held. No, all in all, Lily felt rather pleased with herself, and a little surprised. Where had that anger come from? Lily was quite intelligent enough to be able to self-analyse her emotions and she did so now. As the taxi travelled at speed along the dual-carriageway, her mind raced along a fast track of thoughts. She was angry with Quentin Howard and his philandering shallow way of life.Then, she was angry with Charlie Woods for going from their bed of love straight into the arms of Sam. Maybe she was angry with life in general and had taken it all out on the thief? The aggressive young man who had looked so briefly

into her eyes as he tried to steal her work.She thought back through the few violent minutes in the café, the struggle as she clung to the strap of the bag holding so much of her hard work. Maybe her anger had exploded from resentment at the attempt to take her work from her... did the young thief threaten to undermine her serious working life? Was he a metaphor? Lily had the ridiculous desire to laugh as she realised how she was over-intellectualising the whole matter. Maybe it was delayed shock, she thought to herself... although she didn't feel shocked... rather the contrary. She had a strong feeling of triumph and even satisfaction. Then she began to think through what would have happened if the man had run off with her work. So much of it was not backed up. And then, of course, the man might have been carrying a knife. She acknowledged her own foolishness and determined to be more careful. She caught a glimpse of her reflection in the window and saw that she was still smiling, almost laughing. She smoothed her tousled hair back from her forehead and nodded at herself. She was smiling because there was no need to worry about what might have happened. It was quite simple. She had not let it happen. She was in control of her life again, alone but capable. Did being alone have to be lonely? Lily frowned and felt a pang of sorrow as she thought about Charlie. How good it had been with him and how she had loved their time together. No thief would have attempted to take her bag if she had been sitting in the café with Charlie. She sighed at the thought... was she to go forward alone in life, lonely as her father had been all those years? Then she remembered Gabriella's kind words. Somewhere out there was the man that would be everything she desired. Lily looked out of the window as the taxi pulled up outside the hotel. Somewhere... but where? Well, she certainly wasn't going to search for this dream man. Right now, it would be far better to settle down to search for information for her book. She had a three days pass admitting her to the reading rooms and libraries of the Pinacoteca di Brera. Her anger had now dissipated into a curious and vaguely unpleasant sense of self-satisfaction.

Filled with a renewed sense of confidence and strength, she stepped out of the taxi and walked into her hotel, holding her head very high.

46

Lily was back in Cambridge and it was raining. She had been back for three days and it had rained for three days. Now, hurrying along the narrow passage that led through to King's Parade, she tried not to think about blue skies, sunshine and... yes, Charlie Woods. It still hurt so much, like a physical pain. It was moments like this, between bouts of reading and writing, when her mind strayed back to the hot days and nights in Pistoia. Lily twirled her yellow umbrella in annoyance as her body yearned for his touch. How could she be so ridiculous? Charlie was now with Sam, and she had heard nothing from him, nor had she contacted him. It was over, but still the ache lingered on. Deciding she couldn't face another hour's work back in her usual library corner, she thought to treat herself to a pot of tea in her usual café.

The café was crowded and steamy with heat. Lily stood for a moment, wondering whether to bother. Then she noticed a couple just leaving from her favourite spot in the window. She left her dripping umbrella in the stand by the door and slipped quickly onto a bar stool. She shrugged off her wet raincoat and hung it on the rack, still clutching her laptop bag. Since her attack in Milan, she had been very aware of keeping it close to her. Then she ordered her usual lemon tea from the girl at the counter. No sign of the romantic mediaeval barista today. Lily puzzled for a moment, wondering why it was that she remembered him so vividly. Of course, it was the striking likeness to the Moroni painting, the portrait that had held the key to her first research for the new book. Something in his burning gaze... yes, that was it, he was just like Moroni's *'Il Sarto'*, there could be no other reason he remained so clearly in her mind's eye. Still thinking about it, Lily made her way back to the bar stool in the window. She saw that the vacant seat next to hers had been taken. Then, her heart missed a beat as she saw the man, dark-haired and broad-shouldered, the

Moroni man, hunched over his coffee. It was surely the same young man. Lily felt the blood rush to her face as she sat down, brushing slightly against the man's dark leather jacket. She perched on the high bar stool and stared ahead at the spectacular view of King's College. She made a careful study of the stone pinnacles, outlined against the gunmetal grey sky. Then the waitress brought her tea and Lily turned to her left. The man turned at the same time, and Lily almost gasped. The man's face was dark and swarthy, a broad flat nose under thick dark eyebrows... he was definitely not the Moroni man. His eyes were dull and his mouth fleshy and full-lipped. Then, she realised he was talking to her, 'This place is so crowded, probably because the view of King's is so amazing. Sorry, can I move my book to make more room for your tea tray?' He shuffled awkwardly on his bar seat, trying to move out the way but at the same time, running his eyes over Lily until he ended by staring at her breasts.

Lily was still attempting to regain her composure.

'Thanks, no, plenty of room.' Her bag was slung awkwardly on her shoulder, and it was true that there was very little room. Then she felt the man's thigh against hers, and she moved away abruptly.

'Do you live here or are you a tourist like me?'

Lily sighed. Why had she come into the bar? 'I'm just waiting for my husband.' She sipped her tea and pulled her mobile out of her pocket and turned away from the man. Was this going to be another bad bar experience? She pretended to talk on her phone to her imaginary husband. To her relief, she heard the man at her side begin to leave. She stayed with her back turned until she caught a glimpse of him leaving the bar. She put her mobile back in her pocket and took another sip of tea. Why was it so difficult to be a woman alone in a bar? It was ridiculous. The rain was now trickling slowly down the window, but there was a shaft of light in the sky above the Senate House. Lily decided to stay awhile now that she had been left in peace. She ordered a cheese panini and a glass of water. Then, took out a book and began to read. For some reason she found it hard to concentrate, still feeling somehow disturbed by the fact that the chatty dark-haired man had not been her Moroni man. The words on the page blurred in front of her, and she closed the book with a sigh. Was she so desperate to have a man in her life that she was clinging on to a memory? Ridiculous again. And yet, she found herself turning to look at the bar, hoping that somehow the barista might appear... pouring coffee, looking at her across the crowded bar with his burning eyes, holding out his hand toward her... but, of course, he wasn't. Even the girl who normally served had disappeared and been replaced by a very stout, motherly woman with dyed blonde hair. Lily left half her panini, finished the glass of water then went to the counter to pay. The woman rang up the bill and then gave Lily her change. Was there something in the way she held out her hand, something in the curve of her arm that reminded Lily of Moroni man. Lily took the money and almost ran from the bar... surely she was going mad?

The rain had stopped and the city, newly washed, was shining brightly under a pale blue sky. Lily strolled along King's Parade, trying to regain her equilibrium and still reluctant to return to her work. She stopped to look at a window display in a Swedish designer clothes shop. She studied the large square shapes of rough linen and loose knit cottons but decided the look was not for her. She looked down at the close-fitting dress she had found time to buy in Milan... yes, Italian was much more her style. She looked at her reflection in the window and saw, standing behind her on the other side of the narrow road, the man from the café. Not the Moroni man but the guy who had pestered her, pressing his thick thigh against her. She stood still for a moment, pretending to look closer at one of the mannequins in the window display. Yes, it was the same man... he was standing still, staring at her. Lily, moved slowly on, holding her laptop bag close to her side and trying to stay calm. She walked past the next few shops and then stopped at a newsagent with a rack of postcards outside. She pulled out her phone and pretended to speak into it. There was no-one she could think of to call. Maybe she could call Quentin... but no, that would open a whole new problem. Anyway, she was probably over-reacting, and this man was just a creep, following her for no particular reason. She picked a postcard at random and went into the shop to pay for it. She waited in a queue of Japanese tourists, all talking excitedly, trying to make up their minds about their purchases. She waited patiently, pleased to have time for the man outside to give up and disappear. When she emerged from the dark little shop, she was momentarily dazzled by the sunlight. The rain clouds had completely disappeared, and the air was warm. She raised her hand to shade her eyes and immediately saw the outline of the man sitting on the low wall across the street. She turned quickly and walked in the direction of her college. It did seem that he was following her. Lily's heart thumped as she realised that the correct word was not following but stalking. Maybe she was still shaken from the incident at Milan station as now she felt her legs strangely weak. She wanted to run but, as though in a real life nightmare, she felt almost unable to move forward. She resisted the desire to look over her shoulder as she turned the corner, away from the mainstream of tourists and made her way down a narrow alley toward the rear entrance to her college. She forced herself onward, trying to walk faster but hearing footsteps close behind her. Now, she wished she had stayed in the main thoroughfare or even phoned Quentin... her head began to swim, and she tried to call out, but her throat was too dry. With the last of her strength, she reached the porter's lodge and there, to her relief she saw Henry standing at the door. She almost fell into the doorway.

'Henry, I'm being followed.' She gasped the few words and then sat on the bench in the shade of the stone arch that led to the quadrangle. She heard Henry go out into the street and then she concentrated on regaining her breath. Slowly the green lawns and stone walls came back into focus. She put her head down into her lap, still feeling as though she could faint. Then Henry returned and she heard the porter's lodge door close with a solid thud.

'Are you all right Doctor Fairfax? What was that all about? I saw the man and he saw me on my mobile and then he scarpered. Do you want me to call the police?'

'Oh no, Henry, I feel stupid really. The man spoke to me in a café and I rather snubbed him, then, when I came out of the café he was waiting outside and began to follow me.' Lily's explanation came out in a rush and Henry patted her on the shoulder.

'What you need is a cup of that lemon tea you drink. Come inside the lodge and I'll put the kettle on... and I have a lemon from the college greenhouse. That'll put you right. You'll be fine now you're back safe within the college walls.'

Lily stood up, still feeling wobbly and slightly dizzy. Henry was still talking,

'Problem is, Prof, you're a bit too young and much too beautiful. You haven't had a chance to understand the ways of the nasty real world we have to live in.'

Lily sat in the comfort of the porter's office, drinking her lemon tea and nibbling a ginger biscuit... thinking carefully through all that Henry had said.

47

Lily remained cloistered within the college precinct for the next few days. She was strangely unnerved by the man following her from the cafe in King's Parade... and yet...

'Why should my daily routine of taking lemon tea in my favourite cafe be destroyed by him?' Lily asked herself the question as she looked out over the neat lawn of the quadrangle below her window. She returned to the work on the desk in front of her, sighing impatiently as she tried to regain concentration for the third time that morning. She was attempting to read through a draft thesis from one of her students. The writing was weak and the response to the title frequently strayed toward inaccuracy. Lily sighed again in exasperation and defeat. She would have to wait until the student returned and take the whole thing apart. There was a watery sun glancing through the small leaded window and she needed some fresh air. She closed the files in front of her and stood up. Maybe she would go to a different café or even walk through to Newnham and over to Grantchester. Yes, she would find a deck chair in a secluded corner of the Orchard tea-rooms and take her tea there. She went into the small shower room that led off from her bedroom and splashed water on her face. She patted her face dry and looked into the mirror as she smoothed sun lotion over her face. Her Italian tan had begun to fade and her eyes looked sadly back at her as she began to brush her hair. Where were the green tiger eyes that Charlie had loved so much? She brushed her long red-gold hair more vigorously as tears clouded her vision. Then, dragging her hair firmly back from her face she secured it with a band and straightened her shoulders. She looked at herself critically in the mirror. Then, suddenly she smiled and almost laughed aloud.

'Why don't you admit it, Lily Fairfax? It's not lemon tea you're after... it's the young man, the Moroni man.' She shook her head at herself, her long mane of hair waving from side to side. Once again furious at being so desperate for a man that she was clinging to a small moment of time at the beginning of the summer. Why couldn't she forget him? Lily turned impatiently away from the mirror. Ridiculous... and yet... half an hour later she was opening the door to the café and joining the short queue at the bar.

He wasn't there. The Moroni man was nowhere to be seen. Once again she gave her order to the brassy-haired woman standing behind the counter. She found a seat in the window and began to sip her lemon tea. One consolation... at least the swarthy man who had stalked her was also conspicuously absent. The bar was filled with summer tourists and noisy language students. Sitting next to her at the long bar in the window was a silky-haired Japanese girl. Lily listened as the girl spoke in rapid but broken English to the young man beside her. He was Australian and slow in his replies. They were talking about the view of King's College opposite. Lily sighed as she eavesdropped on their inane conversation. It was even worse than the student's essay that she had left on her desk. Why would anyone bother to travel and yet be so ill-informed? Unable to ignore their voices she decided to leave. The cafe was impossible in the tourist season. Maybe she would walk over to Grantchester after all. She stood outside on the pavement, tired of the constant stream of people gawping up at the famous Gothic spires rising to the light blue Cambridge sky. She knew she was privileged to be where she was and should be happy to share it for the summer but... but she longed to get away. Why hadn't she stayed on in Pistoia? Lily crossed the street, dodging between the taxis that were dropping off more and more sightseers onto the cobbled pavements. She walked quickly down Senate House Passage and, with a quick word of greeting from the doorman, she was soon in the quiet of the Fellows Gardens. She took a sigh of relief as she slowed her pace and walked slowly along the path beside the immaculately mown green lawns. Even here she could see a group of tourists being shepherded around on a guided tour. She decided that it would be even worse at the tea rooms in Grantchester. She stood still for a moment, looking across the grassy stretches of the Backs and down to the river. She wandered across the bridge over the Cam and stopped again, leaning on the parapet and looking down at the river and the people punting in both directions. Everyone appeared happy and to be on holiday. Most of them seemed to be young and in love. Lily felt engulfed in loneliness and at the same moment a cloud passed in front of the sun and a few raindrops fell. She hurried on and then decided to find refuge in the University Library. There, one could be alone and silent for a reason. Yes, she would take the opportunity of continuing some research and order some books she needed. A soft rain was now falling, and she ran across Queen's Road, through the stagnant line of traffic and into the grounds of Clare College. She arrived at the library, short of breath and covered in light rain drops. She ran up the steep steps and into the entrance hall. She quickly greeted the girl at the desk and then went to find a locker for her raincoat. She shook out her hair and then went back to the reception.

'Hi Susie, how are you?'

'Good Morning, Doctor Fairfax. I'm fine... you look rather bedraggled. Is it raining now?'

'Yes, just a summer shower but I was right over in the Fellows' Gardens. How's your research coming along?'

'Slowly, I'm afraid. I never seem to have time. Working part time here and with the kids home for school hols... I'll get into it again in September when the kids go back.'

'I know, it must be hard to concentrate. I'm suffering some sort of mind block and I have no excuse at all.' Lily laughed and went on through the turnstile. She thought about her words as she climbed the staircase. It was true, she had no excuse at all. Somehow, since she had been with Charlie, she had lost her usual concentration and single-minded application to putting her thoughts into words. It was as though the extremes of bodily pleasure had somehow fogged her mind. Certainly, he had unleashed a part of her that she had never known existed. A stab of pain surged up within her as she thought of Charlie. She reached the top of the staircase and looked up at the ceiling. She knew the building well but always stopped to admire the heavy panelled wooden ceiling at the entrance to the reading room. Her head swam a little as she looked up and she reached for the banister. Just the thought of being in Charlie's arms made her body ache. She stood still for a moment to gather herself together again. Charlie was thousands of miles away and getting on with his life... and so must she. And her life was here in Cambridge, in one of the finest libraries in the world. There was no point at all in thinking back. If she told herself that often enough it would just have to be true. Lily walked toward the reading room and then, she had no idea why, she decided to go up to the Munby Rare Books room on the third floor. She carried on up the staircase and then along the blue carpeted corridor. Here the silence was complete and she began to relax. She smiled at the reception desk and was greeted with a silent nod as the turnstile was opened for her. She was well-known by most of the library staff and rarely had to show her membership card. Lily looked down the long room and suddenly stood rooted to the spot. It was all she could do to stop herself crying out in amazement. There, at the far end of the room under a bright moon of light was the young Moroni man. Lily's heart was beating fast as she sat in the nearest empty chair. She moved aside a heavy linen book cushion and laid her laptop case quietly on the table in front of her. She stared at the table top, looking in detail at the familiar book request cards, trying desperately to behave normally. She opened a paper file of her work and stared at the pages of writing without seeing a word. Her ears were buzzing with a strange high sound, and she swallowed several times. It was the feeling she sometimes had in an aeroplane when the pressure changed. She turned over a few pages, determined not to look down the row of tables to where she had seen her Moroni man. Was he a vision? Was she in such a heightened state of emotion that she had conjured him up from nowhere? She was terrified to look and yet she longed to. She tried taking a few deep breaths and began to shuffle the pages of her work into order. But it was no good, she simply had to look. Summoning up all her courage she raised her hand to her head and, resting her elbow on the table, she took a quick peep through the fronds of her hair. It was him, most definitely. Lily looked quickly back at the table. This was ridiculous. Her heart was now beating so fast she thought she would faint. She turned again to look down the room and saw he was looking straight at her. He was smiling, that same mocking smile. He nodded at her, as though in recognition. Lily looked quickly back down at the table and began to open her laptop. Why had he nodded? He couldn't possibly remember her. She stared at the blank screen in front of her. Then, she was aware of someone coming to sit at her table, sitting directly opposite her. Still she tried not to look up but every part of her body was aware that the Moroni man had moved to sit at her table. Unable to bear the tension any longer, Lily raised her head and looked up, directly into the smiling gold-flecked hazel eyes of her Moroni barista man. He was exactly as she had remembered him. His eyes were full of mocking humour and his mouth, full-lipped and sensuous, was stretched in a one-sided teasing smile. Lily found herself smiling back at him and then he silently raised his hand and made the gesture of drinking from a cup. He raised his dark eyebrows and tilted his head slightly to one side, questioning. Lily looked at him, bewitched, seeing the likeness to the Moroni portrait painting again. Then she nodded and began to close her laptop and gather together her unread pages of work.

48

They walked slowly and without speaking, side by side, along the shadowy corridor that led away from the rare books room. Silence surrounded them as they walked between the long rows of bookshelves... even their footsteps were hushed by the blue felt of the carpet. Lily felt a dreamlike, surreal peace descend upon her and wondered if the corridor would ever end. Finally, she had met him and now, they walked together in perfect harmony, their pace matching exactly. But the corridor did end and when they reached the head of the staircase the young man turned toward Lily and held out his hand.

'My name is Leo Torrone, I have seen you before in my café. Do you remember?'

'Oh yes, I remember you... did you say your name was Moroni?' Lily replied quietly, her senses reeling at the sound of his soft voice.

'No, Torrone... not Moroni... ah, Battista Moroni, the painter.' He smiled, that same smile, warm but ironic and now his eyes burned into her. Lily took a pace back as though from the heat of a fire.

'Do you know of the portrait painter, Moroni then?' Lily asked, 'When I saw you in the cafe I though how much you resembled the tailor in his portrait.'

'Ah, '*Il Sarto, il Tagliapanni*'... but, of course, I know it. I am Italian and it is part of my heritage even though it hangs in London in your National Gallery. Come to think of it, you remind me of Tintoretto's portrait of Veronica Franco... do you know it?'

'Yes, yes I do.' Lily blushed as she replied. She knew the painting well, she had studied it in detail. In fact, it was the very portrait she was basing most of her research for her next book, 'The Tuscany Strumpet'... the fascinating life of Veronica Franca, a mediaeval poet and courtesan. The oil painting was a vibrant, quasi-erotic portrayal of a sensuous woman dressed in rich clothes, with pearls and jewels around the milky pale skin of her neck and bosom. Lily blushed a deeper red as she remembered that the woman was stretching the ruffled edge of an under-bodice to expose the very edge of one nipple, one pink-tipped finger pointing directly to it. But Leo was still talking...

'With your beautiful red golden hair pulled back from your face... yes, very like Veronica Franco. I think she has a pearl necklace... your hair looks studded with diamonds... and gold... but, of course, it is raindrops.'
He reached out as he spoke and lightly touched Lily's hair. Lily felt the fizz of an electric shock of contact, and she gave a small gasp. Leo pulled his hand back quickly, 'Excuse me, forgive me... I am carried away by actually meeting you.' He took a step away from her and gave a small bow with his head, 'Will you join me for a coffee in the canteen here?'

Lily looked down at the floor, unable to stand the heat of his gaze. She would be happy to join him anywhere he wanted... in fact, she wanted to pull him down on top of her on the blue felted carpets of the library. Her whole body was aching for him to hold her. Her stomach muscles tightened, her breasts swelled against her silk blouse, her knees seemed to have turned to water... Lily took a deep breath and swallowed, trying desperately to regain her equilibrium, then she managed to reply in a voice husky with emotion, 'That would be good. Yes, why not?'

Why not indeed? Lily walked down the staircase ahead of Leo Torrone. Her heart seemed to have been beating twice as fast ever since she had first seen him in the reading room. She struggled to calm herself and, as they reached the reception hall, she smiled at Susie, who was still behind the reception desk. It seemed a lifetime since she had walked into the library and passed through the turnstile. Then she had been lonely and seeking shelter in the familiar comfort of the book-lined rooms. Now, her blood was racing and all she wanted was the company, the very close company of this young Italian, Leo Torrone, her Moroni man.

Leo held the swing door open for Lily as they arrived at the canteen. There were several free tables and Lily walked straight toward the self-service bar at the far end. She often met students here, but now she was relieved to see that there was no-one she recognised. Right now she wanted to talk to Leo Torrone and find out everything about him.

Leo stood beside her and took two white china cups from the rack, 'Can I pour you a coffee or would you prefer tea?'

'Oh, just lemon tea for me. I always take one of those slices of lemon in hot water and then pay as though I had used a teabag.

They're used to me here!' Lily laughed, a small nervous laugh and her voice had still not returned to its usual timbre. 'I should have remembered you're a lemon tea drinker at our cafe. I'll do the same then... the coffee here is dire, anyway.' They each paid for their drinks and Lily walked ahead,

choosing a table at the side of the long room. 'Shall we sit here?' Now her voice had recovered and she risked turning to look at Leo. He was staring hard at her back and he nodded quickly.

'Anywhere, anywhere you want.' Now his voice was hoarse and... did Lily imagine it, or was his hand holding the cup and saucer actually trembling?

They sat across the table to each other and sipped from their cups, an awkward moment of silence now between them. Then they both spoke at once.

'So, are you studying in Cambridge?' Lily asked. 'Are you a student in Cambridge?' Leo said at the same time and then they both laughed and Leo added, 'You first, *prima le signore*!'

'Very well, I shall introduce myself. My name is Lily Fairfax and...'
'Oh my god, you can't be Doctor Lily Fairfax, the author, you're much too young!'
'Guilty! I have always been too young to do anything that I have achieved.'
'Oh my god, I've read everything you have written but I always imagined you so much older and... well, not so beautiful.'

'Well, thanks for the compliment but I just stuck into my studies early on.'
'Didn't that stop you having a good time when you were a kid...or a teenager?'
Lily was silent for a moment before she replied slowly, 'Yes, I think it did although I had a very happy childhood... but yes, I suppose I did miss out on fun in general. I've been making up for it lately!'
'So how old are you? Oh, sorry, one is not supposed to ask a woman's age... but then you look so amazingly young.'
'I'm nearly twenty-nine... and you?'
'I was twenty-eight last month. My academic progress was the direct opposite to yours.'

'You mean you had a riotous youth and ignored your studies then?'

Leo laughed and his dark face was alight with humour and now his smile seemed self-mocking, 'If only! No, I left school at sixteen as my father had a heart attack and he was running a chain of cafés here and in Oxford. I just had to step up and take over. My mother works in the business too, but she was busy caring for Papa... so...'

'That must have been hard... or did you want to leave school?'

'No, I loved school and had dreams of going to uni back then... anyway, it all worked out in the end. My father made a good recovery and I took my first degree online with the Open University while still helping with the family business. It's a typical immigrant Italian family saga really.' Again he laughed and then returned to sipping his tea.

'And now... you are studying at the moment?'

'Yes, I'm working toward my Ph.D.... with some difficulty recently.'

'I see, well, it can be like that. I've been messing around with the research for my next book... I've promised my publishers but... well, I'm not exactly blocked as I know exactly where I want to take it... but, I don't know... this summer my concentration hasn't been the same as usual.'

'I know exactly what you mean. I've been putting it down to a general summer holiday feeling. I shall get back to it all in mid- September.'

'Yes, me too. What is the subject of your thesis?'

'Well, so far the working title is Imagery and Symbolism in Shakespeare's Comedies'... I may modify that.'

Lily stretched her eyes wide in surprise, 'Really, how interesting. Some of my research may cross over your work. I'm looking at how outward appearance affects our perception... using mediaeval portraiture as a chief reference, of course, as that is my field of expertise. Symbolism is part of that idea... I am following up the theme of my book 'The Florentine Virgin.'

'That must be a hard act to follow... I mean, to have such an outstanding success with your first book... isn't it rather daunting?'

Lily thought for a moment before answering. No-one had asked her that before and she hadn't considered it herself. 'Actually, I have to say no. I can't really say it has occurred to me as a problem.'

'That must be because you are completely confident in your ability. *Bravissima*, Doctor Fairfax! So, tell me, do you have a title yet?'
'Yes, well, I'm wavering between 'The Tuscan Strumpet' or 'The Tuscan Harlot'... can't quite decide.'
'Oh, I think you should go for Strumpet...such a great word, origin Middle English, of course... well, I suppose harlot is too... but strumpet is much more explicit somehow... maybe because it rhymes with crumpet?' Leo laughed aloud and rocked back on his chair. How about 'The Tuscan Crumpet!'

Lily began to giggle, his laugh was infectious, and she felt the tension strain from her body. 'Now if I do title it 'The Tuscan Strumpet', I shall always think of the word crumpet.'

'Well, you could always end your book with a Shakespearean style rhyming couplet... something based on his take on your idea of appearances being deceptive?' Leo suddenly leant over the table toward her and spoke quietly, *'Love looks not with the eyes, but with the mind; And therefore, is winged Cupid painted blind.'*

Lily found herself staring in fascination at the close-up view of Leo's hazel eyes, flecked with gold and fringed with soot-black lashes.
She replied automatically, 'A Midsummer Night's Dream,

Helena in Act I, Scene I.' Then, with hardly a pause, she added, 'I'm not sure I can take much more of this conversation.'

Leo drew away from her and sat back in his chair, 'I'm sorry, I'm taking this all too fast... I am just so...so... *scusa, ma parlo troppo quando mi emoziono*! Lily, I promise I shall be quiet and boring... please, don't go!'
Lily giggled again and said, 'I'm not going. I just suddenly felt overwhelmed. We have only just met and yet... yet it is as if we...'

'Have known each other all our lives? Please don't say that because it's just not true. We need to know everything about each other. Yes, we share some intellectual ideas but we need to know so much more... have you read about emotional contagion... fostering emotional synchrony between individuals. Schoenewolf's theory of...' Suddenly he stopped, gave his charming smile and held up both hands in submission, 'Sorry, I'm doing it again, aren't I? I'm talking too much. Tell me what you want me to do.'

Lily took a deep breath. There was so much she wanted him to do, but none of it appropriate for the moment. She looked around the canteen, the solid oak chairs and white Formica tables. If only she could wave a magic wand and transfer them to a romantic bedroom with a four-poster bed. Her thoughts made her heart beat faster, and she struggled to bring herself back to the reality of the room. Then, she looked toward the door, and her racing heart missed a beat. Quentin Howard, alone and carrying an armful of books, was making his way toward the queue at the coffee machine. Lily ducked her head down and said quietly, 'I was going to walk over to Grantchester. Would you like that if the rain has stopped?'

'Are you hiding from someone?'
'How did you guess?'

'I'm not stupid!'

'I think I've guessed that already! It's just someone I don't want to see right now.'

Leo looked around the room and then back at Lily.

'You do realise that with your mop of red-gold hair that it is quite impossible for you to hide, don't you? Who is it anyway?'

Lily giggled. It seemed she was finding it very easy to giggle. 'It's Quentin Howard, another lecturer, and he's just come in through the door. I really don't want to see him. He's waiting for me to make up my mind about some lectures. Quick, he's in the queue now, let's go!'

Lily stood up and grabbed Leo's hand. They made their way out of the canteen together. They were still hand in hand when they reached the entrance hall. Susie looked up from her desk, her face showing astonishment at seeing Lily rushing out of the library with Leo. Lily turned at the main doors and looked back at Susie and waved, before following Leo Torrone out into the fresh sunshine that had broken over Cambridge.

49

'I just had to call you, Father! I'm so happy and excited I could explode!'

'Goodness, Lily, this is not like you... whatever has happened? Are you back with Charlie?'

Lily stared into space as she held the phone and the connection between herself and her father in Australia. Suddenly she didn't know how to begin, how to explain that she was in love. So very much in love that it almost hurt.

'No Dad, no, it's not Charlie. I've met someone new and... '

'Someone new? This is all a bit sudden, isn't it. I don't know, Lily, you live like a cloistered nun for years surrounded by your dusty books and now... well, first Quentin and then Charlie... and now... '

Lily heard her father sigh down the other end of the phone and on the other side of the world.

'Dad, is Gabriella there? If I could talk to her...I think she'd understand and then she could tell you.'

'Yes, yes, she's right here... I think you may be right. Good idea... all this romance stuff is quite beyond me.'

Lily smiled at the sound of worried confusion in his voice, 'Don't worry, Dad, it's all good news and I love you lots.'

'Hmm, well, you look after yourself. Remember *"This above all: to thine own self be true"*.

'OK, Father, Hamlet, Act I, Scene III. Now pass me over to Gabriella, this call is costing a fortune!'

Lily heard another deep sigh and then Gabriella spoke, '*Ciao*, Lily! How are you? What's happening in Cambridge?' 'Hi, Gabriella! I just wanted to tell you that you were so right.'
'*Cosa*? What do you mean?'

'You know, when you said that I would meet the man who was all I desired... well, I met him yesterday.'

'*Dio mio*, Lily, I didn't expect you to do so immediately. Are you sure?'

'Oh yes, I have never been more certain of anything in my life.'
'Well, tell me... who is this perfect man?'

'His name is Leo Torrone...'
'Ah, he is Italian?'
'Yes, but he was born in England and went to school here.

He's an absolutely brilliant scholar. He's working on his thesis in Cambridge now.'

'So, is he younger than you?'

'Not much, but you know I graduated very early and he took his degree late as he had to help in his family business when his father was ill. He's an only son... he had to leave school at sixteen.'

'Family business? In Cambridge?'

'Yes... and Oxford and Bath. His father has a chain of Italian cafés... I think they franchise or something. Anyway, Leo went back to his studies and managed to land an honours degree in English Literature then... '

'So he is an academic... I am beginning to get the picture. But, *di mi, cara, e un uomo di bell'aspetto, anche*?'

'Oh yes,' Lily breathed out as she pictured Leo, 'He's very good-looking, dark and serious... until he smiles and then his face lights up... he has a wicked sense of humour. He's about the same height as father...probably just under six foot and very muscular... sort of powerful!'

'*Va bene*, I get the picture now!' Gabriella gave one of her rippling laughs, 'So, where did you meet?'

'In the University library...it was such good luck. I had no intention of going there really... I was wandering around, trying to avoid the mad throng of tourists. The library in West Road is members only, so it is very quiet out of term time. Well, of course, it's very quiet all the time, but you know what I mean. Anyway, we went to the canteen together... he even drinks lemon tea just like me... '

'*Calma, calma* Lily! Calm down, you sound very excited. Nothing wrong with that, of course, but do be careful. Your father is hopping up and down beside me now, trying to listen in and telling me to warn you not to be rash.'

'I know, he's right of course, but to be honest, Gabriella, I feel that it is just meant to be. I'll try not to be impetuous but, well, I don't think I can help myself.'

'Well, I may not tell your father that... but, *di mi*, tell me what is happening next so that we can begin to worry about that.'

'Well, yesterday we ended up walking to Grantchester and back. The rain had stopped, and we just walked and talked non-stop. We sat on the river bank on his old mac... I had left my own raincoat at the library, I was in such a rush to get out into the fresh air.' Lily paused briefly, wondering whether to tell Gabriella she had dragged Leo away from the library to avoid Quentin. 'Anyway, that's not important, we just sat watching the river flow by... it was heaven, Gabriella. We were discussing paintings and then we arranged to go to the National Gallery today, and then to the Globe in the evening. Leo has two tickets for 'As You Like It'. I'm so excited, Gabriella. I've been up since six!'

'Sounds like a wonderful day... what will you wear?'

'Strangely enough I haven't even thought about it. I don't know... I think just usual stuff.'

'That's a good sign... you feel easy in this Leo's company then. Good, that's very good. But how did he have two tickets?'

Lily was silent for a moment as she realised she had thought about it. 'I don't know, I suppose he was going with a friend?'

'Hmm, well, I hope his friend doesn't mind, then. Anyway, have a great day, Lily. You had better get off the phone, it will be costing you a fortune. Do you want to speak to your father again?'

'No, you pass on all my news and tell him not to worry.'

'*Va bene!* I shall do my best, but we'll phone you tomorrow to see how it went. *Divertiti*!'

'*Ciao, ciao*, Gabriella, *e grazie*! It's good to talk to you. Best love to you and Dad. *Abbracci e baci*!'

50

Lily and Leo stood side by side and in silence in front of the oil painting of Moroni's *'Il Sarto'*. Lily stole a sideways glance at Leo, thinking how very strange it was to be actually in the presence of both the man and the image that had haunted her since that day in the Cambridge café. Then, Leo turned to her and smiled... the smile that so enchanted her.

'I see what you mean, Lily, it is strangely like looking at a portrait of myself as I would have been in the sixteenth century. Fabulous clothes... but then he was a tailor... his trousers are rather puffy, though, don't you think? I'll stick to my jeans.'

Lily laughed, 'I think you'd look great in his white doublet and huge padded breeches... and that sweet little lacy ruffle around his wrists and neck... yes, I think it would suit you very well.'

Lily moved nearer to the painting to examine the surface and the fine brush strokes. She also wanted a moment to recover her thoughts. She had been thinking how well Leo would look in absolutely anything... or nothing. This was their second day together and, apart from holding hands when she had dragged him from the library, they hadn't touched. She was sure that Leo was flirting with his eyes, but the way he looked at her was becoming confusing. Was he playing the perfect gentleman, was it possibly his strict Italian upbringing... or was he shy? Lily could easily sympathise with that... it was only recently that she had begun to conquer her own timid reticence. But then, the worst option of all... did he just not think of her in a romantic way? They talked endlessly, and their minds flew along the same path, they laughed at the same jokes, played the quotation game and could already finish each other's sentences. It was as if they were born to share their knowledge and love of art, literature and every subject under the sun and moon. But still, she longed for him to hold her, even put his arm around her shoulders or hold her hand in his. She sensed he had moved from standing behind her and across the gallery to look at another painting. With a small impatient sigh, she turned and followed him. He was standing in front of another painting by Giovanni Battista Moroni, a 'Portrait of a Lady'.

Leo turned to her as she approached, 'Beautiful, isn't it? '*La Dama in Rosso*'. I wish she had been hung next to the tailor. They could flirt and give their diagonal glances at each other. Moroni can paint eyes that really look at you from the canvas. The tailor's eyes, in particular, seem to be summing you up.'

'Well, that's the very look you gave me when I first saw you in the café. A look of shrewd appraisal.'

'Really, I had no idea I did that... he looks quite conceited.'
'And you're not, of course?' Lily laughed.
'I probably am pretty big-headed I suppose. But he looks as though he is estimating just how much cloth it would need to make you a dress and that no-one could make it better...'

'And your look is summing up just how clever someone might be... is that it?'

'Probably not in your case. I'm sure I was just dazzled by you and probably too shy to look you full in the eye.'

Lily blushed at his praise. So he was dazzled by her appearance at least... and he admitted to being shy. Did he hide his feelings under a barrage of intellectual talk? He was still talking now, 'Just look at the way he holds those huge scissors... almost menacing in a way. There's symbolic imagery for you!'

'True, it's such an interesting painting of its time... great psychological penetration, following more the schools of Giorgione and Titian, in the High Renaissance, Venetian tradition.'

Leo was looking at Lily intently, listening to her every word. She was experienced enough as a lecturer to realise that, for once, she seemed to be ahead of Leo in their exchange of information game. He was absorbing her knowledge in the same way that she had listened to him about literature. She looked back at the painting in front of them now, The Portrait of a Lady. It was another work that she had been considering in the research for her book... it was an interesting comparison to Tintoretto's Portrait of a Lady, the sexual courtesan and poet, Veronica Franca. Lily closed her eyes briefly to remove the image of the courtesan exposing one nipple. Her ears buzzed, and her heart raced at the thought of Leo undressing her. When... or rather, would it ever happen? She took a deep breath and carried on talking as an expert of Renaissance art should talk,

'I love this painting, too... but it is much more typical of the sixteenth century. She is obviously a very rich woman of Renaissance times. The jewels in her hair and the costly silk dress, every detail shown by Moroni's superb skill... the stitch-work, most probably gold thread. And then the red is such a strong symbolic

colour, so visceral.' Lily paused and looked closely at the painting and then turned to face Leo. 'I have an appointment in October with an expert costumier who works at the National and I shall find out more about the painting then.'

'Can I come?' Leo looked at Lily with the eagerness of a young boy.

'Yes, I'm sure you can... I'll check the date later.' She smiled, partly at Leo's unending enthusiasm and partly at the thought that they would still be together... at least in the near future.

'Great... hearing from an expert costumier will be very interesting. I guess she will know all about the fabrics and needlework of the Renaissance. For me, standing here right now, all I can think is how well Moroni can paint silk... quite amazing. The Contessa does have beautiful reddish golden hair, drawn back like yours... but her face is so severe. I would rather be looking at the painting of Veronica Franca. The painting we talked about before.' Suddenly Leo took hold of Lily's shoulders and looked down at her, his dark eyes smouldering, 'One day I would love to see you dressed like Veronica Franca... you're so very beautiful Lily that I hardly dare to touch you. But I want to, I want to so much.'

Lily closed her eyes and there, in the central hall of the National Gallery, the shy Doctor Lily Fairfax kissed Leo Torrone, her Moroni man, full on the mouth.

51

Lily awoke to the sound of her phone ringing. She sat up slowly, untwining herself from Leo's arms and reached for her mobile. She saw her father's number and pressed to answer.

'Good morning, Father. How are you?' Lily's voice was heavy with sleep. Leo stirred beside her and looked at her, then blew her a kiss. He threw back the tangled sheets and stood up and stretched, his muscular body outlined against the sun filtering through the thin curtains of Lily's bedroom. Lily watched him as he walked out of the room. She sighed and realised her father was talking.

'... so I just wanted to make sure you were back in Cambridge safe and sound.'

'Of course, Father, of course, I am. But it was very late, we just caught the last train from King's Cross.'

'Hold on a minute, dear, Gabriella wants a word.'
'OK, speak soon, Father. I'll try to Skype later.' '*Pronto*, Lily, are you still there?' Gabriella's rich voice sounded across the miles from Australia, loud and clear, 'Did our call wake you? I told your father it was too early in England, but he was worried about you.'

'Don't worry, Gabriella, I was just waking anyway.' Lily smiled and shrugged at Leo as he came back into the bedroom carrying two glasses of orange juice. He carefully set one on the table beside Lily where she was sitting in bed. He raised the other glass in the air towards her and mouthed 'Good Morning' and then drank the entire glass. Lily sipped from hers. Fresh-pressed orange juice... had Leo found oranges in the fridge and pressed them in such a short time? Was there nothing this man could not do? Lily raised her glass to him and gratefully drank the rest. Certainly there was not much he hadn't done last night and into the small hours of the morning. It must have been nearly six before they had both fallen asleep, spent, happy and completely exhausted. Lily rubbed the back of her neck as she listened to Gabriella.

'Your father has been worrying all night as he couldn't get you on your mobile. I told him you had theatre tickets.'

'So sorry, Gabriella, of course, I turned my mobile off in the theatre and then forgot to turn it back on.'

'Of course, I kept telling him that's what it would be. Anyway, how was the performance? It was at the Globe, wasn't it?'

'Yes, it was wonderful. An excellent performance.' Lily turned her back to Leo, who had climbed back into bed and was laughing at the double meaning of her words. He began to beat his chest and then clasped his hands above his head in a champion's pose. 'It was longer than usual, but the tempo was maintained to the end. Very exciting action.' Lily was now trying not to giggle.

'It was 'As You Like It', wasn't it' Gabriella sounded puzzled. 'I never thought of it as an action-packed thrilling play.'

'Yes, 'As You Like It'. It was stimulating, a brilliant performance and I liked it very much indeed!' Lily allowed herself a small laugh and Leo moved closer to her. 'It was one of those productions that stay with you after it has ended.'

'Really, I must read a review. Nothing like that going on here, rather a cultural desert, I'm afraid.'

'But there must be some culture stuff in Sydney, surely?'

'Oh, we're not in Sydney now, we're travelling through the vast vineyards of Western Australia. Yesterday we were flying in a small plane... I was terrified.'

'Goodness, how is Father coping with it all?' Lily asked the question but was distracted by Leo, who was holding her shoulders firmly and had turned her so that her back was to him. He began to massage her neck and his hands were gentle but firm... Lily closed her eyes, remembering the power of his body, his energy... his... but Gabriella was still talking.

'Your father loves every minute of it. I am so happy for him. The Australian wine growers have all read his books and we are wined and dined everywhere we go.'

'I'm so glad.' Lily's answer was short and she drew in her breath sharply as Leo's hands moved smoothly down her back, massaging her aching muscles.

'Lily... are you alone?' Gabriella's voice was almost a whisper.

'Well, no... actually ... no.' Lily struggled to answer as now Leo had begun to kiss the back of her neck and his hands were cupping her breasts. There was a peal of laughter over the phone line then Gabriella said,

'I thought not. Sorry to disturb you, Lily dear, and give my apologies to your young man. Your father is out on the balcony now so I'll keep him out of the loop for a while. He has been worrying quite enough about you already and I am sure there is no need. This sudden new love affair is too much for him to take in. We'll speak again very soon. *Ciao, ciao*!'

'*Ciao, ciao,* Gabriella.' Lily's words were almost a murmur as her breath now came short and fast. She fumbled to switch off the phone and threw it on the floor. She arched her back and leaned against Leo, her arms reaching behind her to pull him closer.

52

'I realise I have been infatuated with you for years. If I close my eyes, I can remember seeing a painting by Bordon... or Bordone as he was called in Venice.'

'Stop right there... I know where you're heading... this is another courtesan showing her breasts, isn't it?'

'How did you guess?' Leo turned to Lily and gently rested his head between her breasts. 'You know, I think I may have some sort of deprivation problem. I read an article once about nipple deprivation... fascinating really... all about survival strategy and oral imprinting. I think I need to imprint myself onto you. Maybe my mother rejected me... ... si, si...mammismo... is that mothers hanging on to their sons or vice versa?' Leo looked up at Lily, his eyes shining with wicked laughter, 'I need therapy, for sure... but the outcome is that I am fascinated by your sweet... ' Leo kissed her left breast, 'high...' a kiss to the right, 'round but pointy...' and then two more kisses and a deep sigh, 'oh, so beautiful bosom. Yes, I am definitely deprived. But then, I love your long, skinny legs, too. Now, what can that mean?'

Lily wriggled away from him and held his head in her hands. 'I think it means you are a sweet-talking Lothario and that you don't want to get up.'

Leo threw himself back on the bed and looked at the ceiling, 'If only I weren't so starving hungry... for food, I mean.'

'We shall have to get up before we are too weak to do so. I have to warn you there's nothing in my fridge, either.'

Leo groaned, 'You are ruining my mamma fantasy now... how can you have nothing in your fridge? Not even a slab of Parmigiano and some dry pasta in your larder?'

'I don't even have a larder.' Lily giggled and rolled on top of Leo, 'So, you Italian foodie, where shall we eat?'

Leo pulled her close to him, his arms circling her waist. 'I'm not that hungry, not quite yet.'

Lily closed her eyes as Leo moved under her, following a rhythm that now belonged to them alone. As they moved, Leo began to recite in time to his movement,
'Shy love, I think of you
As the morning air brushes the window pane,

And how much time of all it takes to know
The movement of your arm,' Leo held Lily's arm and kissed it... *'the steps you take,*
The curves along your head, your ears, your hair,'
Now he ran his fingers through her hair and held it back, looking up at her, his eyes burning like gold,
'For all of this, each hand, each finger,'
He put her fingers, one by one into his mouth, still moving slowly under her,
'Each lip, each breath, each sigh,
Each word and sound of voice or tongue,'
His own voice was low now and breathless as he moved faster,
'I would require an age to contemplate.
But for your heart, your mind, your thoughts, all these,
To love them all I need at least five...' he paused a moment and they both cried out together, a primeval cry drawn from them both at the same instant.
'Centuries.'

He ended the sonnet and Lily lay quite still on top of him and then mumbled, her face pressed into Leo's chest,

'It's a sonnet by Shakespeare, but I have no idea what number it is.'

Leo stroked her back in silence and then said quietly, 'Never mind, I'll recite the rest another time.' He yawned and his voice petered out.

Exhausted and completely sated, they both fell asleep, still wrapped in each other's arms.

53

'I didn't intend to go.' Lily looked at the invitation card in her hand. 'I was invited last year, too, but I just sent the money.'

'The charity ball at Queen's... isn't that the one organised by the young lawyers. It's a grand event... why wouldn't you go?'

Lily hesitated and passed Leo the card. She didn't want to admit that she had never had anyone she wanted to go with... plenty of offers that she had easily refused. 'We could go, I suppose, and the theme is 'Renaissance'.'

'Is it fancy dress, then? Masks and costumes... that would be great. I could dress you up as my fantasy courtesan.'

'Hopefully without exposing my breasts?'

'Well, maybe just a little before we go... then a dainty camisole cover-up... then when we get back to your place... maybe...'

'Stop, Leo, you're a depraved Renaissance pervert trying to corrupt my innocence.'

'Oh yes?' Leo looked at her, 'you weren't so very innocent last night... or again this morning.'

Lily blushed and looked around the café as Leo took her hand and kissed it. They were sitting in the Orchard Tearooms, sheltering from a shower of rain. The café was busy with tourists and foreign language students, but no-one she recognised. Life was still a holiday although the summer was coming to an end. Lily looked at the card again,

'It calls it an autumn ball and yet it's only the beginning of September. I'm not sure I can bear the thought of the summer ending.'

'I agree,' Leo sighed, 'I must get back into my studies soon, but all I can think about is being with you... in you, too.'

'Do you think we shall go mad with love, Leo?'

'Probably, "*There is only one difference between a madman and me. The madman thinks he is sane. I know I am mad.*" Now there's a quotation you'll not know.' Leo looked at Lily, his dark eyebrows raised in question and his face alight with triumph. He had entered into Lily's quotation game that she had always played with her father... and entered it with apparent expert and endless knowledge.

Lily closed her eyes and thought hard for a moment, searching through the possibilities before she would have to admit that she had no idea. Should she make a wild guess or accept defeat? She was about to reply when her mobile rang. She gave a small smile when she saw it was her father calling.

'Excuse me a moment, Leo, it's Father, I have to take his call.' She stood up and moved away from the table, then, noticing that the rain had stopped she went outside into the orchard. The apple trees were dripping with rain, but people were already finding deck chairs and sitting in groups around the low, green tables.

'Hi, Father, how are you... and Gabriella?'

'We're very well indeed, thank you. And you and your... your young man?'

'I'm very well indeed, too. My young man is called Leo, I told you, Father. I can't wait for you to meet him.'

'Well, we're over here for another two months so I hope you don't... what is it called... dump him before we return. I can't keep up with you this summer, Lily.'

'OK, Dad, I deserve that, I know, but this is serious and absolutely the right thing. This does seem to have been my summer of madness, Talking of madness, do you know this quote? *"There is only one difference between a madman and me. The madman thinks he is sane. I know I am mad."* I can't think who said that, do you know, Dad?'

'Of course, that was Salvador Dali, I'm surprised you don't know that, Lily.'

'Of course, I might have made a stab at that but I really didn't know. Leo is so good at quotes and he knows reams of poetry off by heart. I can assure you he will still be around when you do get back from Australia. How is your work going?'

'Well, very well. But I've been mad at myself all week. I packed in rather a hurry and forgot the one notebook that I really needed. All my previous tasting notes on the wines of this region. It would have served me well here and saved me so much work. Nothing to be done, though.'

'One of those black moleskin notebooks you always work in?'

'Yes, I picked up a bunch of them, all in chronological order and forgot that I had been looking through one and left it on my desk. So annoying. I blame Gabriella for addling my brain.'

Lily laughed, 'It's good to blame someone else, isn't it. Rather a first for you, in my experience. Can't you get someone to send it to you?'

'I tried... I left my key with Marisa, of course, and she cleans and keeps an eye on the place... but she can't find it anywhere.'

'But you're sure you don't have it with you?'

'Yes, of course, I am. Don't you start, Gabriella has made me look through my luggage three times already. No, it's just frustrating and very annoying.'

'I'll go and get it for you, Dad. I bet I could find it.'

'You can't leave your work and go back to Italy. No, Lily, I shall have to struggle on without it.'

'But I have another ten days before I need to seriously get down to college work. I can write anywhere... or rather, I should be able to... my brain is addled, too. *"O, what a noble mind is here o'erthrown!"*, how about that, Father?'
'That's too easy, Lily! Ophelia in Hamlet, of course, Act III, Scene I.' 'Yes, exactly... and look how she ended up.'

'Well, don't go too near the river banks of the Cam, Lily.'

Lily laughed, 'Actually we are in Grantchester right now and about to walk back along the edge of the river... but don't worry, I have no intention of throwing myself in... and if I did, I am quite sure my Leo would jump in and rescue me. He's more the romantic hero than a mad Hamlet.'

'Well, I'm very glad to hear that.'

'And don't worry about your old notebook. Leo and I will take it as an excuse to end the summer with a few days in Tuscany.'

'Are you quite sure, Lily? It does seem like madness to go all that way.'

'Well, that will have to be the end of my summer madness and I shall get back to work when we return. No problem, Dad. Now, it's beginning to rain again so I'll go back and tell Leo. Speak soon, love to Gabriella. *Ciao, Ciao.*'

Lily looked up at the sky and saw the rain clouds gathering. She looked back at the long windows of the tea-rooms and saw Leo watching her. She waved at him and then ran back inside.

'I've ordered you another pot of tea... and some scones. I thought we ought to eat while we can.'

Lily kissed the top of his head and then sat down beside him. He reached out and brushed her hair away from her face.

'Is it raining again? I can't believe how beautiful your hair looks with raindrops in it... really, just like diamonds.'

'If you're back on your courtesan fetish then I may as well tell you that I think we should go to the ball. Why not? If you want to go, that is... and the day after we can go to Pisa. What do you think?'

Leo was looking at Lily, his eyes soft and dreamy as he touched her hair. Suddenly he sat up straight, 'Did you say we are going to Pisa?'

'If you'd like to... I'll explain it all after I've had my tea and eaten at least two of these huge scones.'

Leo began to cut open a scone and spread it liberally with clotted cream and strawberry jam. Then, he held it out to Lily and she took a large bite. She ate slowly for a moment, her eyes closed in pleasure. Then, speaking with her mouth half full, she said, 'So, you shall go to the ball, Cinders and you, my darling Buttons must be dressed in a white doublet and huge puffy red trousers.'

Leo looked up at her in alarm as he buttered another scone, 'I don't have to dress up as Moroni's Tailor, not the wretched *Tagliapanni,* please, Lily.'

'Well, if you want me to go as a courtesan then...'

'I concede immediately. The victory is yours, Lily. I'll go to the ball with or without red puffy trousers if you dress as a courtesan.'

'Don't tempt me, anyway, there's method in my madness...'
'Oh, much too easy, Lily, Hamlet, of course!'
'Should it be... *"Though this be madness, yet there is method in 't."* Is that actually how it goes?'
'Yes, it was Polonius in Act II, Scene II. Often misquoted of course. Then he says, *"Will you walk out of the air, my lord?"*. So shall we go, milady*?'*
'Yes, of course, that's it. Well, before we walk out into the rain, my lord, I'll tell you my idea. My agent has been pestering me for days now about various publicity stunts. I thought we should go to the ball and she can get all the publicity and media exposure she wants if I go as 'The Tuscan Strumpet', what do you think?'

'That's a truly brilliant idea, Lily. Maybe your brain is coming back into action?'

'Oh no, I don't think so... I am already dreaming about being in my father's peaceful little villa all on my own with you.'

'Shall we go back to your place now, rain or not?' Leo was looking at her as though his eyes were undressing her. Lily smiled and stretched luxuriously.
'Good idea... by the way, it was Salvador Dali.'

Leo laughed aloud, 'I thought you had forgotten or pretended to as you didn't know the answer.'

'Oh no, I never forget a question but this is probably the first time I have ever needed to cheat. I asked my father!'

54

'I'd be pleased to help but how long do you have before this ball?'

Lily was speaking to the costumier she knew at the National Gallery and Leo was sitting beside her listening in to the conversation.

'Well, that's the problem... it's this Saturday. I hadn't intended to go but now, well, I had a change of heart and my publishers are going to use it as a media thingy. Not really my style but... well, I have to keep them happy sometimes.'

'I'm sure I can arrange something. The Royal Shakespeare Company owe me a favour. I help them out with research, and they have thousands of costumes... really high quality, too.'

'That would be amazing. Thank you.'

'My contact there is Susan James. She can be rather a prickly lady, but she certainly knows everything there is to know about costume. I'll text you her name and number. Mention my name, Janice Sheldon, and see what they can do. Don't forget to link me in to any press coverage you get. The National can always do with some free publicity.'

'Of course, I'd be delighted. Especially as my partner will be going as 'Il Sarto', one of your key treasures.'

'Wonderful... he will have to find some very large pleated pantaloons and a white doublet. I'll send the image of the painting to you and to the Royal Shakespeare costume department... that will help. What about yourself?'

'Well, my next book title is to be 'The Tuscan Strumpet' so I am going as a courtesan. Maybe Tintoretto's 'Veronica Franca' or Boron's 'Portrait of a Lady'.'

'Hmm, well, that will be more difficult but I am sure they will come up with something. Ask them about a costume they made for Juliet in a production five years ago... I have an idea that might suit or at least be a starting point.'

'I can't thank you enough.'

'Well, I hope you find your costumes... by the way, they've moved the costume collection out of London to Stratford on Avon... you will have to go there.'

'Oh, we can do that easily. Thanks again.' Lily closed her phone and looked at Leo with a wide smile, feeling very pleased with herself.
'What do you think? It sounds like we need a day out in Stratford on Avon.'
'Sounds like I am doomed to huge puffy red trousers, too.'
'Never mind, you'll look wonderful and you get a chance to visit your bard's birthplace.'
'True, even with the hordes of tourists there is always a magic in the air... something about the bard lingers on. We could stay the night... I know a nice hotel on the river.'

'Sounds a lovely idea. I'll make my phone calls and see what can be arranged.'

'I'll go and forage for food. I intend to stock your fridge and tiny store cupboard with some basic essentials. Then, I'll cook you lunch and then... we'll think of something to do.'

Lily watched as he strode out of the flat, obviously pleased with his mission. She smiled at the thought that it was all becoming very domesticated. Since the first night together there had been no thought or mention of being apart. It seemed perfectly natural that they should just be together. They had even managed a few hours work that morning. Lily had looked through the outline of Leo's thesis and could easily tell it was heading toward publication. While she was reading through his detailed notes, Leo had read the synopsis of her book. He read in silence, although Lily knew he looked at her several times as though anxious of her opinion. Fortunately, she could give nothing but praise as criticism would possibly have been difficult between them. Leo made a few useful comments on historical points in her work and then they had begun to think about the ball. Lily had emailed her acceptance and now they were half way to finding their costumes.

An hour later, Leo returned with two large bags of shopping and disappeared into the small kitchen. Lily was on her last phone call,
'Yes, Janice, I just wanted to thank you again.'
'When are you going?'
'I've arranged to go down this afternoon. We may stay over in Stratford... Susan James seemed quite confident that we would find something suitable.'

'I'm sure you will... they do have over thirty-thousand costumes.'

'Goodness me, we should be able to find some red baggy breeches then! My boyfriend is not too keen on the look.'

'Well, it was a time for quickly changing fashions. Tell Leo he should be glad he's not wearing split tights and a codpiece to cover his vital parts or even pumpkin drawers!'

The two young women laughed together as women so often do when talking about men.

'I'll tell him! Pumpkin drawers... that's priceless. The things you know about.'

'Oh, you'd be surprised... I often think how men must have been so vain and conceited then... such elaborate styles and changing so frequently.'

'Nothing much different now then. Leo spent nearly two hours looking for a pair of sunglasses yesterday in Cambridge.'

'I know, my boyfriend spends longer getting ready to go out than I do.'

Both women were laughing again as Leo came back into the room. He looked at Lily warily. 'Are you laughing about my red baggy trousers?'

'How did you guess?' Lily could hardly stop laughing now, especially at the look of indignation on Leo's face. 'Janice suggested you might find a codpiece and some split tights, preferably red, of course.'

Leo frowned at Lily, 'Do you want to eat the most divine linguine with pumpkin sauce... or not. Behave yourself, Doctor Fairfax.'

'Sorry, Janice, I'd better go. Leo has been cooking pumpkins!' Both girls were now helpless with laughter.

'Bye, Janice... thanks again. Oh my, I must go... I have tears pouring down my cheeks.'

55

'I can see where Janice is coming from with her idea of a Juliet costume. I think she is probably thinking about a beautiful silk dress that the actress, Francesca Annis, wore in a 1976 production. It was inspired by an early Italian Renaissance fresco but... it's a soft- flowing figured silk... it has cross-braiding on the bodice ... but no, I don't think it will do. Follow me, I have an idea.'

Lily and Leo had met Susan James, a stern middle-aged woman and head of the costume collection, promptly at four in the afternoon. They had rushed around and left Cambridge straight after the lunch that Leo had cooked. Lily had been surprised to discover that Leo owned an aged but well-maintained Alfa Romeo Spider. He told her it was his passion and Lily thought how her father would appreciate it. Then, she had a fleeting memory of arriving at her father's villa with Charlie in the flamboyant new Alfa lent to him by his basketball sponsor. She had heard nothing more from Charlie and didn't really expect to now. Both their lives had moved on so rapidly. She sat next to Leo in his car and somehow it seemed as though they had always been together. Maybe it was just that they should have been? She thought dreamily about the idea and then fell into a light sleep. When she awoke, Leo was pulling into a car park.

'Wake up, my sleeping beauty. We're here in Stratford upon Avon and only just in time to make our appointment at four.'

Lily brushed her hair quickly, looking in the little mirror in the car sun visor. She was refreshed from her sleep and looking forward to viewing the costumes.

'Sorry, I wasn't much company on the drive. Are you ready to go?'
'I was born ready, my lovely Lily. Come on, I have the feeling that Mrs. Susan James is not a lady to be kept in waiting. Half an hour later they were listening in amazement

to Susan James as she described the behind the scene work of her department. 'I had no idea there was such a vast collection of costumes.'

Lily said, trying to keep up with Susan James, who was striding quickly along a darkly lit corridor.

'Not just costumes, props too... some from the seventeenth century... then there are paintings, drawings, prints. Only the costumes come under my command. Here we are, now what do you think about this dress?'

Susan slid a long dress from the rack and lifted the calico cover. Lily gasped as she saw the beautiful dress hanging in front of her.
'Why, it's superb. I've never seen anything like it.' Lily reached out a hand and gently touched the heavily embroidered and beaded rosy pink fabric.

'Hmm, well, it has the added advantage of being a very small size. You said you are a size eight... this would fit, I think, and as the bodice laces up the back, it's should fit very well. We'll supply the typical sixteenth-century cotton camicia, that's the ruffled under- shirt. The neckline is sufficiently décolleté... very low cut to almost expose the nipples. The image that Janice sent shows one nipple, but I'm assuming you won't be doing that, Doctor Fairfax?'

'Oh, please call me, Lily, and thank you so much, the dress looks absolutely perfect.' Lily blushed as she replied and avoided answering in full. Leo was standing close behind her and admiring the dress closely. He turned to look at Lily and raised his dark eyebrows, then smiled, a soft rather wicked smile that went unnoticed by Susan. She was now busily looking through a set of lockers that were ranged along the length of one wall.

'Well, of course, we can easily add the pearl choker for your neck and the long string of beads that she wears, Roman style, diagonally across one breast... and then there is the small, dark velvet wrap... that will be useful on an English September night. Oh, and you need a fine lace overlay across your shoulders. That should do it, I think. You'll have to excuse the way I am rushing you through, but I have a tremendous amount to do today. We'd better move on to the Tailor's costume. Follow me.'

Once again Susan was ahead of them, walking purposefully and fast through the rows and rows of hanging costumes.

'Thank you so much for your time, Susan. We're so grateful you could fit us in at all.'

'Oh well, I owe Janice at the National so many favours it's not true. I'm going away tomorrow so that adds to my rushing around. It was lucky you could get here today. Now, let's see, Signor Moroni in white and red. I thought this doublet with the buttoned front.' She pulled a costume from the rack and held it out to Leo. 'But you're very muscular... very broad shouldered...' Susan patted Leo's shoulders and squeezed the top of his arm, 'Hmm, very well built... not many actors have muscles like yours... we often use a lot of padding.'

Leo interrupted, looking self-conscious, 'Well, I row every day in term time... in fact, I'm quite out of shape at the moment.'

'I don't know about that... you still get plenty of exercise, Leo.' Lily smiled innocently at him, enjoying his discomfort and, at the same time, surprised to learn something new about him, another side to his life that he had never mentioned. Rowing in Cambridge was a serious sport, and it was no wonder that he was so fit. Susan, held her head to one side, appraising Leo's size in a professional way. Lily smiled as she thought how similar it was to the way the tailor in the portrait looked out of the frame, summing up his customer. But Susan was still talking,

'Anyway, the doublet may be a tight fit. You could try it without all the under-padding, perhaps?'

'Is that the bombast?' Leo took the jacket from Susan and smiled at her.'

'My goodness, not many people know that word. Do you work in costumes?'

'No, no... I just read a lot. When I heard what I was in for I did some research.'

'I'm impressed. Now, how about the breeches, red of course and pleated.'

'I've been seriously worried about the puffy sort of trousers. I can't say I'm keen.'

'Oh, you'll be surprised, you're tall enough to carry it off. I think you'll look very fine. And here's a narrow leather sword belt just like the tailor wears in the painting.'

Leo took the belt in his hand, 'Lovely leather, I think I'll hang some big scissors on it instead of a sword. What do you think,

Susan?'
Susan looked closely at the image of the painting, 'Yes, I see what you mean... yes, the scissors are really an essential. I'm afraid we don't have any spare here.'

'I think my mother has an old pair of cutting out shears. They'll be fine. Yes, I do like the belt.'

'You have a good, long slim waist... hmm, I think you will look wonderful. Here, these bright red breeches with vertical pleats should do handsomely.' Susan held the breeches up against Leo and stroked the fabric. Leo stared wide-eyed at Lily over Susan's head as she fitted the fabric into his crotch and stretched the fabric down to his knee. 'Yes, perfect length. I thought so, you have good long thighs, too, very muscular. The breeches will be fine, with or without bombast.'

Susan straightened up and handed the breeches to Leo, quite oblivious of his embarrassment. Lily was trying not to laugh as she watched.

'Maybe Leo has enough natural bombast? As you said, he is very well-muscled.'

'I quite agree. And the breeches will hang well and be much more comfortable and cooler without the padding. But you, Lily, you will need a bum roll under the dress.'

'Oh yes, definitely, a bum roll.' Leo spoke quickly, 'I read up about those, too. It accentuates the waist, doesn't it? Although Lily does have a tiny waist, naturally, but for authenticity I would think she does need a bum roll or a rump... or even a cul?'

Susan looked at Leo with interest. 'You've certainly done your homework.'

'Oh yes, I love finding out new facts and new words. I read the history of early bum rolls, rumps and culs... later in the eighteenth century they gave way to hoops and paniers... if I remember correctly?'

'Exactly so... would you like a job here, Leo?'

Leo laughed and dodged the glare that Lily was directing at him. They continued walking along the corridor, Lily trailing behind as Leo continued to dazzle Susan with his newly acquired knowledge.
When they finally reached the entrance hall, Susan turned back to Lily.

'Well, my assistant will handle the rest. Tell her your shoe sizes and she'll find something suitable for you both. Can't ruin the effect with modern shoes. Then, as you say you are staying the night at the Swan's Nest, I'll have everything sent over to you by six this evening. If you try it on and see if it all has the right effect then fine... if not, come back tomorrow morning and one of my staff will try and sort something out.'

'Oh, I'm sure everything will have absolutely the right effect.' Leo said and he smiled at Lily and then held out his hand to Susan. She blushed in surprise as Leo bowed his head and kissed her hand. '*Grazie mille*, *Signora* James, on behalf of Moroni's '*Il Tagliapanni*' and myself, Leo Torrone. *Molto piacere*.'

56

They checked into the Swan's Nest Hotel and ordered lemon tea to be brought to their room.

'I'm exhausted, Leo. Please pour me a tea and let me just gaze at the gentle Avon flowing past our window. Try not to speak for at least five minutes. I need to recover from all your talk of bum rolls and rumps... how you flirted with that woman.'

'Flirted! Don't be ridiculous, I was just being civil.'

'Then God forbid I should ever witness you trying to chat up a woman.'

'Now that just wouldn't happen, would it Lily. Why would I ever flirt with another woman when I have you by my side?'

'Does that mean you would if I wasn't there?'

'You're digging a hole and backing me into it... you know that's not what I meant. Now, stop, Lily, stop sulking just because I suggested you should wear a bum roll. Anyway, I can't stay quiet for two reasons.

'Two reasons?'

'Yes, one is that I can never stay silent and two... aha... I have a surprise to tell you.'

Lily jumped up from her chair on the balcony and threw her arms around Leo's neck, 'Tell me, do tell me... I hate secrets.'

'But you wanted me to stay silent... I can but try.'
'Don't tease, Leo... tell me, please, please.'
'Very well, I shall forgive your petulant behaviour and tell you that I have two tickets for Congreve's Restoration

comedy, 'Love for Love'. At The Swan tonight at seven thirty.'

Lily clapped her hands in delight, 'When did you find time to do that?'

'I dropped in at my parent's house when I went...er... shopping for our lunch and booked online on Papa's computer. Now, aren't you pleased with me?'

'Yes, of course, but... I didn't realise your parents lived in Cambridge.'

'Well, where did you think they lived? They live up in Newnham.'

'But we walked right through Newnham when we went to Grantchester and you didn't say a word.'

'Well, I hardly knew you and I guess it would have been a bit odd to say... hey, come and meet my folks, honey.'

'Yes, I suppose so,' Lily answered slowly, 'I keep feeling that I have been with you forever and then finding I really know nothing about you.'

'There's not a lot to know... I'm really just a very dull, studious type.' Leo reached up and pulled Lily onto his lap and began to kiss her. Lily pulled away from him and looked into the depths of his hazel eyes.

'Leo, something else, why did you have two tickets for The Globe... the first night we went out together... I mean, you already had two tickets. Who were you going with?'

'Shouldn't that be 'with whom'? Really, Doctor Fairfax, your English is appalling.'

'Don't dodge the answer... why two tickets, Leo?'

'Well, it's of no importance anyway. I had bought the tickets a few weeks back when I was going out with an Italian student.'

Lily felt a surge of anger and jealousy, 'What does 'going out' mean, exactly?'

'Lily, Lily... don't be ridiculous... you don't think I lived as a monk waiting for you to appear out of the blue?'

'No, I suppose not, but...'

'Anyway, you weren't a virgin when we got together but I just don't want to know anything about any men in your past life. We're together now and forever... the future is ours. As far as I'm concerned that's settled, settled forever'

Lily's heart was beating fast at Leo's words and she put her arms around his neck and kissed him hard on the mouth. He put his arms around her and hugged her close and then... then the room telephone rang, sharp and shrill.

Leo sighed and Lily stood up from sitting on Leo's lap and went back to her chair in the window. Leo shook his head and smiled at Lily, then crossed the room to answer the call.

'Thank you, yes, please send it up... and a bottle of Bollinger and a few sandwiches would be good. Yes, wholemeal, yes... some egg and some smoked salmon. Thanks.' He replaced the phone on the receiver and then smiled at Lily,

'The ever-so-efficient Ms Susan James has sent our costumes over. What a truly wonderful and gorgeous woman she is!'

'It's all right, you don't need to tease me. I'm really not jealous of Susan James and I agree she is a very efficient woman. Did I hear you order sandwiches, too? I'm starving.'

'Me too, there's only one thing I want more right now.' Leo moved to stand behind Lily and rested his hands on her shoulders and kissed the top of her head. 'Can you guess what that might be?'

'Probably have some idea,' Lily answered, her voice soft with desire as his hands moved down from her shoulders and began to unbutton her blouse. 'But room service will be here any moment...' Before she could finish the sentence, there was a tap on the door. Leo gave another exasperated sigh and stood up straight,

'Was there ever a quicker smoked salmon sarnie?'
He went to the door and unlocked it. A young man hurried in with a silver tray and set it down on the table in front of Lily. He was followed into the room by two young girls carrying very large cardboard boxes fastened with leather straps. They stood for a moment, unsure where to place them. Leo went quickly to them and took the boxes, one by one and placed them on the floor at the end of the bed. 'Thank you very much, here... can you share this out?' He slipped a note into the ready hand of the nearest girl and she blushed with delight.

'Thank you, sir, thank you very much.' They hurried from the room, followed more slowly by the young man. Lily hastily pulled her blouse together, realising the young man had been staring at her.

'Oh dear, I hadn't realised my blouse was half undone... the young bell-boy was bright red.' Lily laughed.

'Well, he shouldn't have stared but, in my heart, I can't blame him. I would have done the same in his place. You look so beautiful in the light from the window... the sun on the river casts dappled light into the room. You could be a modern version of our dear courtesan, Veronica Franca. Your blouse just pulled apart and your hand raised to your heart.' Leo moved back to stand over Lily and slowly undid more buttons until the blouse fell open and he slipped it from her shoulders. 'Do you think we should try on our costumes now, Lily?'

'I do,' Lily replied quietly as she began to unzip Leo's jeans. 'I can't wait to see you in those red breeches...' She laughed but her voice was low and husky. As Leo pulled his t-shirt over his head, she rested her cheek against his bare chest and felt his heart beating.

Then she stood up and they began to pull each other's clothes off as fast as they could, laughing with excitement.

'You're not still telling me that we have to put on our stupid fancy dress clothes, are you, Lily? Please?' Leo stood in front of her, naked, his hands reached out to her in supplication.

'Lily dodged past him and ran to the boxes at the end of the bed. Quickly she unbuckled the leather strap from the first box. She turned to Leo, brandishing the strap like a whip, 'Behave yourself, Signor Tagliapanni. I'm going to try on my costume, even if you're not.'

'I'm definitely not... the sight of those red breeches might kill any desire you have for me.'

'I don't think so, but it's up to you... anyway... oh my!' Lily had opened the first box and was gazing in amazement at the rosy gold taffeta that lay under a layer of black tissue paper. She pulled the dress from the box and ran to the mirror, holding it against herself.

Leo went over to the box and pulled out a delicate white cotton underslip. 'Look at this... it's the camicia... how thin and fine it is... and look, Lily, beads and posh shoes.'

Lily laid the dress carefully on the bed and took the beads from Leo and hung them round her neck. The string of pearls circled her neck closely and a long string of sparkling beads swung between her breasts. Then she took the shoes from Leo. 'Such beautiful shoes... they're the same silk as the dress and embroidered with flowers and beads.' She slipped them on her feet and, wearing nothing else, walked slowly over to the mirror, adjusting to the new height the shoes gave her. She heard Leo move close behind her and then he slipped the camicia over her head and smoothed it down her body. 'I never thought I would want to put clothes on you rather than take them off but... oh, and the beads should be across one breast...' He gave a deep sigh as he looped the long sparkling necklace across Lily's left breast and looked into the mirror.

'Bring the dress, Leo, I'm longing to try it on now.'
Leo went back to the bed and carefully carried the long silk dress to Lily and then slipped it over her head. She pushed her arms into the wide puffed sleeves and then held the bodice up to her breasts. 'You'll have to lace up the back, please Leo.' He sighed again, and began to pull on the strings down the back of the bodice, all the time looking at Lily in the mirror. As the silk tightened around her body, her breasts were pushed upwards until, as Leo tied a tight bow at the top, they swelled and strained against the silk. Leo stroked her shoulders gently, 'Your skin is so smooth, Lily, so beautiful..' He dropped his gaze from the mirror and began to cover her neck and shoulder with small kisses. Lily reached one hand up to his head and stroked his dark hair, then, with the other, she put her hand diagonally across her body and pulled the bodice down a little on one side. 'Look in the mirror, now, Leo.' Lily whispered as she pointed one finger to her nipple. 'Now I am the painting.'

'Much more beautiful, Lily, *si bella, bellissima. Ho bisogna dei tuoi baci dolcissimi*... kiss me, Lily, hold me.'

Lily turned from the mirror and held Leo close and kissed him as she felt his fingers fumbling to pull at the lacing on the back of her bodice.

'*Mi piace come mi baci*, Lily your kisses drive me wild but how can I get you out of the damned dress... now I know what bodice-ripping is all about. Turn round, turn round.'

Lily began to giggle as she turned round and Leo struggled to untie the top of the lacing, 'For goodness sake, don't tear the silk, you will have Susan James to answer to... why did you tie such a tight knot?' She turned to look over her shoulder and both her breasts came free from the top of the bodice. 'Oh my, this dress is very risky.'

Leo groaned as he looked into the mirror and saw her breasts hanging free over the top of the rose silk bodice. 'This is agony, Lily... I wish I had my tailor's scissors right now. Ah, there, I've undone it at last.' The bodice fell open and Leo lifted the dress over Lily's shoulders, ducking his head under the wide skirt to kiss her again and again. Then, throwing the dress on the floor, he swept Lily off her feet and carried her to the bed. Lily lay on her back and opened her arms wide, the cotton camicia pulled up high around her waist.

'Come to me quickly, Leo, I love you.'

Leo stood still at the end of the bed, looking down at Lily for a moment in silence and then replied,

'I love you, too, my beautiful Lily.' Then he fell on top of her. They made fast and fierce love, both unable to restrain their urgent need for each other.
Then passion quickly spent, they lay on their backs, still breathing fast but silent after the violence of their love-making. Leo spoke first,

'What's happening? Will our love kill us? That was so... so... well, savage.' His voice shook with emotion, 'Did I hurt you?' 'No, no and no. It was... beautiful and wild and... there's no way to describe it... let's just drink champagne.' Leo leapt out of the bed and took the bottle from the ice bucket and quickly popped the cork. He poured two glasses carefully, his hands shaking.

Lily sat up in bed and took the glass from him and laughed to see that her hand shook too. She raised her glass to Leo and then to the sunset.

'To us and to love and to Shakespeare and the sunset and ... everything.'

Leo clinked his glass against hers and said. 'To our love and the future together.'

They slowly sipped the cold sparkling champagne in silence. Then Leo went to refill their glasses and brought the plate of sandwiches over to the bed.

'Do you want a salmon sarnie now?'

'Do I? I'm starving, yes please.' Lily took a large bite from the delicate sandwich and then continued talking with her mouth full, 'This is the most perfect day, isn't it? I'm so glad we had to come to Stratford to collect the costumes. Mmm, pass me another sandwich, Leo?'

'I'm surprised you can eat so much after the wonderful pasta I cooked for you at lunch time.'

'Lunch time seems like another day now. Well, I'll eat the last one if you don't want it. Anyway, you'd better not put on any more bombast or your breeches won't fit you.' Lily picked up the last sandwich and laughed at Leo. The golden sun was gleaming on his olive skin as he looked across at the water. 'What are you thinking about, Leo? You look quite serious.'

'I'm thinking I have a confession to make to you, Lily.'

Lily looked at him in alarm, 'What do you mean, confession? Don't scare me, Leo.'

Leo burst out laughing, 'Your face, Lily, your green eyes go a shade darker sometimes. What did you think... that I was going to tell you that I was married with five children or something?' He rocked back on his chair, laughing even more, ' Don't worry, Lily. I just wanted to confess that I hadn't made that pumpkin sauce. My Mamma gave it to me from her fridge and the pasta from her larder. Oh Lily, you're such a scream.'

'Scream? I'll give you scream. You're a horrid, rotten beast.'

'*Ma, tesoro, se mi guardi con quegli occhioni verdi, puoi chiamarmi come ti pare...* call me anything you like but kiss me, please kiss me and say you forgive me.'

'I'm not sure I do forgive you, taking all that praise for the lunch... but I may have to kiss you because...well, I just can't help it.' Lily gave Leo a light kiss and then dipped her hand into the ice bucket and sprinkled Leo with the cold water. 'But, Leo Torrone- Moroni, it's time we got ready to go to the theatre.'

Leo jumped up, shocked by the icy water dripping down his face and then laughed.

'OK, I shall take my punishment like a man... you're right, we'll be late if we don't go straight away.'

'You haven't even tried on your costume yet.'

'I'll save that pleasure for later. Anyway, you haven't tried on your bum roll either... or the lace shawl and that velvet scarf thingy... I have plenty of ideas for all that we can do later, Lily. But right now... it's theatre time.'

Half an hour later, they were running across the footbridge, hand in hand, as twilight fell.

'This is ridiculously romantic, isn't it, Lily? There should be a cameraman behind us filming the closing shot for some cheesy romantic film.'

'Or we've slipped into a scene in a romantic novel. Can real life really be so sweet?'

'As long as we are together, I would put my shirt on it?'
'Even your red breeches?'
'Definitely!

57

'It was a brilliant production...I think I prefer the atmosphere in the Swan Theatre to the larger Royal Shakespeare. And maybe Farquhar is as good, if not better than Congreve?' Lily yawned. They hadn't slept much and now they were driving back to Cambridge.

'Are you tired, Lily? Are you sure you can face lunch with my Ma and Pa?'

'I'm not really tired, of course, I'm looking forward to meeting them.'

'I have a feeling they will love you... almost as much as I do. But in a motherly fatherly way, of course. Do you think your father and Gabriella will like me?' Leo glanced swiftly at Lily when she didn't reply and then smiled as he saw she was sound asleep.

'*Sogni d'oro, cara mia*, sweet dreams.' he said quietly.

Two hours later Leo turned off the motorway and drove slowly through the country lanes from Grantchester and into Newnham. He pulled into the driveway of his parent's home and turned off the engine. Lily awoke and stretched,

'Oh my, we're here, are we? You should have woken me, I haven't time to brush my hair or anything.'

'You look lovely, couldn't look lovelier. My parents aren't posh, anyway.'

'Well, the house is very grand and what a beautiful location, overlooking the water meadows.'
Before she could say any more the front door opened and a woman rushed out, her arms wide,

'*Finalmente,, benvenuti, benvenuti*!' Lily got slowly out of the car and watched as Leo was embraced vigorously by the woman she had instantly recognised as the brassy-haired woman who had served her in the café. Leo disentangled himself gently from the embrace of his mother and turned to Lily.

'Lily... meet my Mamma!'

'*Mio dio! E possibile? Guarda! Ma...* but is the beautiful girl in my café? *Leo, perché non ai detto prima?*' Leo's mother turned to him in surprised anger and attempted to cuff him on the head.

Leo ducked and grinned, '*Ma, Mamma, comé...* how could I tell you what I didn't know? How was I to know you had met Lily in the café?'

Suddenly, Leo's mother ran back into the house calling out, '*Piero, dové stai tu? E l'ombrello giallo...*' She disappeared into the house and Leo looked at Lily and shrugged.

'I should have warned you. Mamma is usually quite mad but I have no idea why she is talking about yellow umbrellas.' He put his arm around Lily and they went into the house together. Lily looked around the hall, admiring the high-ceilinged Victorian architecture.

'It's a beautiful house, Leo...' Before she could say any more, Leo's mother came rushing into the hall, carrying a yellow umbrella. Lily looked at it in surprise, 'My umbrella... is it my umbrella?'

'*Si, si...* you left in café. I see you again and I not think. That day you ran quick from the café and I see some ... *come se dici, un ragazzo cattivo...* bad type follow you. I see you forget umbrella in rushing and I give to the wash-up boy. He go after you but he say you go into college...private door and he not in time ... and *il cattivo* go off. I tell wash-up boy he is stupid slow but what can I do? *Mamma mia!* Now... *invece sei qui... e eccolo*...your beautiful yellow umbrella.' She passed the umbrella to Lily, who took it and looked at it, still surprised.

'Why, Signora Torrone, thank you so much, *mille grazie*. I can hardly believe it! I hadn't missed it yet... so much has happened since.'
'Please, Lila, call me Maria and now meet my husband, *il]mio marito*, Piero Torrone, *il padrone*!'
Lily realised that a man had joined them in the hall and was standing in the background, smiling. He came forward and shook Lily's hand.

'Welcome to our house, Doctor Fairfax, we are honoured.'
'Oh please, call me Lily ... and thank you for inviting me.'
Maria Torrone interrupted, 'Why we stand all in the 'all, please, come in. Leo, your manners... show Lila to the *salone*.' Leo gave an exaggerated bow to Lily and ushered her into the first door on the left of the hall. 'Here we are, Lila, come into a room we hardly ever use. It is reserved for our most honoured guests and is truly uncomfortable.'

'What you saying now, Leo?' Maria followed them into the room which was, indeed, sombre and furnished with heavy leather sofas. 'You not want sit here?'

'Well, Mamma, it really is so much nicer in the conservatory, where we generally sit around.'

Maria sighed and looked at Lily with a sad conspiratorial smile, 'You see, I try, but always he wants to sit lazy in the loggia. Well, if you happy then...' She walked ahead of them, muttering, removing her apron and shrugging her shoulders as though she despaired.

Leo followed Lily and gave her a quick kiss as they turned into the corridor that led to the garden room.

'Leo Torrone, *basta che ti comporti bene mentre sei qui.* Be'ave yourself. I have eyes in the bottom of my head.'

Lily tried not to giggle as they entered a long conservatory at the rear of the house. Here the furniture was mostly comfortable rattan chairs with bright coloured linen cushions. Piero Torrone was already there, examining the long rows of tomato plants that edged the whole room.

'Why, this is a lovely room.' Lily said and went to admire the ripening tomatoes. Piero picked a small tomato and offered it to Lily. She took it and put it into her mouth.

'Mmm! Delicious, so sweet. It reminds me of the tomatoes I ate as a child... and the smell too.' She gently stroked the leaves of one of the plants and sniffed appreciatively. 'How lovely, I should love to grow tomatoes like this.'

Piero smiled shyly and nodded, 'I can show you perhaps, Lila, one day.'

Lily nodded back and looked into his eyes, so similar to Leo's hazel eyes, flecked with gold. She was aware that there was a mention of a long term future in his few words.

58

The taxi dropped them at the Silver Street entrance to Queens College. There had been wild talk about hiring a horse and carriage but the idea had finally been dismissed. Rachael West had been in a feverish whirl of excitement over the last few days. Lily had informed her that she had accepted the invitation to the ball and that she was going in the costume of a mediaeval courtesan, escorted by a young man dressed as Moroni's *'Il Sarto'*. Rachael had been ecstatic... not least because she had begun to fear that Lily would never accept the idea of inviting media coverage. Then, Lily had told Rachael that she had also accepted the television producer, Vince Wright's offer and signed the contract to work on the history of art series with Quentin Howard. Rachael's excitement knew no bounds and Lily had been pestered with texts and emails ever since. Now, the night of the ball had finally arrived. It was a fine, warm night and the moon and stars were clear in the sky above the ancient chimneys of the college.

'On such a night...' Leo whispered to Lily as he held the taxi door and she stepped down, carefully holding the long skirt of her dress to one side, 'On such a night... should I be seen wearing puffy red breeches?'

Lily laughed and kissed his cheek, 'You look...' Before she could finish her sentence there was a flash of a camera and then another and another. Lily turned to Leo, 'It looks as though Rachael has been busy. We had better strut our stuff.'

'And me in these pantaloons... I'll strut as well as I can, I suppose and think of England or something.'

'Think of me.'
'Well, that's not difficult as I certainly wouldn't be here, breeches or not, without you, my love.'

They moved arm in arm into the college portal and found themselves in a crowd of people already drinking champagne. The grounds were floodlit in bright colours, showing the red clunch bricks in a strange green mercury light. They moved through the first crowd of people and made their way to the Old Court. Lily had agreed to a short TV interview to be held there and they were already running late.

'You go ahead, Lily, I'll pick up a couple of glasses of bubbly and see you there. It will look better if you have a glass in your hand while you talk.'

'True, I'm supposed to be enjoying myself.' Lily sighed and walked ahead, swishing her long skirt and pulling her lace shawl closer over her shoulders. Suddenly, without Leo beside her she felt shy and very aware of the low cut of her dress. She took a deep breath and walked toward the group of journalists and a cameraman who were waiting under the famous moon dial in the Old Court. The interview took longer than she thought... chiefly because she was joined by Quentin Howard who talked at length of their future work together. Leo had passed Lily a glass of champagne and then stood aside while the questions were asked. Finally when it was drawing to an end, Lily turned to Leo and took his arm.

'I shall be asking Leo Torrone's advice on the mediaeval literature essential to my research. He has already been invaluable in helping me with the framework of my next book, 'The Tuscan Strumpet'. Thank you everyone.'

Leo put his hand on Lily's bare shoulder and smiled at her and then straight into the camera, '*è stato un piacere lavorare con te* ... and I look forward to the future together.'

Quentin stood the other side of Lily and leaned in towards her as the interview closed. Everyone took a sigh of relief and began to talk at once. As usual, it was Quentin's voice that ruled,

'I don't think I've met Leo Torrone? I didn't know you were researching already for your book, Lily. I thought you were on holiday with your father in Tuscany.'

'Oh yes, I was... in fact, we're going back there the day after tomorrow.'

'But I heard he is in Australia..' Quentin looked down at Lily and then across to Leo. His handsome face was unusually creased and concerned.

'You're right again. He is in Western Australia but Leo and I are going to the villa for a few days before term starts.'

'Oh, I see. Well, have a good time, won't you.' Quentin turned quickly away from the group and walked off.

Lily thanked the TV team again and then took Leo's arm as they walked away.

'Isn't the Moon Dial simply fabulous in tonight's moonlight?' Lily looked up at the intricate lines and figures on the dial between the arched windows. 'So beautiful, isn't it.'

Leo looked up at the dial, shining brightly, 'Do you know how to tell the time by it? You see the metal rod that comes out from the centre of the sun, not the other metal rods that are just supporting rods... follow the shadow to the Roman numerals in blue then... actually Lily... I don't want to talk about the Moon Dial. I want to know what's going on with this Quentin guy?'

'What do you mean? Going on? Nothing's going on.' 'Well, he seemed to think there was... pompous creep.' Lily laughed, 'Well, you know what you said when I asked about your ex Italian student girlfriend. That was the past and now we are together, nothing else is important.'

Leo smiled and snatched up Lily's hand and kissed it hard. There was another flash of a camera and they both looked at each other in surprise and then laughed. 'So, the moment is recorded for posterity. I don't need to worry about the handsome Quentin leaning all over you, I don't need to punch his lights out... or put my tailors scissors to good use, trim his long hair or something more? Even in my puffy red breeches I am quite ready to fight for you, my fair lady.'

'No need at all. My red-breeched Moroni man. Definitely no need. Do you know what? The breeches really do suit you.'

'Oh please, just when I was beginning to believe everything you said. Ah well, the breeches are now ready for dancing. May I ask for your hand in the next dance, my beautiful crumpet-strumpet?' 'Cheeky... I'm not your crumpet or your strumpet. But as it seems you already have my hand, yes, let's dance.'

'The dance floor has been laid the other side of the river. We can cross the Mathematical Bridge to get there. I love that bridge. Did you know that it wasn't really Newton's design at all?'

'No, I didn't but I have a feeling you're going to say you've read all about it and...'

'How did you guess? Do you want to know all about it?'

'Well, I do know that the students call it the Wooden Bridge and say that it crosses from the dark side to the light side.'

'Exactly right... but more than that...' suddenly he stopped talking and smiled at Lily. 'I'm somewhat distracted, Lily, it looks as though you are about to pop out of the top of your bodice.'

Lily looked down quickly and hastily drew near to Leo while she tugged at the top of her dress. 'Thank goodness you noticed. Really, I shall be pleased to be back in my usual clothes.'

'Oh, I don't know... I'm happy in my baggy breeches, especially if you're wearing that dress. Do you know what? We could forget about the dancing, what do you think?'

Lily drew closer to Leo, 'I think you are a wicked fiend and that we are definitely here to dance.'

'You're right, of course. We should dance..first... then...'

'I can see why your mother cuffs you round the head, Leo Torrone.'

'You mean, she tries to. You have to catch me first.' He ducked under Lily's arm and ran across the famous bridge. Lily picked up her skirts and ran after him, as fast as her silken shoes would allow.

59

Lily and Leo were sitting drinking lemon tea in the departure lounge of Stansted airport, the table in front of them covered with newspapers and magazines.

'Rachael certainly seems to know how to do her work. Lily, there's an article and photo in every Sunday paper that I've seen so far.'
'I like this one in Harpers Bazaar, look at the way you're smiling right into the camera. You look like an A list movie star.' 'Rubbish, I look like a loony, smiling inanely, just the handbag on your arm. You're the star, Lily, just look at you in that dress.'
'Thank goodness my bodice hadn't slipped down.'
'Don't worry, I was keeping a very close eye on it... just in case. Oh no, look at this one in the Mail on Sunday... it's that shot taken when we were kissing near the Mathematical Bridge. Just look at my breeches.'

'It's actually a brilliant photo... the famous bridge in the background and the sort of blur of lighting. I think you look so great.' ' Really? Even as eye candy I have to be a failure... but have you read the caption?' Leo passed it to Lily, laughing.

'Doctor Lily Fairfax, the hottest name on the academic scene with her new man, Leo Torrone. Is it true love?' Lily read the caption aloud, 'Oh god, my students will love this... then it goes on to talk about my new book title, so Rachael will be pleased. And a mention of the National Gallery and the charity, too.' Lily looked at Leo and smiled, 'I never thought I'd be in the Mail... kissing.'

'I'd kiss you right now but you never know... the paparazzi might be hiding behind the book stall. By the way, Lily, it was very sweet of you to mention my name in helping with the research.'

'Well, you have helped. Talking about it and adding your special knowledge of the literature of the time has been great. When we both get down to work next week, I hope I can help you, too.'

'No doubt of that. It's no good, Lily, I just have to give you a little kiss right now.' Leo leaned over the table and kissed Lily lightly on the end of her nose. 'It's OK, no-one around with a camera.'

'I'm sure the fuss Rachael made will all die down quickly. I hope so, anyway.'

'Well, I don't know... your new TV series with the long-haired lover boy Quentin will bring you into the limelight.'

'Well, it won't start until the new year so I shan't worry about that yet.'

'I suppose it will involve travelling?'
'Well, yes, but never for long stretches.'
'If we were married, Lily, I could come with you, couldn't I?'
'Married... er, yes, but you could come with me anyway if you were free.'
'Would you think about the marriage bit, Lily? Just think about it?'
'Leo, what are you saying? Is this a proposal?'
'I've wanted to ask you to marry me since we had our first lemon tea together in the library. Haven't you guessed?'
Lily nodded slowly, 'I think I have felt the same... I mean I just don't imagine life without you in it... but...'
'That's a horrid word, 'but' and anyway...'
At that moment, their flight number was announced and they realised they were late to board.
Leo grabbed both their bags and they ran to the escalator and down to the boarding gate. The air stewardess checked their passports and frowned at them. 'You're the last to board, please hurry.'

'I'm so sorry. But this man was asking me to marry him... and I was being so stupid ... hesitating and not saying yes straight away... I don't know why.'

Lily turned to Leo and threw her arms around him. 'Of course I want to marry you, yes, yes!'

Leo dropped the bags and hugged Lily whilst the stewardess looked on speechless. Then she picked up their bags and marched down the corridor to the plane entrance. 'Follow me, please!' She looked over her shoulder and suddenly gave a wide smile, 'Congratulations!'

Lily and Leo ran after the stewardess, their arms still around each other.

'Another winning shot for the end of a cheesy film!' Leo said to Lily as he kissed her again.

'No, the film can't end just yet... we have a week in Tuscany ahead... and we're engaged!'

60

'Hi, Dad, I've found it! Your little notebook... it was with your recipe books in the kitchen.'

'Oh my, how stupid of me... of course, I remember now. I was looking through it in the kitchen when I saw Gabriella coming up the drive. I slipped it on the kitchen bookshelf. Fancy not remembering that. Thank you, dear.'

'No problem at all, Father, we'll go into town and post it later this morning. You'd better give me an address where it will reach you safely.'

'I'll text you with our next port of call. Send it registered, please or by a courier.'

'Yes, maybe a courier would be better. I thought I could scan the pages before I post it, just in case.'

'Could you? Won't it take you ages?'

'No, we can do that for back up. In fact, I could then email you the images as well. Actually that was Leo's idea. I can't wait for you to meet him, Dad.'

'Well, we shall be back sometime toward the end of November. So, it's serious, is it?'

'Actually, Dad, Leo has asked me to marry him.'

'Oh my goodness, Lily... so soon? You've only known him a few weeks. What did you say?'

'I made rather a mess of my answer at first... I hesitated, I have no idea why... but it sort of came out of the blue ... and then I couldn't wait to say yes. But Dad, I just know it's right. You'll see when you meet him.'

'Well, it's not like you to be rash, Lily. And you have so much on with your career at the moment.'

'Well, Leo has his thesis to finish, too. But we can help each other so much and I am so happy that I feel I could fly to the moon, never mind write another book.'

'Well, of course, you know your own mind, you always have, Lily. But do think carefully.'

'Yes, Father, I will, I promise.'

'And thanks again for going all that way to find my book. You're the best daughter a man could possibly have. Lots of love,

Lily, and be careful... "*It is too rash, too unadvised, too sudden, too like the lightning"*... be careful.'
'Alright, Dad, that's Juliet in Act I, Scene II... don't worry, I won't end up like her.'

Lily's father laughed at the end of the phone, many thousand miles away, 'I'm glad to hear it. I always thought Juliet rather a silly young ninny. But, Lily, you're slipping ... it's Act II not Act I.'

'Oh my, you're right, dammit! This love stuff can rot the brain.'
'I'm afraid that might be why I forgot my book.'
'So, it's going well with you and Gabriella?'
'Better than I could ever have dreamt. I'm so glad you like her, Lily.'
'I do, I really do. And I'm sure you'll like Leo, too. He's pie hot at our quotation game and he drives an old Alfa Spider.'
'Ah, you should have told me that before... a Spider, now that tells me a lot. Yes, I look forward to meeting this brave young man.'

'Well, if you want to see a photo of him you should get hold of some English Sunday papers.' 'Why's that?'

'I'm not telling you but take a look.'

'Very well, we will. We've been travelling down the Swan Valley, but we're in Perth now and should be able to pick up the papers. I'll send you that address, too.'

'OK, Father, we'll speak soon. Best love and to Gabriella, too.'
'Bye, darling.'

Lily put down the phone and went out to join Leo on the terrace. She went up and put her arms round Leo, 'Dad's worried about me being rash... I told him we were engaged to be married.'

Leo stood up quickly, 'Goodness, Lily, he must be so shocked. I haven't even met him yet. I was just sitting here thinking how special his home is... it has a really wonderful feeling to it... peaceful, full of books and a great kitchen. I'm beginning to imagine what he is like. I do hope he will like me.'

'Don't worry, I'm sure he will approve of you. I told him you drove a Spider and that got a first tick of approval.'

'I just had a look at his Lancia in the garage... what a car... it's a Zagato, isn't it?'

Lily looked across the stretch of blue water in the pool, shining brightly in the sunshine... suddenly remembering how Charlie, too, had admired her father's old car. For another brief moment she thought about Charlie... the day he had mended the swimming pool jet stream. Was it the next day that he had left the villa, the last time she had seen him? She blinked rapidly and turned away from the sun, 'Come on, we'd better get going. The post office in Pienza will close at noon and I told Dad we'd scan the pages first.'

Less than an hour later they were wandering around the piazza in Pienza, the parcel already posted and thinking about looking for a restaurant for lunch.

'I've been to a small trattoria in a back street somewhere with my father.'

'Sounds good, I'm guessing he's a man who would know where to eat well. Let's go and look for it. It can't be far off.'

They walked through the shady arcades along the side of the piazza and soon found the trattoria in a narrow side street.

'This is the one. Shall we see if they have a table?' Lily peered in through the window to the busy restaurant. Leo was reading the menu on the board outside.

'Definitely, this is a serious menu... typical Toscana... I'm so hungry.'

The tables in the restaurant were all occupied but the proprietor led them between the tables and out into a small courtyard at the back.

'This is splendid... what a beautiful courtyard and such a great view.' Leo turned to the proprietor and continued talking volubly in Italian. The proprietor was delighted to find that Leo was an Italian and soon they were drinking ice cold glasses of Prosecco and being told what they should eat.

'It seems best to go with his recommendations, don't you think, Lily?'

'Definitely, I don't think we have a choice anyway. Did I hear you say your family came originally from Siena?'

'Yes, well, nearby anyway. My father's father moved the family to London when my Papa was a teenager. It was Nonno who began the café business... in Chalk Farm.'

'So you were born in England... it's seems strange to hear you're so very Italian here and now. I hadn't really thought about it before. I mean you seem so English, too.'

'Most of the time I feel completely English... but you've heard my mother... obviously we speak Italian at home all the time. She was very impressed with your Italian, anyway.'

'Was she? Well, it does come quite easily to me but I'm not bi-lingual like you.'

'Lily, have you nearly finished your tiramisu... shall we get back to the villa? I do love you so much and...' Leo rested his hand gently on Lily's knee under the table, 'I was just thinking we should have a siesta this afternoon...it's so... so... hot.'

61

Lily woke slowly, the room was dark and she had no idea how long she had been asleep. She reached out her arm and found the bed empty next to her. She sat up and looked at the time and was amazed to find it was nearly eight o'clock. She lay back in bed and closed her eyes, thinking about Leo. They had spent the entire afternoon in bed, making slow leisurely love and talking about the future. Now, her body felt tender from Leo's caresses and the weight of his body. She remembered that Leo had recited the rest of the love sonnet and then she must have fallen asleep. She stretched her arms above her head and yawned. There was a glorious luxury in the weight of her limbs and she breathed slowly, enjoying the sensation of utter satisfaction. She heard Leo moving around in the kitchen below and idly wondered what he was up to. Then, she fell asleep again into a light, dreamless sleep.

'Lily, Lily are you ever going to wake up, my sleeping beauty?'

Lily opened her eyes and saw that Leo was standing over her. There was a shaft of moonlight glancing through the open shutters and falling across the white sheets of the bed.

'Goodness, what time is it? I must have been asleep for hours and hours.'

'It's just gone nine o'clock and time for a very late picnic dinner. Come on... I have it all ready. It's the most beautiful warm moonlit night.'

'A picnic?' Lily looked at him in surprise. 'OK, I'll take a quick shower and be down in a moment.'

Less than half an hour later, Lily went down to the terrace and found Leo waiting, a rug over his shoulder and a large basket by his side.

'There you are at last. I've been waiting for you to wake up for hours. Come on, I have it all planned.'

Leo took Lily's hand and they walked down the drive and up through the vineyards to the top of the hill. Leo spread out a large rug on the top of the slope and put down the basket. 'Isn't the view amazing from up here, Lily? The vineyards stretching away to the east and then the fields and hills stretching away as far as the eye can see. So warm still.'

'Just a soft breeze as though the summer may end soon... but the moonlight, it's as bright as day.'

'It's a full moon tonight... perfect, not a cloud in the sky but a billion stars.

Lily sat on the rug and looked up at the moon and stars above,

"How sweet the moonlight sleeps upon this bank Here we will sit..."

Leo sat beside Lily and kissed her, 'Too easy, Lily, it's Lorenzo in The Merchant, of course, Act V, Scene I. But this is no time for romantic verse, my girl, my picnic will go cold.'

'Why, what do you have in your basket?'

'I have all sorts of treats. Firstly, champagne and two glasses.' He popped the champagne and the cork flew up into the night air. They sipped from the glasses and then looked at each other and laughed. 'I know what you're thinking, Lily.'

'No, you don't, you can't possibly.'

'You're thinking this is yet another soppy romantic end to a film, aren't you, admit it?'

Lily giggled, 'You're right, I was... it's just all too perfect.'

'Well, I haven't even begun.' Leo triumphantly pulled out a neatly packed pizza and began to pull it apart.'

'When and where did you get that? It can't have come from your Mamma's kitchen this time.'

'Ha ha, Lily. No, but I spotted a pizzeria in the piazza in Piena... mio dio, that's quite hard to say after a glass of champagne... anyway, I drove in and picked it up while you were still sleeping and sleeping on and on. Quick, eat it while it's still hot. I had it in your father's oven waiting.'

'I am surprisingly hungry.' Lily rolled up a thin slice of the pizza and took a large bite. 'Mmm, scrummy... there's nothing like it when you're really hungry. What else do you have in your basket?'

'Greedy girl, do you expect more? Well, I have napkins and, oh yes, a little punnet of wild strawberries.' Leo poured Lily another glass of champagne and they sat, eating the rest of the pizza in companionable silence.

'Moonlight is so much whiter than sunlight, isn't it. The fields could almost be covered with snow.'

'Did you know that there are two lumens of radiant light from a full moon.... whereas the sun...'

'No, Leo, I didn't know and right now I don't care... here, have a strawberry.' Lily laughed and pushed a strawberry into Leo's mouth, 'and another... and, just for once, stop being so clever.'

'Oh, these strawberries are so delicious, I don't think I can remember what I was going to say anyway. Here, try one yourself.' Leo put a strawberry into Lily's mouth and then kissed her. 'Oh, I remember now, I have one more thing in my basket.' He turned away from Lily and searched in the bottom of the basket, then passed a small parcel to Lily.

She took it from him and examined the package, neatly wrapped in white tissue paper and tied with a pink ribbon. She untied the bow and slowly pulled the paper aside to find a small velvet box. She looked up at Leo and then back at the box, then she opened it. Inside, resting in cream silk was a ring. Lily gasped and carefully took it from the box. Leo took it from her and placed it on her ring finger.

'Oh, Leo, it fits perfectly and it's so very beautiful. It looks very old and precious. Leo, I love it.'

'So, will you marry me, Lily?'

Lily looked up and realised that Leo was resting on one knee on the picnic rug.

'Oh yes, Leo, yes I will.'

Leo moved close to Lily and held her tight. 'I love you, Doctor Lily Fairfax.'

'I love you, Leo Torrone, my Moroni man.' Lily looked down at the ring on her finger, 'The ring is so marvellous, wherever did you find it? The stone gives off a magical glow in the moonlight.'

'I bought it in Cambridge, in that antique jewellery shop in King's Parade, right near our café. It's a mediaeval silver ring with a ruby insert. As soon as I saw it I knew it was for you. I've been longing to give it to you.'

'It's the most beautiful and mysterious ring I have ever seen... but, I don't have anything for you.' Lily looked at Leo in dismay.

'My beautiful Lily, you have given me everything I could ever wish for, don't be crazy.'

'Leo, do you know the moment when I was completely sure that I loved you and would love you forever?' 'No, tell me.'

'When you agreed to wear those baggy red breeches to accompany me to that silly ball at Queen's.'

Leo laughed aloud, throwing his head back. 'Lily, you're hilarious. I knew I loved you and would do forever from the moment I gave you your change in my café. All I had to do was to find you again.'

'So, is this finally the end of the saccharine romantic novel or the sentimental film... can the credits now roll as the moon shines whitely down upon us both?'

'Oh no, Lily, this is just the beginning, just the beginning.'

THE END

Shy love, I think of you
As the morning air brushes the window pane,

And how much time of all it takes to know

The movement of your arm, the steps you take,

The curves along your head, your ears, your hair.

For all of this, each hand, each finger,

Each lip, each breath, each sigh,
Each word and sound of voice or tongue,

I would require an age to contemplate.
But for your heart your mind your thoughts, all these,

To love them all I need at least five centuries.

Sometimes I think
Our heads might be enclosed
Closer together upon the pillow's space,

And how into the dark deeps of your eyes

I'd look and think of angels.

Then your breath And all the aura of your body's breathing

Intoxicatedly would overwhelm me
And I would die. For it is too much

That such a thing should be and I should live.

Surely the thought is greater than reality,

The sum of you and love outsteps infinity.

If happiness were like
The flowers of June then I would take

The best of them, roses and columbine,

The lilies, and bind them in your hair.

They are not more beautiful but they add

Meaning to my love.

For all our words

Are short and lame of breath and stumble,

And you surpass them though I know not why.

Shy love I think of you as the day wanes

And as the sun sinks deep into the ocean

And as the stars turn round above in silent motion.

This is the sonnet by Shakespeare that Leo recited to Lily.

Have you read my other titles?

Perfume of Provence Dreams of Tuscany Provence Love
Legacy Provence Flame Provence Starlight Provence Snow
Moonlight in Tuscany Provencal Landscape of Love Love
on an Italian Lake Too Many Men
and
The Wine Dark Mysteries 12 romantic thrillers

all to be sampled and bought from my website
katefitzroy.co.uk
Now, just for fun, here is a question for you... Does Kate
Fitzroy prefer:

- a) gin and tonic

- b) dry white wine

- c) cold lager
  ?

email your answer to fitzroykate@gmail.com

and win a short story written and not yet published by Kate

Printed in Great Britain
by Amazon

32551389R00165